OH MY GOD, SOMEONE'S LICKING THE BLOOD FROM MY KNEE!

A twinge of pain shot through his leg, up from the knee he had cut while crossing the stream. That seemed so long ago, another age, another life. . . . He could hear a soft lapping sound, like a cat drinking milk. As the pain in his leg receded he could feel the tongue, wet and cool, rolling over his wounded knee.

The soft slurping sound stopped briefly . . . and then began again. Two of the figures glided closer. He could hear them giggling, like children. A third child moved next to him and touched his chest. The child's fingers crossed his shoulder and skittered down his arm. A quiet mewling sound came from the child. All the children were now touching him, their fingers flying over his skin.

When they began to lick and suck his skin it tickled, sending thrills of goosebumps over his body. He didn't even mind when each of them bit into his flesh. They sucked at his open veins, the strange little mewling sounds creating a sweet chorus of pure childlike music.

He let himself sink into it . . . he couldn't have resisted if he had wanted to . . .

PINNACLE'S HORROR SHOW

BLOOD BEAST (17-096, $3.95)
by Don D'Ammassa

No one knew where the gargoyle had come from. It was just an ugly stone creature high up on the walls of the old Sheffield Library. Little Jimmy Nicholson liked to go and stare at the gargoyle. It seemed to look straight at him, as if it knew his most secret desires. And he knew that it would give him everything he'd ever wanted. But first he had to do its bidding, no matter how evil.

LIFE BLOOD (17-110, $3.95)
by Lee Duigon

Millboro, New Jersey was just the kind of place Dr. Winslow Emerson had in mind. A small township of Yuppie couples who spent little time at home. Children shuttled between an overburdened school system and every kind of after-school activity. A town ripe for the kind of evil Dr. Emerson specialized in. For Emerson was no ordinary doctor, and no ordinary mortal. He was a creature of ancient legend of mankind's darkest nightmare. And for the citizens of Millboro, he had arrived where they least expected it: in their own backyards.

DARK ADVENT (17-088, $3.95)
by Brian Hodge

A plague of unknown origin swept through modern civilization almost overnight, destroying good and evil alike. Leaving only a handful of survivors to make their way through an empty landscape, and face the unknown horrors that lay hidden in a savage new world. In a deserted midwestern department store, a few people banded together for survival. Beyond their temporary haven, an evil was stirring. Soon all that would stand between the world and a reign of insanity was this unlikely fortress of humanity, armed with what could be found on a department store shelf and what courage they could muster to battle a monstrous, merciless scourge.

Available wherever paperbacks are sold, or order direct from the Publisher. Send cover price plus 50¢ per copy for mailing and handling to Pinnacle Books, Dept. 17-399, 475 Park Avenue South, New York, N.Y. 10016. Residents of New York, New Jersey and Pennsylvania must include sales tax. DO NOT SEND CASH.

THE TWELFTH CHILD

RAYMOND VAN OVER

PINNACLE BOOKS
WINDSOR PUBLISHING CORP.

PINNACLE BOOKS

are published by

Windsor Publishing Corp.
475 Park Avenue South
New York, NY 10016

Copyright© 1990 by Raymond van Over

All rights reserved. No part of this book may be reproduced in any form or by any means without the prior written consent of the Publisher, excepting brief quotes used in reviews.

First printing: September, 1990

Printed in the United States of America

For Lynda

If there is anything good in this book it is because of her. Without her being there the hours and days would have been longer, less fulfilling, and the book harder to create.

ACKNOWLEDGMENTS

For the medical accuracy amidst the blood-sucking phraseology, I must thank Dr. Paul del Giudice, who was so generous with his time. Any errors or mistakes that finally made it into the manuscript are, of course, mine.

And had it not been for the generosity and technology provided by Georgetown University's Tegucigalpa office when my computer broke down while living in Honduras, this book would probably still be in the writing with pen and yellow pad. Thanks especially go to Ray Garufi, Steve Liapis, and Roberto Barahona, who were "strengthening democratic institutions" while I was writing horror, for their kindness and consideration during those traumatic times in Tegucigalpa.

Chapter One

It must be a full moon, he had heard one of the nurses say as he finished closing the incision. It was a favorite comment whenever things got insane at the hospital. And while he didn't know Mars from Martians when it came to astrology, he had to admit that almost every month the OB ward went crazy.

Mallory had just finished his third C-section in the last twelve hours and he was exhausted. He wearily pulled the surgical mask down from his face and let it hang around his neck. The first section, an enormously overweight thirty-nine year old woman, had been waiting for him when he came on duty at six that morning. As soon as he had cut through the skin the fat had jumped out at him. He had to scoop through it to find the abdominal muscles, peritoneum, and uterus. The next section hit him almost immediately after he had finished closing. But perhaps he should be thankful that he had a relatively normal six hours until the third one.

He stripped the bloody latex gloves from his hands and tossed them into the wastebin as he walked out of surgery. He rubbed his face and neck hard as he walked. His shift was over at six o'clock. He glanced at his watch. Just twenty minutes more. But first he needed a cup of coffee before he showered.

It was visiting hours and Mallory didn't want to deal with the crowded elevators, the forced smiles and the pale strained faces of anxious relatives, so he decided to walk. He pushed through the *EXIT* door and clumped down the two flights of stairs, his blood-stained Dutch clogs slipping off his feet at every step.

Even before he opened the second floor stairwell door he could smell the over-cooked vegetables and grease-laden recirculated air. Whenever he entered the cafeteria it was hard to believe he was in a place of healing.

The cafeteria was nearly empty so Mallory walked quickly down the line. He slid his tray along the three aluminum tubes in front of the food display windows and grabbed a vanilla Dannon yogurt and a cup of coffee.

The room was typically institutional, large and square, with red plastic laminated tables and ten year old beige paint on the walls. He chose a booth near the window, which looked out onto a roof and an air-conditioning unit, and gingerly sipped his coffee. At least it was hot, but as usual it tasted like old socks spiced with caffeine.

Mallory was numb . . . more tired than he had been in months. He cradled his head in both his hands and closed his eyes.

Boring . . . routine . . . exhaustion, all words that seemed to describe his life right now. It wasn't at all what he had expected in medical school. Then his greatest passion had been to do research in human reproduction cycles. To try and understand the basic biology of cells—and especially the cycles of cell division. With little money to continue specialized post-graduate training, he had ended up in obstetrics and gynecology. Not the ideal place to sustain his poetic vision of Gaea and the eternal female.

Before he could start feeling too sorry for himself, the subdued but insistent loudspeaker cut through the fog of his fatigue.

"Dr. David Mallory . . . OB surgery . . . Dr. David Mallory . . ."

"Shit!" Mallory said aloud . . . so loud in fact that the others in the cafeteria looked up at him.

He took one last quick gulp of coffee and headed for the elevator.

Mallory walked into OB. "Where is she?" he asked a plump, red-haired nurse preparing an IV.

"Room 4," she said, motioning toward a door to her left.

It was a typically small Hitchcock Memorial Hospital delivery room. No bigger than a nun's cell, it was one of four birthing rooms in the obstetrics section of perhaps the best medical center in New England. Nurses had hung a poster on the wall with baby unicorns, surrounded by hearts and playing in a sunlit field. All the colors in the room were pastel. A triple-level birthing bed that was still flat, with the head slightly elevated, dominated the room. A fetal monitor and an "IV." connected to an electronic-drip monitor were the two main pieces of equipment next to the bed.

One glance told him that the patient was in serious trouble. Her head was thrown back, limp on the pillow, lying flaccidly to one side. Her skin was sallow; a sheen of sweat covered her face and neck. She was clearly comatose.

"Okay, fill me in, Jeff," he said to the doctor checking her blood pressure. Jeff Goldman was the OB resident on duty that night and as smart as they come.

Mallory had worked with him often over the last year, and they had become friends soon after Jeff had arrived at Hitchcock from Dartmouth Medical School. He had a wild, irreverent sense of humor mixed with an innocence that appealed to Mallory. Mallory liked and trusted him even though he was more into computers than medicine. He was a slight, prematurely balding young man with wire-rimmed glasses and a perpetually quizzical look on his face. He could have been a stand-in for Woody Allen.

"Five minutes ago she suddenly went unconscious," Goldman said. "Everything was fine until then."

"Seizure? Hypoglycemia? Shock?" he asked.

"Don't know. But she's hypertensive."

Mallory lifted her eyelids and studied the pupils. He shined his penlight into her eyes.

"Pupils are reactive, symmetrical." He turned to Goldman. "Always check for intracranial bleeding with a hypertensive patient in coma."

He touched her forehead and cheeks. "Clammy skin. What're her vitals?" he asked, pulling a stethoscope from his pocket and pressing it against her chest and ribs.

"Her BP is two-ten over one-forty. Heart rate holding at around ninety-five."

"Well, her heart and lungs sound clear," Mallory said, stuffing the stethoscope back into his pocket.

"How's the fetus?" he asked.

"So far good. No distress at all."

Mallory pressed on the lower portion of the uterus just above the pelvic arch, then along the fundus. He looked over at Goldman. "Yeah, well this kid is breech."

"No," Goldman said. "I just checked. It was fine, in good position."

"Well, it's turned," Mallory said as he glanced at the heart waves on the paper tracings coming out of the fetal monitor. The audible, regular beeping of the fetus's heart over the monitor's speaker was reassuring ... strong and steady.

"Dilation?" Mallory asked, pulling a latex surgical glove on his right hand and coating two fingers with gel.

"I checked fifteen minutes ago. She's been at seven centimeters for one hour. We put her on Pit . . ." the resident glanced at the wall clock . . . "forty minutes ago. Contractions are strong every four minutes."

A nurse lifted the unconscious woman's knees and held them open as Mallory inserted his two lubricated fingers into her vagina. He felt the soft, thinning cervix and pressed his fingers into the opening.

"She's fully effaced and ten centimeters now," he said, extracting his hand and pulling off the glove in one fluid motion. He threw the glove into a wastebasket.

"Jeff, did you type and cross her yet?"

Goldman shook his head. "Negative. Not enough time."

"Okay, I want a CBC, fibrinogen, and a coagulation screen. Type and cross her for four units of blood. Who's the attending physician?"

"Paul Bardfield, but he's delayed with another critical patient. Said he'd be here in an hour or two."

"Great," he said sarcastically, "do we know anything about her? Have her charts handy?"

Goldman shook his head. "She was a late admission, been here for little over an hour. When she came in she told us her name is Betty Milner and she lives in New Hampshire, a few miles up the Connecticut River just outside Orford. I got the impression she was very happily pregnant, even with her husband away on a business trip. Bardfield said she was in good general health. No allergies. Beyond that . . . nada . . . no medical history. He's bringing over her file."

"Fantastic," Mallory said under his breath. "Why are we so lucky?"

Stabilize and terminate the pregnancy . . . that's what the ward manual called for, Mallory thought. But there wasn't time to stabilize the blood pressure. There wasn't time for anything. The kid was breech, and the mother ten centimeters dilated, and he didn't have the foggiest idea how long before she'd deliver. One hour? Two? He considered briefly trying to turn the baby and intensifying contractions by upping her Pitocin, but Jeff said she'd already been on it for forty minutes and it would probably take too much time. She was already moribund and there was a possibility of her kidneys failing and if renal failure wasn't enough, there was danger of abruptio . . . and if the placenta separated from the uterus he could lose both the baby *and* the mother.

Strangest of all, there was no fetal distress. With all this going on, the baby's heart beat was as healthy as they come, and since it was well within the parameters of safety, he wasn't going to question such blessings. Yet, the mother, for some reason he couldn't fathom, was on the verge of collapse. Why such a breakdown of her physical condition? He didn't know what was going on, but one thing was certain. He had to get that baby out . . . and quickly.

"Jeff, get her into the section room now . . . stat! And don't bother scrubbing, just glove and put on your gown."

He turned to one of the two nurses who had just walked in and was relieved to see that it was Lili Shikome, one of the best OB nurses he'd ever worked with. She was also one of the most attractive women he'd ever seen. Every doctor in the place had hit on her since she had arrived three weeks ago from California, but she seemed to be all business. She took her job seriously, and he liked that.

"Lili, I'm glad you're here. I'm going to need all the help I can get. Now listen carefully. First, get pediatrics and anesthesia in here stat. Have the other nurse call them and you open the section tray. But first draw up twenty milligrams of Hydrazaline and push it 'IV.' Then call hemo and sit on them. Get me those four units of blood."

"Okay, let's move, people," he said as he spun on his heel and raced down the hall to surgery.

Mallory felt panic rise up from his gut and he fought to calm himself. There were relatively few crises in obstetrics that required panic-speed. True fetal distress, perhaps, or a prolapsed umbilical cord. But at the top of the horror list was abruptio, a sudden separation of the placenta from the uterine wall. It could be instantly fatal to the baby . . . and catastrophic for the mother, who could begin hemorrhaging and bleed to death before much could be done. But as much as he tried to control his anxiety, his mouth felt like sandpaper and his heart was pounding in his chest as he pushed through the large swinging door into the OB surgery washroom. He had never gotten used to holding someone's life in his hands. He constantly dreaded that one simple mistake that could cause an unnecessary death. Thank God he had never yet been responsible for a patient's death.

A nurse was waiting for him. It was the plump redhead. Her name tag read "C. Carpenter." She immediately helped him slip into his gown. "Get a Foley catheter in her stat," he said as she held open his gloves and he shoved his hands inside. "I want to see that bladder drained and out of the way when I'm inside."

"And Carpenter, check for proteins in the urine," he yelled over his shoulder as she hurried out of the room.

He'd like to get an estriol count and find out what kind of hormones the fetus was kicking out into the placenta, but the procedure wasn't done anymore. Progress! With hypertension he had to assume an initial diagnosis of eclampsia or toxemia. The door opened and Goldman entered, already in his gown.

"Well, is the good doctor ready to perform his miracles?" Goldman said wryly.

"Very funny," Mallory said as another nurse tied a surgical mask around his face. "Listen, Jeff, I know you get a smart-mouth when you're nervous, but let's cut the humor and stick to business."

When Mallory and Goldman stepped into surgery the young woman was already prepped, her stomach stained from pelvis to rib cage with antiseptic. Her pubic hair hadn't been shaved, but that wasn't important now.

Lili was standing next to the open section tray. Mallory noted with satisfaction that the four units of blood were in place . . . and so was the anesthesiologist, a nerd named Wally. Mallory couldn't remember his last name, but like most anesthesiologists he grinned a lot. Mallory had never figured out why surgeons seemed not to give a damn if they were well-liked, and anesthesiologists wanted everyone to like them. He was sure it had something to do with their jobs, but he couldn't figure out what . . . or why.

"Are you ready, Wally?" he asked curtly, relieved that he at least remembered his first name.

"I'm giving her oxygen now. I'll have her tubed in a minute," Wally said, his fingers fumbling with the latex tubes he was trying to adjust.

"Okay, but keep her light. She's already in coma."

He turned to Lili, who was assisting him. "Lili, call down and get me four more units of blood, just in case we need it."

"Wally," Mallory said dryly, "can I start yet?"

"Give me five more seconds," he said nervously, inserting the endotracheal tube down the young woman's throat.

"Go," Wally said, watching his gauges.

"Scalpel," Mallory said, his open hand extended toward Lili.

She slapped it smartly into his palm. He made a firm, strong slash down the abdomen, from a few inches below the navel to just above the pelvis. Quickly but carefully he pared away the layers of subcutaneous tissue and muscle.

"I've reached the peritoneum," he said.

In less than two minutes the thick muscle of the uterus lay exposed. He glanced up at the fetal monitor. Still strong and regular. No distress. *This kid is a powerhouse,* Mallory thought.

He made a deep transverse incision in the uterine wall, and the dark-red muscle parted open like swollen lips, exposing the bag of waters and the baby floating inside.

"Damn," he gasped, startled.

The baby's face was pressed against the clear membrane of the water sac, and for one weird and giddy second it seemed its eyes were open and staring up at him.

"Something wrong?" Goldman asked.

"No, no," Mallory mumbled. "I'm just over-tired."

Mallory ruptured the membrane with a forceps. Pink liquid gushed out, running down over the woman's body and staining the operating table.

"Bloody amnio," Mallory said to no one in particular. Everyone could clearly see it.

"Jeff," Mallory said, pointing to a vein, "get that bleeder. Clamp it, damn it."

After Goldman had clamped the vein, Mallory

inserted his hand into the uterus, just below the baby's head, and began to gently lift the head up and out.

"Press on the fundus," he ordered.

Goldman pressed on the top of the uterus while Mallory tried to lift the baby's head free.

"More, give me more fundal pressure."

The baby's head came up through the incision and Goldman immediately suctioned the nose and throat.

Mallory lifted first one shoulder free, then the other, and pulled the baby out.

"It's a boy," he said.

"Delivery time?" a nurse asked.

"Six minutes after six."

"I've got the bulb," Mallory said to Goldman. "Here ... clamp the cord."

Goldman put two Kelly-clamps on the umbilical cord about six inches apart and Mallory cut between them.

"Get that cord blood."

He handed the baby to Lili, whose beautiful half-American, half-Japanese face was flushed and beaming. She took the child, wrapped it in a swaddling cloth and cradled it in her arms, cooing to it. Mallory, who noticed the ecstatic expression on her face, thought that with her love of children she was in the perfect job.

Enrapt and smiling, and ignoring the isolette where newborns are usually examined for their Apgar scale, she headed for the nursery, talking softly to the baby.

Goldman was shocked that Lili took the baby without first examining it. It wasn't normal procedure as he'd learned it. He checked an impulse to follow her and do the Apgar scale, but Mallory was under too much pressure and might need him to help close.

Mallory took a deep breath ... he had to hurry and finish. He held apart the uterine incision and examined the placenta. About the size of a partially deflated football, the placenta didn't have its usual purple, blood-gorged look, but was pink-gray in color. It was already partly separated. While Goldman held the incision open he reached in, pressed his fingers behind the afterbirth and gently peeled it away from the uterine wall.

He lifted the placenta out and tossed it into a tray.

"Placenta time?" Carpenter asked.

"Six-o-twelve," another nurse noted and jotted it down.

"Okay, let's close," Mallory said.

Mallory held out his hand, and the plump redhead slapped the first stitch and suture holder into it.

"Wally, how's she doing?" he asked. There was surprisingly little blood, and Mallory began to close up the uterus.

"Wally, did you hear me?"

The anesthesiologist was checking gauges anxiously at the top of the operating table. He looked up, worry written across his chubby face. "Hurry and close, Mallory, her BP is sixty-five over zero."

"That's nuts," Mallory said, startled. "It was over two hundred systolic a few minutes ago."

"I know," Wally said, "but I checked it three times. Look at the cardiac monitor, her pulse is almost one-ninety."

Mallory stared unbelievingly at the blips on the screen, then quickly turned back to his suturing. He was sweating heavily now, and not just because of the operating lights. He felt it tickling down his spine. Carpenter reached over and wiped his eyebrows and forehead.

"Pressure?" he asked, sewing as quickly as he could. He was almost finished with the uterus. "Damn it, Wally, what's her blood pressure?"

"A weak fifty over zero and dropping," Wally

answered, his eyes wide open and abnormally magnified behind his glasses.

Mallory continued sewing. An icy sick feeling rose from his gut. He knew he was in a race now. The woman was . . .

The room abruptly became deathly silent.

The cardiac monitor . . . the damned monitor had started to beat erratically and slowly. The only thing Mallory could hear was his own dry, rapid breathing into his mask.

The sudden silence just before the cardiac alarm went off affected everyone simultaneously. Every face in the room was turned to the monitor . . . waiting. Without realizing it, each person had unconsciously attuned himself to the constant beeping of the patient's heartbeat. When it stopped, the effect was mesmerizing. All eyes watched the very slow brachycordia line running across the monitor screen.

Then suddenly it stopped.

"God damn it to hell," Mallory cursed, "it's happened."

"Somebody call a code," he said. "Wally, are you ventilating?"

"Yeah," Wally said, his voice hoarse. "And the tubes're right in place."

"Jeff, you and Wally bag her and pump her chest while I finish suturing."

Wally continued pumping oxygen into the young woman's lungs as Goldman gave closed cardiac massage. A nurse had dashed from the room and within ten seconds the loudspeaker was announcing a cardiac arrest in OB surgery.

In less than a minute three residents burst into the room pushing the arrest cart, a small pharmacy and instrument tray on wheels. A fourth resident, a slightly overweight woman in her late twenties, followed a few seconds later. She was puffing from her run down the hall.

Each doctor took up his assigned role. Talk was rapid and to the point. While Mallory closed, Wally answered their questions about blood pressure before the arrest, pulse, and the duration of the arrest.

As they talked one attached additional electrocardiogram leads to the patient, another took over Goldman's place, rhythmically compressing the sternum. Every thirty seconds the monitor was checked for some sign of spontaneous heart activity.

The tracing remained flat, and the monitor was now screaming as they worked. A nurse snapped off the alarm.

His own heart pounding, Mallory kept sewing. In his mind he was racing against death.

"She's got cardiac activity..." the young woman resident said.

"Rhythm?"

"V-fib," she answered the team leader, a tall, sandy-haired resident named Jack Logan.

"Stand back, everybody," Logan ordered. "Get paddles ready. We're going to shock her."

Logan placed two cardiac defibrillation paddles on the young woman's chest wall. He triggered the paddles, and the body seemed to leap several inches off the table.

"Rhythm?" Logan asked.

"Still V-fib."

"Okay, turn up the juice," Logan said.

Logan triggered the current again and the body went rigid, then convulsed violently its whole length.

All eyes were on the monitor, which still showed an erratic, jagged heart wave.

Logan triggered the paddles again... and again. And each time the body jerked spastically, the massive spasming back and chest muscles forcing the body to arch upward, and the pale-gray flaccid limbs jerking in a mimicking paroxysm of life. But the expressionless face remained unmoving.

Mallory was standing several feet back from the operating table, still clutching the suture holder and stitches. He wasn't watching the cardiac monitor any longer, he was staring at the face of the young woman, trying to remember her name. What was it? Betty ... Yes ... Betty Milner. She was pretty, with a scattered wave of tiny freckles running over the bridge of her nose and onto her cheeks. Her reddish-brown hair was curly, but flat now, with a few strands sticking to the cold sweat on her forehead.

Helplessly, Mallory stood there, immune now to the noise and ordered chaos swirling around him, staring, a useless statue with a bloody white bib holding a few threads of stitches and a curved needle for suturing as the pretty young woman died before her time.

The sounds of activity receded farther, and Mallory felt his heart sink. In some mysterious place deep within himself, a place he didn't want to be aware of, his deepest fears were inexorably rising. And even as they rose, flowering like a cancerous black blossom, he could only stare at Betty Milner's pale face.

Surprisingly, perhaps because the violent spasms of electric current racing through her had displaced the endotrachial tube, the young woman groaned softly once as he watched, her eyelids fluttered and the long dark lashes began beating erratically, like the wings of a frightened bird taking flight. Her eyes wandered under the dark, purple-tinged flesh of her lids ... roaming aimlessly ... as if looking for a place to escape; then her eyes suddenly snapped open. They became still and she stared blindly ahead. Dilating, the black pupils pressed outward until the cobalt blue of her living eye all but disappeared. The tired, gravestone-pale face abruptly relaxed. She was dead.

Mallory was overwhelmed with melancholy and hot tears burned at the edges of his eyes. But even though he didn't realize it until much later . . . something of far greater significance had occurred.

The twelfth child had been born.

Chapter Two

Mallory entered the doctor's locker room and immediately stripped and broiled himself raw in a shower. He stayed under a long time, letting the hot water beat on the back of his neck and shoulders until it hurt. When he came out two other staff doctors were changing. One was Richard Weston, a prematurely graying, handsome jock who spent as much time in front of the mirror as at the operating table. The other doctor Mallory had seen around the hospital but didn't know. He nodded to them both.

"Sorry to hear about your C-section," Weston said, combing his hair. "That's tough."

"Yeah," Mallory said softly. He didn't want to encourage conversation . . . and especially with Weston.

"I had one like that last year," Weston said, talking into the mirror as he adjusted his tie. "Everything going smoothly. It was just a simple appendectomy. Young man, about 22. He just closed down. Heart stopped for no reason."

He turned to Mallory. "You wouldn't have believed the hysterics when I told the parents and his fiancee. Tranquilizers on the spot. And even worse, there was a threatened lawsuit. We had to do some fancy talking to put them off."

Mallory, not able to listen to Weston's stupid, insensitive monologue anymore, quickly tied his shoelaces and stood up.

"Well, my shift's over," he said. "I'm going home."

"Good idea . . . and forget the whole thing."

A hot flash of anger suddenly raced through Mallory, and he turned on Weston.

"Forget? Listen, you asshole. I can't forget it. It happened . . . don't you understand? I'm delivering a baby and the woman dies . . . for no reason. That's not the kind of thing a doctor with a conscience can easily forget."

Weston's face flushed at the implied insult. He'd never really liked Mallory. Too much of a self-righteous know-it-all. A golden boy from med school who believed his professors' bullshit.

Controlling his irritation, Weston tried to keep his voice low and even, professional. "Dr. Mallory, you've only been out of residency what, a few years? Why don't you take some advice from those with more experience? If you push this too far, and there's an inquiry, somebody may be found to have made a mistake. And it may have been you, smart-ass. Do you realize what that means? If *you* were the one who made the mistake? You think your insurance rates are high now, they'll go through the roof if you're found negligent. Then kiss your career goodbye.

"Take it from me," Weston said. "I've been through this scene before. Don't rock the boat, let the thing rest."

Mallory, his lips compressed into a thin line, paused, his hand on the door. He turned and looked at Weston. Very slowly and distinctly he said, "I have just one thing to say to you, Dr. Weston. . . . Take your insurance policy and your scalpel and stuff them up your ass."

Before Weston could reply Mallory walked out of the room, slamming the door behind him. It wasn't a very elegant or stylish exit, but it made him feel damn good.

Mallory didn't speak to anyone as he walked toward the elevators. The white face of Betty Milner kept reappearing, floating like a ghostly mirage in the hazy heat of his exhausted mind.

Burned out. If he never really understood that pop culture jargon before, he understood it now. He felt hot and tired, and decided that going directly home would be ridiculous. He didn't want to sit around alone feeling depressed or watching television until his brain was gorged and swollen from its useless feeding on late night TV. If he saw David Letterman grinning stupidly and sucking his teeth one more time he would put his foot through the screen.

There were too many questions about Betty Milner's death to waste the night in self-pity and depression, too much confusion in his mind about what caused her rapid degeneration. One minute she was "happily pregnant" and in "good general health" (weren't those the words Jeff Goldman had used to describe her?), and the next she falls into coma and is moribund—in a matter of minutes.

What had caused the coma? The partial abruptio? The hypertensive shifts in blood pressure? The final heart failure was the most understandable. The healthiest heart could fail under such an assault.

He was also puzzled by the peculiar lack of bleeding and by the sudden drop in her blood pressure. He'd lost count on how many C-sections he had performed and none of them had bled so little. And her blood and tissue had seemed... what was the word... thin? pale? anemic? As the questions and the few medical facts at his disposal raced through his mind, one common thread kept reasserting itself. Her blood. The blood pressure kept shifting, first astronomically high, then plummeting. And its appearance. He couldn't put his finger on it, but something in him was disturbed by how it looked.

He wanted to get out of the hospital, take a walk, breathe some clean air free of the smell of antiseptic, urine and bile and detergents. But before he did he would give Carl Jeffords a call and ask him to do an analysis on her blood. Just the thought of exploring a few leads made him feel a little better.

He took the elevator to the first floor and stopped by the admissions and information desk and called Jeffords. It was all arranged in a few minutes. Jeffords, who Mallory thought was one of the best hematologists in the business, had just come on duty. He had a light work load and would get right on Milner's blood and get back to Mallory in an hour or two.

Mallory wanted to wait for Jeffords' analysis, so he decided to take a walk around Occam Pond. It was only a few blocks away, and the complete circuit around the small man-made lake was exactly one mile from the entrance of the Mary Hitchcock Memorial. He had taken the walk many times before and knew every tree and rock along the one lane blacktop that circled it. Whenever he needed a breather from the hospital or a little exercise, he would either jog or walk the circuit several times. It had provided some of the rare moments of peace during the last few years. After he had hired on at Hitchcock direct from medical school, work had consumed him almost every waking hour. He never seemed to realize that he needed a break or change of pace until exhaustion suddenly hit him like a baseball bat to the back of his head.

The benefits of his hot shower had worn off, making him feel even more tired than before.

As he walked Mallory sucked in the clean, cold air. He felt it rush through his lungs, and his body began to come more alive. It was a quiet night, the distant sounds of Hanover, a mile and a half away, muted and inoffensive. He walked with his hands in his pockets, a habit he had had since childhood. Whenever he had been troubled or frightened, he had slumped down inside himself, his body coiling inward while his mind raced, searching for understanding.

He went over all the facts again. And came up with the same non-answers.

For an hour he plodded around the pond, hardly aware of the occasional car or another late-night walker passing by.

This conversation with himself was getting nowhere. He didn't know enough to ask any more questions. He needed help. Whatever happened to that woman was beyond him ... at least for the moment. But one thing was clear to him. Running around in his head, amidst the confusion and the painful memory of the young woman's death, was a mystery. And he was going to solve it. There was no such thing as an unsolvable medical event. Everything had a cause ... and an answer ... if you just knew where to look, and if you understood enough to ask the right questions. Obviously, he hadn't been asking the right questions.

He turned and headed back toward Hitchcock. Maybe Jeffords would come up with something.

He walked into the cafeteria, where he and Jeffords had planned to meet, and took a small cottage cheese salad and a black coffee to a free table.

Someone had left a rumpled *Boston Globe* scattered over the seat next to him. He picked it up and thumbed through it while he ate the salad.

Twenty minutes later Carl Jeffords entered the cafeteria. He glanced around the room, spotted Mallory, and walked over to the table.

"David, I'm glad you're here," he said, his face somber. He pulled out a chair and lowered his tall, skinny body into the seat across from Mallory. He placed a large manila envelope on the table in front of him.

"Well, what's up?" Mallory asked, searching Jeffords' face for some clue.

"David, I don't know how to say this," Jeffords began. "It's the most bizarre thing that's happened to me in ten years of medicine." Jeffords took a deep breath. "The only thing . . . no, that's not accurate," he said, shaking his head. "There are two surprising facts here."

The hematologist reached into the envelope and pulled out a small plastic vial. He held it up. "Look at this. Do you recognize it from medical school?"

Mallory studied the contents of the tube carefully. It was a yellowish-brown liquid that he recognized as hemosiderin, a granular pigment formed from the breakdown of hemoglobin composed essentially of iron, or colloidal ferric oxide.

He looked up at Jeffords. "Hemoglobinemia?" he asked.

"Good for you. I'm sure at least half of the obstetricians on staff here wouldn't know what the hell they were looking at. This . . ." Jeffords said slowly, "is basically all that's left of your patient's blood."

"You mean the blood you analyzed . . ." He stopped, speechless.

"Yeah, that's it. Or what's left of it after a few tests."

Jeffords paused and took a sip of Mallory's coffee and made a face. "Disgusting. I don't know why anyone drinks this crap."

He put the styrofoam cup down and slipped a computer readout toward Mallory.

"But the biggest shock was her hematocrit. I just don't know how to account for this. I ran her blood through a hemacytometer and counted her red blood cells. Do you know what her RBC count was?"

He looked at Mallory, as if he actually expected him to answer.

"You realize that four to five million per 100cc is a normal red cell count?" Jeffords asked.

Mallory shook his head. "Of course."

"Well, your patient's is less than 200,000, the lowest red blood cell count that I've ever seen . . . or ever expect to see."

"Jesus," Mallory whistled. "What in hell would cause that?"

Jeffords smiled wanly. "Well," he said slowly. "That's what I've been asking myself for the last hour. And I haven't found any answers."

Helplessly, like a little boy who has been asked an impossible question by the teacher, Jeffords shrugged and raised both of his hands, palms up. "Nothing. I've checked with several colleagues, the best hematologists I know, and none of us has an explanation.

"There is only one clear fact in all this," Jeffords went on. "Whatever is going on, or rather *was* going on in your patient's body, it's either a hemolytic or hematophagous disease. Something utterly destroyed her red blood cells."

The two men stared at each other in silence for a moment. Then Mallory stood up.

"Thanks anyway, Carl. Somehow I didn't think there'd be any easy answers to this one."

Mallory walked away, his hands stuffed in his pockets. Jeffords watched him until his back disappeared through the doorway. Absently he picked up Mallory's cold coffee and took a sip, staring at the empty door. Jeffords was a totally rational man, completely dedicated to science. He didn't have an intuitive bone in his body, but for some inexplicable reason he felt a sudden and overwhelming melancholy, perhaps even a sense of impending doom, and it was directly related to Mallory.

Chapter Three

Mallory had rented a small house on the outskirts of Hanover, three miles north of the Hitchcock Medical Center. He drove the narrow, tree lined river road slowly, his mind still on the mystery of Betty Milner's death, and pulled into his drive just after ten o'clock. The night sky had the quality of soft black satin and was filled with hard and bright stars.

The house was a small, white Cape Cod with an attached two-car garage. It sat on a knoll overlooking the Connecticut River, which at this point was only about one hundred yards wide. The Vermont side of the river, with its softly-rounded, pine-covered mountains was now only a darker shadow against the night sky. An occasional car on the Vermont side, its lights flashing between the dense growth of trees, moved along Route 5 like some giant animal's shining, night-foraging eyes.

The house had been rented to him by a surgeon who practiced in Boston and used to drive the two hours to Hanover for quick mini-vacations several times a year. But the doctor's wife had become seriously ill with liver cancer and was undergoing extensive therapy at Mass General in Boston. Mallory had been given a two-year lease, for it was unlikely that the wife would be traveling again. She had only months to live.

Mallory switched off the engine and stared at the dark house. He had never felt comfortable there. It was big and silent, much like the house he had grown up in. A wry smile crossed his lips. Most people would think of him as fortunate. A sheltered, upper middle-class childhood with a doting mother and a successful local doctor for a father. But "privilege" was a two-edged sword, one side razor sharp with high expectations and the other dull, dull, dull. His mother had been suffocatingly attentive. And if the hard truth were demanded, she was also an emotionally blind, shallow, ever-hungry philistine. And his father, St. Simon of Scarsdale, had been so involved in being the town saint that he'd failed miserably in caring for his own family. If Mallory saw him for more than an hour a month he had felt privileged.

He got out of the car and walked around to the back of the house. He couldn't sleep now and had to clear his head.

The house had two entrances. The front door at the top of a long curving drive off the river road, and the back with a small stone patio and two wide flagstone steps facing the river. A broad lawn sloped gently toward the water, which was about thirty yards from the house. The ground was now dotted with patches of snow lingering from the last big storm.

He walked down and stood at the edge, listening to the wind and other night sounds. The air smelled of mud and wet trees. A heavy mist shrouded the water; it seemed the cold breath of some unseen monster rushing over the surface. He loved the river at night when he could sense rather than see its velvet, fast-flowing waters.

A sudden chill had come into the air and bit into his

exposed skin like tiny teeth. He clutched his jacket against his chest. Often in February, as winter struggled to hold onto its grip, a cold breeze would rush down from the north, cutting between the mountains and through the tops of the pines lining the river. Sometimes in autumn he would see the freshly fallen leaves skipping over the water, blown like gold dust down the dark face of the river. Tonight the sound of the wind whistling and humming through the wet trees was a preternatural musical sound, yet it seemed almost human, much like babies crying in the distance.

Mallory couldn't shake the dark mood that had overwhelmed him after he left Jeffords. He had gone to his office and worked on his computer for a while, filled out his report on Betty Milner's death . . . and stared out the window. He felt totally alone, wrapped in an isolation that seemed not simply the understandable loneliness of a man who had been working too hard, who had sacrificed friendship and affection for the hard discipline of medicine. He knew all these truths about himself. And he had learned to recognize and deal with that kind of loneliness in med school. No, his present isolation was heavier, more pervasive than that. Surrounded by the black forest, and the muted howling of the northeaster swirling around him, Mallory felt more trapped and alone than at any time in his life. And he couldn't figure out why. Yes, he'd lost his first patient. Yes, he felt a failure and inadequate to be a doctor—especially in the saintly mode of his father. Yes, he was lonely, with no one to talk to . . . except maybe Jeff Goldman. But he didn't want to deceive himself . . . it was more than these recognizable echoes of an overly ambitious young man.

He walked along the river with his hands in his pockets, his shoulders slumped forward, head down, watching his feet directly in front of him, seeing little, absorbed in his thoughts.

In a way he felt deserted for the first time by science, by the rational method he had followed his whole adult life. All those years of schooling seemed to come to nothing. Or almost nothing, for his training hadn't prepared him for the medical dilemma he was now confronting.

But one thing was certain, there was nothing he could do about it now . . . except maybe drive himself crazy. He turned and started back, no closer to understanding what had happened to Betty Milner, or what accounted for this black feeling that was eating into his spirit.

Ten minutes later he was in a hot tub, his head back, the bathroom lights off. He had put on a tape in the bedroom and the quiet sounds of a Mozart quintet drifted over him, its complex, subtle harmonies calming him. Oblivious to the tub water cooling, he let the music float through his head, like an echo of evensong heard from cathedral catacombs. Finally at rest, and almost asleep, he was shocked back to reality by the goddamn happy-tune door chimes.

He sat up in the tub and shook his head. "What the hell is this? Will this day never end?"

He glanced at his wristwatch, which he had placed on the chair next to the tub. Eleven-forty. He stepped from the tub, threw on his terrycloth bathrobe, and stalked barefoot across the living room to the front door. He pulled aside the curtains and looked through the window but could see no one, only a dark shape standing on the front porch.

When he opened the door he was stunned to see Lili Shikome standing there, a slight, shy smile on her face. Her expression was a peculiar mixture of melancholy and contentment.

"Dr. Mallory," she said. "Forgive me for interrupting

you so late at night. I didn't call first because I was afraid you wouldn't see me."

Mallory was speechless. He stood there like a tongue-tied schoolboy.

After a moment of uncomfortable silence, Lili spoke. "It's important. May I come in?" The northeaster had done its job and brought an arctic blast of air with it. The temperature must have been well below zero, and her breath crystallized into stray clouds of mist.

"Of course," he stammered, stepping back. He held the door open for her. "Let me take your coat."

She slipped it off her shoulders and handed it to him. He hung it in the hall closet.

Mallory's mind was racing. He couldn't figure out what in the world Lili Shikome could want at almost twelve o'clock at night. She was standing quietly in the middle of the living room as he entered. She was wearing a blue silk oriental dress with a slit at the knee that ran to the lower thigh. It clung to her body, outlining every curve. It was a modest dress that had an immodest impact.

"Sit down, please," Mallory said, snapping on a table lamp.

Lili walked over and sat on the small couch next to the fireplace. Sounds of Mozart floated in from the bedroom.

Mallory took the easy chair opposite her. Still uncomfortable, he smiled. "Well, what can I do for you?"

She stared at him for a moment, amused, as she rubbed her hands together lightly. "Could I first trouble you for a cup of tea? I'm frozen," she said.

"Of course, I'm sorry. I should have offered," he said getting up. "I was just going to make some for myself," he lied, not knowing why. For some peculiar reason he felt like a child when he was around Lili.

Which was ridiculous. Everything was turned around. She was his nurse, and younger than he by a good five or six years. Even though he found her attractive, he had never been shy or uncomfortable around women before. Mallory padded into the kitchen to make tea, acutely conscious of his bare feet, of his nakedness under his bathrobe, and of the fact that Lili was watching him. It occurred to him that she was the first woman who had ever been in his home.

When he returned with the tea, he put the tray on the coffee table and sat next to her on the couch. He started to pour the tea when she gently put her hand on his arm.

"Let me," she said, and took the teapot.

Neither spoke as Lili served the tea and handed Mallory his cup. She did it with a grace of movement that Mallory watched with pleasure. It reminded him of how precise and graceful she was in surgery . . . and why he liked working with her. Beauty and efficiency. A heady combination.

For several minutes they sat in silence, Mallory because he didn't know what to say, and Lili because she seemed to be enjoying the tea. Several times she turned the cup, warming her hands as she did so and drinking delicately from opposite sides. The movement reminded Mallory of Japanese tea ceremonies he had seen.

She put the cup down and sighed. "Ahh, that's better. You know I've been here for almost a month, and I'm still not used to the cold."

She smiled and looked up, her incredible smokey gray-green almond eyes locking with his.

"I'm sure you're wondering why I'm here so late. For most of the evening I've been trying to figure out what to do."

Abruptly she stood and walked over to the fireplace,

35

her back to Mallory, her long lynx body stunning in the clinging silk dress. For a moment he stared, an upsurge of long-repressed feelings rushing through him. She seemed completely unaware of her beauty, her sexuality. It was one of the things that attracted him the most about her. She didn't use her beauty as a weapon.

He put it out of his mind. A hot affair with his nurse was the last thing he needed right now. He had avoided complications like that for almost two years, and this would be the worst time to get involved.

"You see," she said, "I've been going over it in my mind, trying to figure out what happened this evening. I've seen many people die in surgery, but we always knew why."

Her statement was phrased as a question, and she stared directly at him, waiting for an answer.

He shrugged. "I don't know," he said simply. "It's been bugging me all night. I haven't been able to sleep. I've been searching for some sensible answer . . . I even had Hitchock run post-mortem blood cultures."

Mallory felt his stomach and chest tighten again and he sucked in a deep breath. He really didn't want to talk about it anymore. He'd been through it too many times. What he really wanted was a good night's sleep and to forget . . . to put it out of his mind for a few hours.

"What did they find?"

"Her red blood cell count was extremely low, which probably accounts for her coma and heart failure, but we have no idea what caused the loss of red cells."

"I see," Lili said. "That is strange. Any theories?"

He was conscious of Lili still staring at him. Her eyes were bright, the luminous color of graying autumn grass in bright sun.

"No, that's where my brain locks up. I don't have the vaguest idea. And it's no comfort that no one else seems to know what the hell's going on either."

"Have you asked other doctors what they think?"

"Yes, the hematologist at Hitchcock is a friend, and he checked out the blood. He's as confused as I am."

"He's the only one you've talked to. . . . I mean if you discussed this with other specialists you might find something."

"Yeah, I've thought about that. And it's something I'm going to try, but I have to draw up a list of names and either call or write letters asking for them to act as consultants on the case. I don't think I'll get too many responses . . . you know how busy most doctors are, especially those doing research and practicing medicine at the same time."

"What about the National Institute of Health? Wouldn't they have a list of similar cases?"

"I thought about that too, and tonight I checked the NIH medical library from my office computer. Nothing. Not even one similar case."

Lili thought for a moment. She had turned and was facing Mallory. He was having a hard time keeping his eyes off her. Why did she wear that damn dress? he thought. Every line of her body was clear. Even from across the room he could see her full breasts moving with every breath.

She walked back to the couch, still preoccupied with her thoughts, the silk of her dress whispering as it moved. She sat down, crossed her ankles, and turned to Mallory.

"If the NIH library medical files won't help, what about their computer central files? They have far more extensive information. Records going back for years."

Mallory bolted upright on the couch.

"Of course," he said. "That's a great idea . . . but I think they're hard to access. They contain private notes from doctors, research protocols that are secret, patient followups that are sometimes too personal. But I'll call them in the morning and ask for permission."

He turned to Lili and smiled. "Thanks for the idea . . . I was at a dead end and being driven crazy."

"I'm glad I could help. That's the other reason I came by tonight. I was worried. When you left the hospital you looked terrible. Really stricken. I asked around and a nurse told me that it was the first time one of your patients had died."

She reached her hand across the short distance between them and lightly touched his leg, a comforting gesture, just above the knee. But he jumped, startled, as if a charged electric wire had been dug into him. It wasn't his imagination. He felt a powerful point of electric heat, a spark that jolted him, sending a tingling heat up his leg to his groin. He felt himself swell, the familiar warmth concentrating between his legs, hardening muscles he had avoided using for more than a year.

"I remember the first time I lost a patient . . . and the guilt . . . but you did everything you could," she was saying, but Mallory had trouble following the quiet rhythms of her voice.

She had left her hand on his leg as she spoke, with just the tips of her fingers, the silver polish on her long, well-shaped nails shimmering as they rested against the cloth of his bathrobe.

Suddenly he felt his utter nakedness under the robe. He became embarrassed as he hardened and he pulled the robe further over his lap to disguise his condition. *My God, what's happening to me,* he thought. *I haven't felt like this since I was sixteen.*

Lili continued to talk to him softly, her voice seeming to come from a great distance. He wasn't sure what she was saying, so absorbed was he by the sudden surge of feeling she generated. And her eyes . . . those incredible, glowing gray-green eyes, like light from under the sea . . . wouldn't blink, wouldn't turn away, but held him in their warm gaze.

Mallory had once taken mescaline as a student and his senses had gone wild. His fingers had started to tingle and the sensation burned up his arms, into his chest and belly and ran throughout his body, like fire spreading over parchment. He felt the same way now, only the heat rose from his groin not his fingers, radiating through his bowels, burrowing into his bones and filling his head with fantasies.

He hadn't willed it, hadn't even thought about it, but suddenly he found himself next to her, their faces almost touching. Through the haze of their closeness he could see her almond eyes, half-closed, and her lips slightly parted, as if she were breathing lightly through her mouth.

"Put your hand here," she whispered, "see how my heart goes . . ."

She lifted his hand and pressed the flat of his palm against the full flesh of her breast . . . he could feel the heat of her body through the smooth silk of her dress, the erect fullness of her nipple pressing into his hand. Their lips, each grazing the other's, were trembling, warm voices breathing into each other's mouth, a murmuring intimacy, bodies seeking alliances and points of contact . . .

In the past, whenever sensuality had raised its flowering head, Mallory had tried to decapitate it so it would cease to trouble him and not get in the way of his work. He had steeled himself against his senses for such a long time, and now it seemed his whole careful construction was melting.

"I need you," he whispered into her mouth. "I didn't

realize how much . . . how hungry I was . . ."

She stopped him with her tongue.

The rest was like a dream.

He explored heated passageways of flesh, shadowed corners of sensation, that left him shuddering with surprise. The drops of perspiration on her neck, under her arms, beneath her breasts, tasted both sweet and bitter, both acid and mild, like nutmeg and honey. Her breath seemed a composite perfume, the pungent odor of summer heat and the richness of the earth after a heavy rain. Everywhere she touched burned his skin.

She guided him and when he pressed into her, the heat amazed him. Like a living sheath, her sex closed around him, velvety soft yet strong and vibrating. He had never experienced such a sensation.

His hands on her hips, he raised her body toward him. Lifting up onto his knees, he thrust deeper into her. She gasped and her head fell back, the arch of her long neck swan-white, her mouth open.

His body trembled, shaking with desire, unconscious of everything but the need to be satisfied. He seemed surcharged with sex and his senses saturated with life. . . .

She opened further with each touch. Then abruptly, with amazing strength, she reached out and took hold of his hips and pulled him to her like a prey. And somewhere in the dark cells of his mind he wondered whether he had entered her or had been simply absorbed into her warm flesh.

Sometime during the long night of their gentle-violent lovemaking, he heard her voice, whispering, inviting, "Let yourself go, David, trust . . . let yourself go . . ."

Much later Lili looked over at Mallory, his face outlined in the moonlight filtering through the window and smiled at his dreaming, half-awake, half-asleep face. She knew he was lost, sated, his male energies subsiding and pulling him along into restless sleep. Already she understood him so well.

When Mallory awoke she was gone. At first he wasn't sure it hadn't been a dream but the smell of her filled the room . . . in the air, on the sheets, even on his hands. He wondered why she had left so early, without waking him. He jumped out of bed and got his briefcase and pulled out the small red phone book of work numbers. He found Lili's and dialed, waiting impatiently while it rang. There was no answer. Maybe she was still in transit, he thought. Or having breakfast somewhere. He would call later, once his hormones and glands had quieted down. God, he was still overwhelmed with the excitement of being with the woman. She was like fire, pure blue-white flame . . . like an acetylene torch burning a hole in him.

As he dressed memories of the night before flooded back. He wondered what she remembered most about their time together. He recalled her incredible sensuality. He had starved himself for so long that it was like a spring rain on parched earth. He could drown in it and still yearn for more.

Everything about Lili was sensual. She was a sensual angel. Not a woman at all, an angel. Obedient to her impulses, her capacity for sensualism, her gift of her self, her complete self.

Amazing, he thought. He could swear that there was not a corner, not a millimeter of herself that she did not offer to him. She seemed blind to the dangers of giving too much, unaware of the pain and disappointment of offering herself completely. It was not just the giving of her body, of her open sexuality, but her feelings were unencumbered and were unhesitatingly involved. They seemed to him a fire out of control within her, and the dryness of his own life spontaneously flamed up when he came near her, a shocking sympathetic combustion that he had not realized he was capable of.

Chapter Four

Mallory was bursting with energy, and he began organizing his research into the mystery of Betty Milner's death. He called the NIH and discovered that he would need to file a request and detailed protocol in order to use their central computer records. He called several doctors and, as he expected, they were intrigued by the low red blood count but were too busy to do anything more than review his research. By the end of the day he was still in the dark . . . still not sure what to do next. The NIH official request would simply take too long.

At the hospital he discovered that this was Lili's day off. He called her for dinner but there was no answer, so he went home to left-overs and tried her number several more times. Still no answer.

As he sat debating his next move he got an idea. It was dangerous . . . maybe even foolish, but it was the only opening left him.

He dialed Jeff Goldman's number. It rang eight times, and he almost hung up when Goldman answered.

"Jeff," Mallory said immediately. "I need your help."

"Sure, name it." Mallory could hear the sound of chewing. He must have interrupted him in a late snack.

"I can't seem to get that young woman out of my mind," he said after a moment.

"That's normal. I get that way sometimes myself," Goldman said lightly.

"No, listen. I'm serious. We lost a patient yesterday, and her face has burned a hole in my brain. I can't get her out of my mind."

Quietly, Goldman said, "I understand. I've been thinking about it a lot, too. What can I do for you?"

"Well, it's delicate and I don't want to talk about it on the phone. Can we meet somewhere?"

"Sure, I'm already for bed though. You want to pop over here?"

"Be there in ten minutes," Mallory said.

Mallory hung up the phone and grabbed his jacket on the way out. He slammed the door behind him, not bothering to lock it.

It was a cold winter night with the kind of crisp, clear New England black sky that never ceased to overwhelm him. He remembered as a child sneaking out of the house when he was supposed to be sleeping, clutching his long, black aluminum 10X power tripod telescope in one hand, a flashlight in the other. He would sprawl on the grass and solemnly run the telescope over the sky for hours gazing in amazement at the massive numbers of glittering stars. The thought that other beings lived on some of those lights was overwhelming to his young mind, yet undeniably logical. He smiled at the memory. Hell, the idea was still overwhelming to his adult mind. The sky had been his first great passion and unlike other eight year old kids, who wanted to be cops or astronauts, he wanted to be an astronomer. How things change.

Tonight, the moon was so silverbright he almost

didn't need headlights to drive; but still, if you paused to look, even with the full moonlight, the sky was an awesome empyreal vault of a billion stars.

He drove quickly through Hanover, turned west and crossed the bridge over the Connecticut River into Vermont. Another mile and he entered Norwich, the kind of small Vermont town pictured on calendars and postcards. He turned right in the center of town onto Route 5 north and drove past the town meeting hall and the white, steepled Congregational church.

Goldman lived in a three-room apartment on the second floor of a big white farmhouse just off Route 5 on the outskirts of Norwich. Goldman's apartment had originally been a part of the home of a local doctor but had changed hands several times since then. The house was now owned by a couple in their seventies who rented the upstairs apartment to supplement their incomes.

Mallory drove up the sloping driveway to the house and parked behind Goldman's car. His apartment had a separate entrance, up a short flight of rickety stairs that led to a small porch and his door. Goldman was still eating. He opened the door with a cup of herbal tea in one hand and a large rice cracker in his mouth. Mallory could smell the perfume of the tea, like a room full of dried wild flowers.

"Like some tea?" Goldman asked, chewing the rice cracker. He was wearing a pair of pale green pajamas and a white oriental bathrobe. His feet were bare. Mallory noticed his big toes angled sharply toward the smaller ones, and the calcium growth on the side of his feet. Bunions. He would need surgery before he was forty.

"No, thanks," Mallory said. "My stomach's a mess right now. I seem to have lost my appetite."

"Chamomile. It's great for stomach distress," Goldman said, taking a seat at the small kitchen table next to the picture window.

"No, I couldn't. Maybe later," Mallory said. He took the seat opposite Goldman. For a moment there was silence as Goldman sipped his tea and crunched on the cracker. He regarded Mallory quietly, his Woody Allen face pensive.

Mallory stared out the window. Inside, with the apartment lights on, he couldn't see any stars. Nothing but blackness.

Without moving, Mallory quietly said, "You're into computers and I need help."

"What kind of help?"

Mallory turned slowly to Goldman.

"To break into the NIH computer central file."

Stunned, Goldman's eyes widened. Then he smiled. "You mean use the NIH medical library, like all the doctors at Hitchcock do every day on their office computers?"

"No, I've already reviewed the NIH general library tapes from my computer. You know that the NIH library files are standard stuff. Literature reviews, case histories, disease classifications. Not what I need. I have to get into the main computer files, and possibly even the private personnel files listing physicians' notes on case histories."

"My God, Mallory. Do you know what you're asking? We could both lose our asses over something like that. Goodbye medical career. Hello prison."

"I know. If we're caught. But I don't think we will be."

"Oh, that assurance makes me feel a lot better."

Both men were silent for another long moment.

"Listen," Goldman said, "you don't have to break into NIH. It's a public facility, created for the use of the medical profession. Why not simply apply for whatever information you need?"

"And wait two months or two years while the red tape tangles me up. No thanks. I want answers now."

"What answers are you looking for?" Goldman asked. "Is it important enough to lose your license or go to jail?"

"For me it is, yes. But I don't expect you to take that kind of gamble. Listen, we can't use our office computers because we reveal our user numbers and work terminal when we log on. That way we can be traced. And besides, our user numbers wouldn't give us clearance into the central files. So I figure if we use other Hitchcock terminals or even go into the Baker Library stacks at Dartmouth and use their terminals, we can log onto the Kiewit Network, and from there get into NIH. We could get access after hours, when everything's closed down."

"Oh, great, then we can get arrested for breaking and entering."

"No, hold on. I can get clearance to use the computer at night on the excuse that I'm too busy during normal hours. We both know how user numbers work in the Kiewit Network. Because we work at Hitchcock and have our own user numbers we can get into the system easily. But since Kiewit will keep tabs on our numbers we'll have to search until we find someone else's so we can't be traced. The only problem will be getting into the NIH program."

"Right, and also getting caught..."

"Look, I'll just say I'd like some computer time to research an idea I have. Once we're in, Kiewit won't know what we're doing."

"Okay, so we may not get arrested for burglary, but unauthorized hacking into a federal computer file like the National Institute of Health's is heavy stuff."

"I understand how you feel. And I'll take the heat.

You just get me into the NIH files and then you can take off . . . and if I'm caught, I'll say I did it all by myself."

"God," Goldman blurted out, "my mother told me never to trust goyim doctors . . . and look what it's got me into."

"Will you do it?"

Goldman shook his head slowly back and forth. "Somehow I just can't see myself in prison clothes, but all right."

"Fantastic," Mallory said, grinning. "I knew I could count on you."

"Yeah, well if I'm putting my ass on the line for you, don't you think I deserve to know what's going on?"

Mallory stared at Goldman, his face suddenly serious.

"Yes, I guess you do," he said. Mallory stood up and walked around the table and stood at the window, his hands sunk into his pockets. He stared out into the darkness.

"I don't have any of the answers yet, Jeff. But something really peculiar, out of the ordinary, happened to that young woman."

"Yeah, she died," Goldman said. "But on second thought that's not too out of the ordinary."

"Will you shut up and listen. I mean something really weird happened to her, something no one has ever heard of before."

Mallory sat down across from Goldman again.

"Her hematocrit was under two hundred thousand. And no one . . . I mean no one I've talked with can make any sense out of it."

Mallory stared at his hands, which were clasped on the table before him. "She shouldn't have died, Jeff."

"What do you mean . . . shouldn't?" Goldman said, suddenly irritated.

He had struggled all night with his own demons, wondering what else he could have done to help the woman. Did he miss seeing some signs indicating what was coming? Could he have somehow prevented her from going into coma? Should he have been aware sooner that the baby was turning breech? He had just succeeded in quieting his own conscience and convincing himself that he had done everything he could, and he wasn't too happy about Mallory raising the same goddamn questions all over again.

"How the hell do you know should and shouldn't?" he said. "Are you suddenly omniscient?" Goldman stopped, embarrassed. "My God, I sound like my mother."

Mallory smiled and reached over and touched Goldman's arm. "Don't feel too bad, Jeff. She sounds like a wise woman. What I meant is that there was no clear medical reason for that death. No original medical cause."

"No original cause? What are you talking about? You sound like Dr. God. She had a cardiac arrest. Heart failure. A million people around the world die of it every year."

"But what caused it? Most cardiac arrests, or heart attacks, we can attribute to any number of specific antecedents."

Mallory's face had flushed; he was clearly miserable.

"High blood pressure, coma, placenta abruptio, are all peripheral. There's only one really odd medical fact here that stands out from all the others. Her incredibly low red blood count. That's what I want to plug into the NIH computer for . . . to find out if any other women in their records are listed as dying during childbirth with that unbelievable RBC."

"Okay, I see your point," Goldman said. "Did you check for an excessive amount of hemolysin?" he offered. "It causes the dissolution of red blood cells."

"Of course, it was one of the first things I asked the hematologist to look for. But it was negligible. In fact, there were no unexpected chemical substances in the blood at all. Nothing to explain such a dramatic loss of red blood cells."

"What about hemolytic anemia?" Goldman asked.

"No, that's anemia caused by excessive destruction of red blood cells due to chemical poisoning, infection or sickle cell. She had none of those factors. Listen, Jeff, I've gone over it in my mind a hundred times. I've asked myself . . . and others . . . every conceivable question. And I come up empty every time. Look, I've gone through the general subject files of the Hitchcock computer records and the NIH library computer and found nothing helpful. The NIH central computer files seem the best bet. They have millions of cases in their files . . . and somewhere we should be able to find an answer."

"Have you considered that there may not be an answer?" Goldman asked. "At least no answer that will satisfy you?"

"That's possible," Mallory said. "But not likely. Medicine functions according to natural law, and there's always an answer. Somewhere."

Chapter Five

The computer room at Hitchcock was a long, rectangular, high-vaulted space with no windows, containing two rows of four desks. From the shadowed, sharply-angled light hanging above the supervisor's desk in the center of the room, each desk looked like a heavy pine box layered with years of thick blackened varnish.

Mallory was mildly amused, for he had expected typical computer-room type desk furnishings; all shining metal and clear plastic, computer generated art on the walls. Or at the very least, aluminum desks painted pale grey with chrome-plated legs cushioned by equally grey rubber stoppers on each foot. Instead, this room had all the charm of the haphazard, of an office thrown together quickly to take advantage of some giant warehouse sale of office fixtures. No doubt all bought at bargain rates.

But the equipment made Goldman whistle. All first rate, brand new IBM hard disc computers, each with the latest 386 micro-processing chip. "Massive memories and blinding speed," is the way Goldman put it.

Lili, who had insisted on coming along *(after all, it was my idea, she had said)* was also impressed, although she was, like Mallory, another computer illiterate.

They decided against turning on all the lights. No point in drawing attention to the fact that they were working here so late. They didn't want to be interrupted and then have to abort and start all over again.

"Might as well use the supervisor's machine," Goldman said, walking between the desks toward the center of the room. Lili and Mallory followed quietly. This was Jeff's expertise.

Goldman sat down, laced his fingers in front of him, palms out, and cracked his knuckles. He grinned up at them and snapped the machine on, waited for the program to run through its check sequence and come on screen.

Within a few minutes he was into the Kiewit Network. "And this is where the fun starts," Goldman said, glancing over his shoulder at Lili and Mallory, who had pulled up two chairs and were watching him closely. "Now we start searching for the NIH codes. It may take a while so just relax. And stop breathing over my shoulder."

For over an hour he worked the keyboard like a concert pianist, punching in every conceivable combination of codes and passwords with no results. Occasionally he would utter a breathless curse.

Lili and Mallory became bored with watching the long lists of words and numbers scrolling down the screen. At first they talked in low voices, then they wandered around the room, nosing into the desks, reading several magazines *(PC, Desk-Top Publishing,* and *Penthouse)* they had found in the toilet. Finally, Mallory had stretched out his legs, crossed his hands on his stomach, put his head back and closed his eyes.

He had just begun to doze off when a loud grunt from Goldman jolted him awake. He glanced over at the small man, who was now bent over the computer, his nose about six inches from the screen. His thick, wire-rimmed glasses reflected the monitor's blue-green light. Mallory grinned. It seemed as if Jeff had two mini-computer screens where his eyes should have been. With a slight sheen of sweat covering his green skin he looked like Woody Allen in make-up playing an android.

Mallory closed his eyes again, listening to the muted rattle of Jeff's fingers punching the keys when suddenly there was absolute silence. He had stopped typing.

"Ahh," Goldman sighed, his voice hoarse. "And now I see with eye serene, the very pulse of the machine."

He touched another key and sat back. He glanced over at Mallory and Lili, a big grin on his face.

"Wordsworth," he said smirking. "His words, but my brain. Mallory, my man, we're in."

"Fantastic," Mallory said, bolting up from the chair. He leaned over Goldman's shoulder and peered at the monitor.

A dotted line ran across the center of the screen, the cursor blinking brightly in the upper left hand corner.

"Okay," Mallory said. "What's next? Do we just start asking questions?"

"That's it, my man. It's a very simple set-up. Runs like an index construction. Type in your subject and you'll get a readout that says either 'we ain't got no such animal,' or it'll pop up your subject heading, along with subject subheads, and wait for further instructions."

"Okay, you can take off, Jeff. And thanks for all your help. I really appreciate it."

"Wait a minute," Goldman said. He spun in his chair and looked directly at Mallory. "You can't get rid of me that quickly." He grinned broadly and patted the computer. "I've developed a personal relationship with Martha, here. And even though we argue a bit, I've grown fond of her. Besides, I'd like to hang around and see what comes of all this."

Mallory thought for a moment. "And what about your license? And the other things we talked about?"

"We have permission to use this computer, right? And there's no way anyone can find out what we're doing unless they come in here and look at the monitor over my shoulder. And I have a fast finger for the cancel switch."

He stretched his small, knotty hands above his head, fingers interlocked, and cracked his knuckles again. "Shall I get started?" he asked.

"Sure," Mallory said, smiling at him, "why not?"

"Okay, first I'll punch in subject, 'Childbirth,' then 'Death,' and then play around with 'contributing complications' for awhile."

Goldman's fingers began typing rapidly, his concentration intense.

He made several bad guesses, and the computer quietly told him he was asking the wrong questions. Finally, he succeeded in getting a list of childbirth deaths with complications of anemia. The screen was inundated with names and dates, scrolling lists of childbirth deaths due to liver, kidney and heart and other blood complications. When he pressed the computer for deaths with low red-blood count anomalies, he hit paydirt.

A list of ten names jumped onto the screen. Both Mallory and Goldman were surprised. They had expected maybe one or two. But ten? Five patients were listed as death caused by kidney or heart-failure with hemolytic complications and three by hemorrhage. Two were listed with "cause of death unknown," but all had an abnormally low red blood cell count below seven percent.

The first thing that struck Mallory was that while the deaths had taken place all across the country, they had occurred like clockwork—at the same period every year—the early part of February. There was only one break in the pattern: in 1988, no death was listed. Goldman had silently placed the tip of his finger against the monitor, pointing to the missing year. Every other year since 1978 a woman had died with a red blood cell count three hundred thousand or lower. Including Betty Milner's, that meant there had been eleven deaths with this mysterious childbirth disease over the last twelve years, all taking place in the month of February.

Mallory and Lili peered over Goldman's shoulder at the monitor screen. They all realized that the statistical probability of this happening was astronomical... almost out of the question.

"God, this is making less sense the more we learn," Mallory said under his breath. "No disease strikes all across the country at the same time every year."

"Some do," Goldman said. "Reyes syndrome hits kids mostly during the months January through March."

"No, Reyes also occurs at other times. And not like this. Not with this kind of clockwork regularity."

Mallory studied the screen for several moments and noticed that the attending physicians' medical notes were in an appendix. He pointed to the appendix listing. "Can you get me a list of all the attending physicians? And punch up their notes for me?"

"No problem," Goldman said, and pressed the control key and the f5 function key. The physicians' names, degrees, and hospitals in which they had worked flashed onto the blue-green monitor screen.

Lili leaned forward and ran her finger down the list of names. The date for each doctor's last employment listing coincided with the dates of the childbirth deaths. It seemed as if the attending obstetricians all left their jobs the same year that their patients died.

"You noticed this?" she asked, pointing to the dates.

"Yeah," Mallory said. "Jeff, see if you can find where any of these doctors are working now. And get me a list of present home addresses."

The next scroll down the monitor took their breaths away. They stared, open-mouthed, at the screen.

After each name except one the word "DECEASED" was etched in bold letters. "My God, that's impossible," Goldman breathed. "That is simply beyond belief."

He looked over at Mallory and Lili. "It's not possible. I don't know what the chances are of this happening, but you couldn't calculate the probabilities of all those doctors dying with such regularity."

"And look at the dates," Lili said. "They all died almost exactly one year following their patients' deaths—all in the month of February! Every one of them."

The dates next to "Deceased" ran consistently down the column, just like the deaths of the birthing women ... 1978 through 1986.

"What happened to the doctors in '87 and '88?" Goldman asked, shaking his head.

"There doesn't seem to be any record of a patient's or doctor's death in '88," Mallory said. "There's a patient's death in '87, but no mention of the doctor. Maybe the obstetrician who delivered in '87 is still alive? Can you get us details on the '87 doctor, Jeff?"

Goldman punched a few keys and a name flashed on the monitor.

"Dr. Wilhelm Bowker, Box 42, Crystal Lane, Paydanarum, Massachusetts."

The medical fact sheet on Bowker said he had retired in 1987 from Bellevue Hospital in New York City, where he was on the obstetrics staff, one month after the death of his patient, Cheryl Walker. He had moved to Massachusetts and no longer practiced medicine.

"Check his medical notes in the appendix, Jeff."

The notes covered three pages, none of which were helpful.

"Standard medical comments," Mallory said, turning away from the screen and running his hand through his long, unruly hair. "Nothing that explains what happened to those women."

"Or the doctors," Goldman muttered quietly, biting his already short, abused thumbnail.

Mallory paced the room for several minutes, preoccupied with his thoughts. Nothing made any sense. All those women dying of apparently similar causes ... at the same time each year, with no real explanation of why. But add to that the fact that every doctor except one who treated the women also died within a year ...

Mallory shook his head. He was getting a splitting headache and he felt sick to his stomach. When he turned back to Goldman and Lili he stopped dead in his tracks.

It was an eerie scene. They were both staring at him, bathed in the chlorophyll glow from the computer screen. Lili was leaning against the computer, the fingers of one hand pressed against the base of her throat. Goldman had twisted around in his chair, his arm curled over the backrest, his thick glasses colored green by the computer light. They looked like cadavers, their computer-tinted skin the color of tree fungus. Both of their expressions were solemn, as if they were examining a terminally ill patient.

"What is it?" he said, his voice echoing in the empty room.

Goldman cleared his throat, a small, tight coughing sound. "It's just ..."

He turned and glanced at the screen. "It's just ...

the fact that all the doctors have died so quickly after their patients, and with such regularity."

Goldman looked embarrassed for a second, as if he'd been caught cheating on a test. "It sort of flashed on me ... I guess I hallucinated your name on the list ... for the year 1989."

He turned quickly back to the computer, his face flushed. "Stupid of me, I know."

For the first time it dawned on him. Of course, his name, and Betty Milner's, would be on the same computer list next year ... or as soon as Hitchcock catalogued and transferred this year's records to Washington. A single icy finger seemed to run joyfully up his back. Would he be listed *dead or alive?*

It was a stupid, superstitious question. He didn't believe in such prophetic nonsense. A ridiculous question, yet it pushed its way into the front of his consciousness. *Dead or alive?*

"Bullshit," he blurted out, and walked back toward Goldman and Lili. "Coincidence, nothing but coincidence. A great string of weird facts. What do you want me to believe, that I'm next?"

Even as the words came out Mallory had the awful sensation, an almost biblical, prophetic feeling that *yes,* he was next. It washed over him, from head to foot, a waterfall of freezing facts suddenly cascading down on him. Panic overwhelmed him. He felt like a child being accused of some terrible misdeed of which he was innocent.

"Well?" he said, his voice too loud and strident, an octave higher than normal.

Neither of them answered. Goldman turned away and studied the screen as if seeing it for the first time. Lili, her eyes full of concern, was still watching Mallory.

She put her hand gently on his arm. "No, I don't

believe that. It's as you say, coincidence."

Mallory smiled thinly at her. "Thanks, but it doesn't help much. I still feel like someone's just started to carve my tombstone."

An irrational tremor of fear continued to vibrate somewhere deep within him. He was not sure which way to move next. *What am I supposed to do now? There had to be "reason" in all this. Medicine didn't work according to coincidence.* He leaned over the large desk and looked down at his hands spread out before him. He could see the large blue arteries pulsing under the skin. In a peculiar way it depressed him, a tangible sign of his vulnerability. Only a microscopically thin barrier of cells between life and death. Cut or puncture the thin membrane protecting his body's internal functions, and it would drain of life like a balloon full of water stuck with a needle. A thin knife, even a piece of stiff wire in the right spot, killed the vulnerable human body as surely as being torn apart.

He felt like a lost and frightened child. It was the same feeling he had had last night standing by the river. His brain seemed stunned, strangely dull and sluggish, as if clogged by the dark, moving mists of his fear. It recalled the time his uncle took him hunting, and he had killed a deer. Like then, he felt lost and alone in an alien, mysterious world.

He must have been no more than eleven or twelve. His uncle, a tall, rangy, handsome young man with a thick head of black hair and whose eyebrows grew together over deep set eyes, had cajoled his mother into letting him go, arguing that it was time for him to see life as it really was. It was time to "toughen up the kid," his uncle had said.

They left, along with two of his uncle's friends, as the fog-shrouded earth came awake. Mallory still recalled walking through the silent forest, the pungent earth steaming with mist. And how excited he became every time they caught sight of the beautiful, nervous animals . . . even if it was across a far meadow—too far for a good shot, his uncle had whispered. They had tracked several deer all morning, and at one point he could actually smell the animals . . . a deep, rich, acid odor, like a mixture of wet fertile earth and urine.

Eventually they hid in a clump of fir trees upwind of a small pond. And after an hour of waiting the first rustling came. A minute later a brown doe, its white fluffy tail bobbing nervously, gingerly stepped from out of the stand of white birches surrounding the pond. His uncle squeezed Mallory's arm, nodded his head toward the deer and pressed the rifle into his hands. Trembling, Mallory tried to remember everything his uncle had told him about sighting, holding his breath and gently squeezing the trigger. He did everything he had been told and as the deer bent its head and put its muzzle into the water, he gently pulled the trigger.

The explosion was deafening, and the rifle's recoil slammed Mallory back into the base of a fir tree. The doe's head jerked up, her large round eyes staring right at him, as if she were ready to scold the young boy who had pulled the trigger. And for a moment Mallory thought he had missed. But her eyes had gone wide with shock and then suddenly she cried, a thin, wavering cry that was eerily human. Her mouth opened, coughing, and she sank to her knees. Mallory saw the scarlet stream rush out, painting her muzzle and pale brown chest. The doe rolled over on her side, legs jerking, still trying to raise its head. The animal's tongue hung loosely from the open, gasping mouth that now bubbled with blood and saliva. It moaned several times, its chest and stomach heaving, coughed wetly, and finally lay still.

Mallory was silent the whole trip home. He avoided

looking at the deer. Its feet were tied criss-cross, and it hung upside down from a pole carried on the shoulders of his uncle's two friends. He remembered clearly how he had hated his uncle for making him do it. And no matter what his uncle said, no matter how he complimented him on his great shot through the lungs, Mallory didn't say a word.

That night, as his uncle and his two friends sat in the kitchen drinking beer, Mallory hid in his room, still sick to his stomach, still trying to ignore the bloody memories. For some reason it was the doe's coughing that bothered him the most. It seemed so . . . human. For hours he could hear the men's voices laughing, and the retelling of the kill over and over again. When his uncle came upstairs to get him, he refused to leave his room. Red-faced and angry, his uncle picked him up and carried him down to the kitchen. The deer's head had been cut off and was sitting upright on newspapers in the sink, a pool of thick blackened blood encircled the severed neck. Its swollen tongue still hung out. His uncle carried him to the sink and held him a few inches from the head, forcing him to look at it. The acrid smell of blood permeated the kitchen, and Mallory shook his head violently back and forth, trying to avoid the awful stench.

He started to cry in great convulsive sobs, barely able to catch his breath, but it did no good. His uncle held him in front of the head for a good three or four minutes, shaking him, yelling at him to grow up. It was then that he also began to hate his father, who was never home, never there when Mallory needed him. Even his mother was out for the night, playing cards with her girlfriends. And the maid, poor shy Agnes, tried to make him stop, but she was no match for his furious uncle.

Finally, disgusted and mumbling how ashamed he

was, his uncle had put him down. The two other men were watching, laughing. Mallory, standing on trembling legs, had then suddenly vomited, with no warning, no contraction of stomach muscles that he was aware of, just an abrupt, solid spew of partially digested food and bilious liquid launched out of his mouth in a vaulting stream. It splattered the kitchen floor and a corner of the table, ran down the cabinets, and covered the seat and legs of one of the kitchen's wicker chairs.

That was the only time Mallory had ever killed anything. And his uncle never took him hunting again. In fact, he rarely spoke to his uncle after that night . . . but then, his uncle really didn't want to talk to the "little coward" anyway. He had rarely felt that helpless and alone again. Until tonight.

"I guess there's only one way to go," Lili said, almost as if she were aware of his indecision and had read his mind. "You have to talk to that doctor . . . what was his name, Bowker?"

"Yeah," Goldman said. "Maybe he'll know something not in his notes."

Mallory couldn't shake the feeling of doom that had come over him. The list of doctors, and the word "deceased" after their names, were cut deep into his consciousness. The *chip-chip-chip* of the mason's hammer chiseling his tombstone seemed to strike with the same pulse as his heartbeat.

"Yeah," he said, repeating Goldman. "Maybe he'll tell us something not in his notes."

Chapter Six

After Mallory and Lili had dropped him off at home, Jeff was still shaken. He couldn't forget the frightened, stricken look on Mallory's face when that list of doctors . . . and their deaths . . . lit up the screen. On the ride back Lili had been wonderful . . . sweet, understanding, comforting. But Mallory had withdrawn. He was sullen and uncommunicative. He was really scared . . . but wouldn't admit it. And there was nothing Jeff could do about it. Nothing he or Lili said seemed to have any effect.

And ironically, Mallory was right. It was all so mysterious, and such a senseless, wasteful death. Maybe something was missing from her file, some medical fact that might help them understand what had happened? Perhaps some physical problem she didn't think important and hadn't told them about?

Well, it's too late now. She couldn't review her medical file for them. And they had gone over Bardfield's file on Betty Milner until they were cross-eyed and had found nothing helpful. *Wait a minute.* Jeff slapped his forehead, almost spilling his mint tea. *Jerks, dumb jerks, that's what they all were. Maybe it isn't too late. There still was Frank Milner. Who should know about Betty Milner's physical condition, and know all the details of her medical history, if not her husband? And he could at least give them the family doctor's name, which Bardfield didn't have.*

The idea was a revelation for him. Mallory was always talking about gathering all the medical facts you could and then knowing how to ask the right questions. Well, here they had a living encyclopedia on Betty Milner's health . . . and they hadn't even bothered to talk to him yet.

"Crazy," he muttered, "crazy and stupid."

Jeff grabbed a telephone book and fanned through the pages. He found Milner's address and number immediately. He dialed the number and waited impatiently, nibbling at his fingernails.

After the tenth ring he replaced the receiver, already decided on what he would do. It was a foolish gamble, but he had nothing to lose. He checked his watch. A little after nine. And there had been no answer. Maybe just out shopping or visiting friends, or some such thing. He could try again in a little while or drive out there. This did seem something that should be handled face to face.

A few doubts crept in as Jeff drove out of Norwich and turned north on Route 5 toward Orford and the Milners'. Perhaps he should call Mallory and explain what he wanted to do? But Mallory might not want to disturb the man so soon after his wife's death. Sometimes he was overly sensitive about his patients . . . and their families. No, better talk to Milner first. If he failed, no problem. If Milner had anything interesting to say, he could go to Mallory with a *fait accompli*. Bring him a few medical tidbits that he could chew on. If Mallory had a few leads to follow it would at least keep his mind off the woman's death.

Goldman hummed a folk song he had learned at

64

summer camp when he was a kid as he drove north along the river.

Orford was on the other side of the river from Norwich, about ten or fifteen miles north of Hanover. A small, rusted, steel-girder bridge painted an olive green arched over the considerably narrowed Connecticut River at Orford, and Jeff turned east off Route 5 and crossed into New Hampshire.

Jeff drove south through the small wealthy town, past the white Orford Parish Congregational Church, the small post office and the village common with its gleaming black cannon and pyramid of cannon balls crouched in the middle of the dark lawn like a metal monster. Jeff had never really enjoyed Orford; it was too manicured and regulated. Almost like one of those perfect little Swiss villages where every fence, house, and roadway was constructed according to local mandate. The Orford city leaders would never survive a week in Brooklyn. They'd have a nervous breakdown walking past the graffiti and through the litter on only one block.

It wasn't hard to find the house; a giant silver mailbox shaped like a miniature of the house at the end of the drive glittered in his headlights. Red phosphorescent numbers flashed brightly... *Box 417*. It was a large three-story place; the top floor had a single dormer at the center of the building. Downstairs was dark but three windows were alight upstairs.

"An expensive house," Jeff thought. "Frank Milner must do all right in his travels."

The drive curved in a half loop, peaking at a two-columned front porch. Jeff parked near the front porch, and hesitated before turning off the engine. For some reason he felt uncomfortable. It wasn't just his doubts about doing the right thing. When he turned off the engine the silence settled over him like a living

thing, and even sitting in the car he suddenly felt foolish
... and nervous. A childish fear. Something he always
felt when everything suddenly became silent and dark.

He laughed quietly. He was a city kid. Raised in
Brooklyn, in a big family. There never was any peace in
his house, and he was comfortable with chaos all
around him. That's why he liked working in emergency
or trauma centers. But he had always felt uneasy and
nervous in the country. When he had first arrived at
Dartmouth Medical School as a freshman, he had
taken a room with a family who lived out in the sticks
near Lyme. The first night, with the wind beating the
branches of a big elm outside his window, and the
house creaking like Bela Lugosi was coming up the
stairs, he had lain awake until dawn, the blankets
drawn up to his chin. Only with the first light did he feel
comfortable enough to fall asleep. He knew from the
Dracula movies that Lugosi would have taken to his
coffin by first light. And strangely, the house had
stopped creaking as the sun rose. He laughed again and
got out of the car. It had become bitter cold, and he
pulled the collar of his coat up.

Not surprisingly, the doorbell evoked a loud musical
chime that seemed to go on forever. He stamped his
feet and rubbed his hands as he waited; the temperature
was probably close to zero. His breath was a stream of
icy mist, and even the metal rims on his glasses felt like
ice on his skin.

He was shocked when the door suddenly opened. He
had expected the porch light to come on, or at least a
downstairs light. But there was no sound, no light, no
preparation. The door snapped open and a tall,
middle-aged woman, her matronly face set, an impatient
expression etched with acid on dark features, dominated the entrance. She looked like a woman who had
stepped out of one of those yellowed, tinted photo-

graphs from another age, a stern European spinster aunt who visited your home once a year to put things right. Even her graying hair was tied in a tight bun at the back of her head.

"Yes," she said.

"I'm sorry to disturb you unannounced like this," Jeff said. "But it's very important. Is Mr. Milner in?"

"What do you want?"

The woman's rudeness was undisguised. But Goldman was practiced at handling irascible older women. He smiled and said, "I'm Dr. Goldman, one of the physicians that attended Mrs. Milner at Hitchcock Memorial Hospital. It's important that I speak to Mr. Milner."

"At this hour?" she asked. "Can't it wait until the morning?"

"No, I'm afraid not," Jeff said quietly. He wasn't going to explain any more than he had to, and he wasn't going to lose his temper and fall into his usual habit of being a smart-mouth. That would get him nowhere with this sour old bag. He had dealt with dozens like her in Brooklyn. She had cousins in every deli, restaurant, and department store in Brooklyn.

She stared at him for a moment with her shiny, pebble-eyes and then said, "You were the doctor that was with Mrs. Milner when she delivered the baby?"

"Yes, or at least one of the doctors."

"I see," she said, her voice softening slightly. "Come in."

She turned on her heel and disappeared into the dark interior of the house. Jeff followed her. He could see a faint light at the top of the staircase, which ran along the wall to the right of the entrance hall. A light switched on in a room to his left. When he entered the woman was standing in the middle of the room, her hands clasped in front of her, watching him.

"Wait here," she said, the edge of irritation still coloring her voice. "I'll see if Mr. Milner can see you."

She left on surprisingly light feet, whispering across the wooden floor in fur-lined slippers.

Jeff looked around. It was a library, but most of the shelves were taken up by dozens of miscellaneous *objet d'art* and expensively bound sets of books . . . *The Complete Works of Thackeray, Emerson,* and classical Greek writings like *Anabasis, The March Up Country,* and *The Peloponnesian War* . . . that Jeff was sure had never been opened. The room was large and square, with high ceilings and expensive furnishings. Yes, indeed, Jeff thought as he wandered around the room, Frank Milner does real well. But he didn't have time to come with his pregnant wife to the hospital. Jeff already didn't like the man.

Voices wafted down from upstairs, and Jeff moved over to the doorway and listened. He couldn't make out what was being said, but the tone was abrupt and sharp. Obviously, he wasn't being well received.

Then it dawned on him. The male voice was subdued, quiet, almost pleading, while the female voice, which Jeff recognized as the maid's, was sharp and imperious.

He smiled. The old bitch had obviously cowed Milner. The thought of an aggressive, nouveau riche businessman being cowed by a maid appealed to him. There was a kind of justice, a social symmetry to it. But maybe she wasn't the maid or housekeeper? Perhaps she really was a relative come to take care of a womanless house and baby?

Jeff wandered into the hallway and the voices became more distinct, yet he still couldn't understand what was being said.

With the exception of the library, and the reflected light from the top of the stairs, the house was still dark.

A faint light seeped out from under the door at the end of the entrance hall below the staircase. Jeff walked over, listened for a moment and gently tapped on the door with his knuckles. There was no answer, no sound at all, and he quietly turned the knob and pushed. It was unlocked.

The soft light, which cast dim violet shadows on everything, came from a nightlight stuck in a baseboard wall outlet.

There was something peculiar about the room that Jeff couldn't quite identify. It had a dark "feeling," as if something vital was missing. His first impression was "sanctuary" . . . like the rabbi's study in the back of the synagogue that he had wandered into one night while his parents talked with the Reb. It was a spooky room, full of dust and mysteries, the power of God's word, and books containing the secret teachings on the meaning of the universe. That room, like this one, reminded him of fearful rabbis who created Dybbuks, of medieval sorcerers who conjured spirits, and of possessed magi who, like Captain Ahab, received omens from "the vasty deep."

The room was cool, as if a window were slightly open. But as his eyes adjusted to the poor light, he saw that it was smaller than the library and that the two windows on the opposite side of the room were closed. And then he saw the toys, row upon row of them placed neatly along the walls. A doll's house, with a Raggedy Ann leaning lopsided against it, was pressed against the right-hand wall. A wooden rocking horse stood quietly awaiting a rider in the middle of the room. Jeff walked over to it and ran his hand over the rippled mane. It was expensive and hand-carved. Every detail exquisitely rendered. Mallory's kid—he had taken to calling the Milner baby "Mallory's Kid"—was one lucky little boy. It looked like he'd have every toy known to man by the time he could walk.

A poster of St. Exupery's "Little Prince," with stars cascading around him, was pinned to the wall over the doll's house.

A child's room. He was puzzled by the contrast between his weird feelings about the place and its obvious intention of comforting and nurturing a baby. Betty Milner had worked hard to prepare this room. The thought saddened him. And oddly, it brought to mind his older sister, Louise, who had done the same thing—for six months in a flushed and excited high-energy rush she had prepared every inch of the baby's room. But in her case, it was the baby who had died one month after birth.

The sensation of coolness, of dust and decay in the room, obviously came from his memory of Louise's baby's death. It had been one of the most traumatic moments of his teenage life. The night after it happened he had wept along with his sister, holding her in his arms. He was only fourteen at the time, and he always believed that it was little Jody's death that had turned his mind to medicine.

But no matter how he analyzed his feelings, he didn't like it here. Perhaps it brought back too many memories for him. He turned to go when he heard it. A murmur, or laughter so soft that he wasn't sure it was real. He stopped, his hand on the doorknob. Everything was silent again, and he could still hear the two voices upstairs. He took another step, and the same soft bubbling laughter came from behind him, from somewhere to his left. He stared hard but it was the darkest part of the room, and he couldn't make out anything clearly. A soft rustle of cloth against cloth came from the velvet-shadowed corner.

Jeff pushed the door wider, to let more light in, and walked toward the sound. As he got closer shapes began to take form, but he was almost on top of it before he recognized the crib. It was an elaborate, ornate crib with a lace-edged canopy arching over the top half. He put his hands on the railing and looked in. Mallory's kid lay there, smiling, wide dark eyes steady and looking up at him. He had none of the normal newborn infant's blank, unfocused stare. In fact, this child's eyes were sharp . . . and staring straight at him. His mouth moved, as if trying to shape words . . . and the child raised his hand toward him.

Jeff was amazed. No newborn, no baby only a few days old, could make such coordinated movements, could focus its eyes so specifically. It was impossible. As he studied the child, Jeff noticed that the baby's eyes glittered with a curious pale light . . . a fire seemed to flicker deep within the dark pupils. It was unreflected, for there was no light nearby, and it seemed to come from within.

A sick thrill ran through him, like when he hit his elbow on a sharp edge, and his stomach did a somersault. There was something really weird happening here, and he didn't like it. Jeff backed away one step, and turned to go when he heard . . . or rather felt . . . someone behind him. He glanced over his shoulder. The tall shadow of the housekeeper filled the open doorway. The hard edge of back light surrounding her sharpened the edges of her image, and he could see her hand raise toward him, a slight gesture, palm up, motioning him to come to her.

As he stared at her a kind of prickly heat flushed over his body, and she became more visible, a pale glow seeming to flow from her. But her image remained opaque in the darkness, as if he was seeing her through a curtain of silk or gauze. It made her face paler than normal. It had become a startling white face framed in the shadows, wavering, coming forward and then retreating languorously into the darkness, like a drowning man sinking into deep waters. For a moment Jeff thought he was drowning ... or drunk ... his head light and reeling, a balloon on a string. He thought he might faint and put out his hands to stop the fall. He didn't fall but simply stood there lightheaded and weak ... oddly tired and lacking any willpower to move ... almost drugged, not knowing what was happening to him. A clear, terrible fear grew within him; he felt it radiate through his body like an icy piece of crystal breaking. He tried to control it, to stop the crackling fear that ran through him, but he began trembling instead, breaking into a cold, clammy sweat.

A frightening sensation of evil filled the air; it crawled over his skin, as if the eyes of the devil had a physical touch ... and he was being watched.

A sudden wind rattled the house, the shutters beat against the outer walls like the bony wings of Satan's fallen angels, and the still air in the room vibrated like a cobweb shaken by an unexpected breeze.

Silence hung around him as if he existed in a thick fog, and he had the sensation of being a child again in the rabbi's sanctuary, surrounded by powers so great that he could only stand wide-eyed and stunned. Then, not wanting to and without knowing why, he began to move. All he could hear was the sound of his feet shuffling on the carpet, his own hard and fast breathing and the bubbling laughter of the child as he walked toward the waiting shadow in the doorway.

Chapter Seven

Mallory had been trying to find Jeff all day. He was supposed to work the afternoon shift at Hitchcock and had not shown up. That wasn't like Jeff, and Mallory was worried. He had called him six times starting at ten that morning. It was now after five, and the New England winter had brought early nightfall. The northeaster was blowing its ice-laden wind again, the third day in a row. He had once heard an old-time Yankee, one of those New England characters straight from a Herman Melville novel, announce in an accent as thick as mud pie that a three day nor'easter always brought bad weather with it.

When he and Lili had left Jeff last night, he seemed fine. Could he possibly have gotten sick? He had called the elderly couple who lived below him, but there was no answer there either.

They had all planned to drive down to Allentown and visit Dr. Bowker tomorrow . . . and they needed to make plans.

Mallory had telephoned Bowker that morning. At first Bowker had sounded polite but cautious. After Mallory had explained that he wanted to talk about Cheryl Walker, Bowker's 1987 patient, the man abruptly became rude and hung up. Mallory had been surprised by the reaction, but then realized that Bowker seemed to be hiding something. Despite the anger and rudeness, Mallory thought he heard a tinge of anxiety or perhaps even fear in the voice. And since the man wouldn't talk to him on the phone, perhaps he had to be confronted head-on? If three medical people showed up on his doorstep, Bowker surely wouldn't refuse to talk with them.

He was sure Jeff wanted to go ... in fact, he had said he wouldn't miss it for the world. Mallory felt a bit like a worried mother hen, but he had to find out where Jeff was. If he was sick or injured ... he may need help. He grabbed his car keys and his coat. He would be in Norwich in ten minutes.

When he arrived Jeff's car was in the driveway. But there was no answer when he knocked. No one downstairs, either. The place seemed deserted. But where would Jeff go without his car? This wasn't Brooklyn where he could hop on a subway or bus.

Mallory peered through a crack in the curtains covering the window. He could see only a corner of the kitchen table. A vase of flowers was on its side, the water and flowers spilled over the table.

Then he saw something that made his heart seem to drop into the pit of his stomach. A trail of blood crossed the floor in a jagged thin line and ran under the table, collecting there in a dark pool around one leg. It was all Mallory could see, but enough to panic him.

He stepped back and kicked the door with his right foot just below the lock. The jam shattered and the door swung open. He rushed in and stopped, horrified.

"Oh, my God," he moaned. His stomach lurched and he fought the nausea rising, choking him like a lump of acid. Revolted, he covered his mouth with his hand.

Jeff's body, a noose around his neck, hung on the

wall from a curtain-rod hook next to the window. He was naked and his chalk-white flesh looked plastic and unreal. Mallory stared, unable to move. Jeff had been dead for some time, his body had stiffened, already growing rigid with rigor mortis. The pitiful, skinny, knobby-kneed legs were lacerated and covered with blood. A black-blood trail streamed down the inner sides of his legs. Mallory could clearly see the slashes that had cut the inner groin arteries. Two pools of blood, now coagulated and turned a dark purple, had stained the yellowed linoleum under him.

Jeff's thick, wire-rimmed glasses had fallen on the floor and were caked with dried blood. Mallory bent over and picked the glasses up by one of the wire arms and stared at it . . . remembering his eyes, full of curiosity and sparkling with humor. He looked up. The eyes were now dry, glassine, and wide open, filled with terror and staring blindly down at the floor, as if he had died watching his tormentors.

His purple tongue, already black around the edges, was swollen to the size of Mallory's wrist and hung from his mouth like a panting dog's.

"Oh, God," Mallory moaned again, looking away from the body, unable to think coherently. *He had to get the body down from there. It looked like bloodless meat . . . hanging. . . .*

Almost in a trance he walked over and put his arms around the cold, rigid legs, his shoulder against the naked stomach. He lifted the body and the loop around the curtain rod slipped off. Slowly, he lowered the body to the floor. He could not look at it and kept his eyes tightly closed, for the distorted neck, twisted at its queer angle, and the tongue hanging out, was too much for him to bear seeing again. Especially now . . . lying grotesquely on the floor. He went into the living room and found an afghan over the back of the couch and covered the body with it.

His knees felt suddenly weak. Shakily, he sat down at the kitchen table. His hands were trembling. He needed time to think, to pull himself together. He had to call the police. Jeff was obviously murdered. He couldn't have hung himself . . . and then slashed his own leg arteries. And the body . . . so pale . . . so little blood. The human body holds six quarts of blood and it should have been all over the floor. It looked as if he had been slaughtered like a piece of meat and all his blood drained from him. . . .

Mallory stared at the floor and saw his own footprints, outlined in red, going into the living room and back again. He looked down at his marked shoes, horrified that he had been walking in Jeff's blood.

He covered his eyes with his hand, trying to hold back the flood of feelings that were sweeping over him. He failed. Before he called the police he wept. And somewhere within the cold misery choking him . . . a hot and implacable hate grew and he swore to find and destroy whoever had done this.

Chapter Eight

By the time Mallory called the police and they came to cordon off the apartment and take Jeff's body away, it was three in the morning. He went with the officers to the police station, a single room on the first floor of the Town Meeting Hall, a large square brick building at the corner of Main Street where Route 5 turned north. Set in any other location the building could be mistaken for a miniature armory, but in a small New England town it was considered a charming example of early America. The single room of the station was entered from a door on the left side of the entrance hallway.

Sick with depression and barely able to keep his eyes open, he talked with two police officers until almost five-thirty a.m. He was exhausted, emotionally whipped and hoarse from going over and over how he had discovered the body.

He sat in the small room, bleak by any standards—a few chairs and two desks, an old wooden one to the left and another painted metallic monster facing the door as you entered. The only decoration was an old boundary map of Norwich at the turn of the century behind the reception desk and a group photo of an unrecognizable softball team. The chief of Norwich's four-man police force was in Montpelier, Vermont's state capital, so Mallory was questioned by two duty officers. The one who talked most was a beefy man named Jack Weidemeier. His beer belly, square, heavy face and jowls and bristly blond hair gave the impression of a former college lineman gone soft. Weidemeier was a man with a lot of raw energy, even at five a.m., and he kept drumming his fingers on his desk as he talked.

No, he didn't know whether Jeff had any enemies, but he couldn't imagine that would have anything to do with it. What did he think "had to do with it?" Nothing, just a figure of speech. No, he had no idea where Jeff had been last night. No, he didn't know whether he was involved with any weird cults.

On and on it went, hour after hour.

The other officer, Charlie Kelly, was a few years younger, about thirty. He was as slim and wiry as Weidemeier was square.

Both men were obviously intelligent and both seemed skeptical of Mallory's story. Why, they wanted to know, was he worried enough about Goldman to drive all the way to his home?

No matter how often he told them that Jeff was conscientious, an intern who rarely missed working his shift, they still came back to it. And he couldn't tell them more. He really didn't know why he had been so anxious about Jeff. Call it intuition, a hunch. Whatever had bothered him enough to go check out Jeff's apartment had no name, and that was not something that the police seemed to accept.

Quiet and observant, Kelly did not say much during the questioning. He leaned his chair back against the wall, put his feet up on the rungs, and listened. Mallory knew he was being studied by Kelly's shrewd, watchful eyes. But he didn't much care. In fact, still stunned by the awful reality of Jeff's murder, he didn't care much about anything. When it was finally over Weidemeier lit a cigarette, thanked Mallory for his patience and turned to his typewriter, an old brown IBM office model. He began typing out his report, his two index fingers chopping over the keys with a kind of clumsy precision.

Kelly stood up and extended his hand. "Thank you, Dr. Mallory. That couldn't have been easy. But you realize we have to ask all those questions. Especially in a capital case."

"I understand," Mallory said, his voice dry and hoarse. He took a sip of the tea they had given him an hour earlier. It was cold and the bitter tannic acid shocked his dry throat. It left an aftertaste like a mouthful of varnished woodchips.

Kelly walked him out of the station. A hundred yards to the right and across the street a few employees were pulling into Dan and Whit's all-purpose general store.

"You're not planning to leave the area any time soon, are you, Dr. Mallory?" Kelly asked.

Mallory turned and stared at him. "No," he said softly, too tired to respond more.

"You're a material witness, Dr. Mallory." He shrugged apologetically. "Others, including my chief, will want to talk with you. And then there's the county and state."

"I see," Mallory said. "I'll be around."

"Okay, try and get some sleep," Kelly said kindly. He turned and walked back to the station.

Yeah, Mallory thought. *Sleep. He didn't think he would ever be able to close his eyes again without seeing Jeff's body hanging from that wall.*

He drove home slowly, his hand trembling no matter

how tightly he squeezed the wheel.

But he was wrong. When he got home he walked into the house and fell onto the bed fully clothed. He was asleep before he had time to wonder why his eyes seemed to be full of tears.

He called Lili just after lunch. She had already heard the news. It was the major topic of conversation all over the hospital. She was just as bewildered as he was. In fact, she was overwhelmed and could barely talk about it. Several times her voice choked as she fought back tears. She called Jeff "a sweet bird," nervous, high-strung, lots of activity to obscure his anxiety. Always ready to fly off in a new direction just for the fun of it.

Mallory asked her about the plan to see Bowker. She had a heavy schedule that day. Two staff nurses were out sick so she couldn't go with him.

"Why not put it off for a few days?" she asked. "Give yourself some time to heal. Put things in perspective."

"That's good advice," he said, "but I want to keep busy and I'm facing two days off. A drive might be diverting. Besides, when I spoke with him I said today. He didn't even want me to come so I better stick to schedule."

The conversation lapsed and Mallory could hear the distant metallic background sounds of the hospital. Intense thin voices came over the line. They all had that familiar adrenalin edge to them, but trying to sound calm and in control. He recognized himself in the disembodied voices, but he felt closer to hysteria than a simple adrenalin high. In fact, he missed being lost in the controlled chaos. At least that didn't give him any time to think, to have the image of Jeff's naked, hanging body, the legs streaming with black blood . . .

the bloated tongue and staring eyes...

He shook his head. "All right," he said to Lili. "I'll call you when I get back and give you a run down on Bowker."

Near the Massachusetts border the late afternoon sky darkened. By the time he turned south on 95 a half hour later the clouds had become ominous. A blackberry sky, they called it in New England because of the great roiling clusters of black clouds that would come rushing over the horizon, bringing with it anything from violent winds to sudden rain of thunderstorm proportions. This time it was winds. He passed the outer edges of Boston and continued south. He was almost there. An hour or so to Providence, and then maybe another forty-five minutes to New Bedford. Bowker lived in Paydanarum, a town not far from New Bedford on the southern coast of Massachusetts, just north of the Rhode Island border.

The rest of the drive was through a darkling sky as night was quickened by the storm. He drove through the eastern edge of the front as he left Providence on 195 toward New Bedford. The winds were blasting across the highway when he turned off and headed toward the coast where he picked up Route 6. A splattering of fat rain drops, like translucent overfed insects, were now exploding on the windshield.

Paydanarum turned out to be an exclusive beach community with several acres of grounds surrounding each of the large and expensive homes. It reminded Mallory of when he was a boy and those rare times when the family was all together in the Hamptons. He and his father would sometimes spend several hours together before he'd disappear into his study, turning the long stretches of empty sand outside their house into a cheerless playground of lost promise.

But Paydanarum smelled of even more privilege and money. The lawns and shrubbery were too neat and clipped to have been touched by less than a professional gardener's hands.

He reached Bowker's house, which was placed at the edge of a pine grove facing a hundred yards of beach, and turned between the square stone pillars. He could smell the salt air and hear the surf, a gentle susurration floating out from the black shroud surrounding the house. The night had a bite to it, and the wind blew angrily through the trees. No moon or stars could be seen; it was as if the violent wind had blown them out. "The breath of gods" Aristophanes had called storm winds.

Mallory smiled. He remembered that in "The Clouds" the Greek playwright had also called rain Zeus's piss that fell to earth after going through a giant sieve.

When he knocked on Bowker's door it was just before nine o'clock. The trip had taken him more than four hours. His hands were still tingling from gripping the steering wheel and the tension of driving in heavy winds.

Bowker opened the door himself. A tall, almost gaunt man with sloping shoulders. His head, angled forward on a long neck, gave Mallory the feeling of a predator. This impression was reinforced by the scowl on the man's pallid face. His thick, scraggy eyebrows ran straight above his eyes, like two fat caterpillars stretched and ready for pinning. His eyes were deepset, hidden now in shadows.

Mallory explained who he was, and for a fleeting moment he thought the man would slam the door in his face. But instead, Bowker stared silently at him and then glanced over Mallory's shoulder with a nervous flick of his eyes.

"I asked you not to come when you called," he said in a voice used to giving orders. It almost seemed as if he were talking to a crowd assembled on the lawn behind Mallory.

"I told you I thought you were foolishly concerned. Deaths in hospitals are as common as bad taste," he said coldly. He turned on his heel and walked inside.

Since he left the door open Mallory assumed it was a sullen invitation and stepped into the house. He closed the door gently, not wanting to irritate the man anymore than necessary.

He passed down a long dimly lit hallway lined with books. A glance told him Bowker's reading habits were highly eclectic. There were a few medical books, mostly out-dated general reference works. In far greater number were books on poetry, religion, myth, psychology and philosophy.

A peculiar library for a doctor only recently retired. Physicians usually retain an intense interest in their profession. If Mallory tried to judge his man simply by his library he'd guess a humanities professor. But even here he would hesitate, for with a closer look he noticed that the titles ranged all the way to the arcane. Even weird. He ran his fingertips over the spines, *The Annals of Ancient Bestiary,* Thomas à Kempis's *Meditations,* and Manley Hall's outsized, rare leather-bound volume, *Encyclopedia of the Occult.*

A peculiar man, Mallory thought as he stepped into the living room. As if to confirm the image, Bowker was sitting on a velvet easy chair, its wine-dark richness sensual in the light from the single golden-shaded lamp nearby. Bowker's arm was thrown over the back. He held a goblet of red wine and watched Mallory with a kind of mordant humor. Gone was the asperity, the irritable flash in his dark eyes. Now his expression was one of amusement, as if a lion were enjoying a kitten's antics before sweeping it away with its paw.

Deliberately, Bowker raised the wine to his lips, watching Mallory over the rim. Pointedly, he didn't offer Mallory a glass, or even a gesture for him to sit down.

This little act was not lost on Mallory. He hated these kinds of social power games. The old man had probably read Korda's book *Power: How to Get It, How to Use It,* and took it seriously. He had, no doubt, been a holy terror at hospital board meetings.

Ignoring the small insults Mallory took off his coat and sat down opposite Bowker.

A brief, genuine smile flickered at the corners of the old man's mouth.

"This, I suspect, is a waste of your time," Bowker said. "And I'm sure it's a waste of mine."

He motioned toward Mallory with the back of his hand, a brush stroke of permission. "Get on with it," he said.

It had rarely ever taken such a short time for Mallory to so thoroughly dislike someone.

"I'm sorry it's so late and may be inconvenient," Mallory said. "But it is very important."

The old man said nothing.

"Do you recall your patient Cheryl Walker?" Mallory asked.

"Of course."

"Do you remember the details of her death?"

"Yes."

Brief and to the point, Mallory thought. *This was going to be like pulling up a cactus by the roots.*

"What was her crit? Both before and after death?"

Bowker pursed his lips, took a sip of wine, and said, "I don't recall before. But the post-mortem was around six percent. Perhaps 300,000."

"Didn't you find that strange?"

The old man stared hard at Mallory. "I don't know how long you've been on staff, Doctor. But from your age I'd say about four or five years? Am I right?"

Mallory nodded.

"Well, I suspect that if you'd had a few more years you would have seen any number of hematocrit readings between six and ten percent. Yes, it's low, but not really exceptional."

"What about an RBC of 100,000?"

"That's a bit more unusual, but nothing to get excited about. 'There are more things in heaven and earth, Horatio' . . . et cetera, et cetera."

Bowker picked up a wooden box with delicate inlaid arabesques on the lid from the table next to him. He opened it and took out a long thin cigar wrapped in foil. Gently, with great care, almost like a surgeon operating on a friend, he unwrapped it.

"There are still so many mysteries in medicine," he went on, focusing on the cigar, "that one more dangling participle on the peculiar grammar of human life is hardly worth noting."

"What about ten dangling participles in a row," Mallory said, his voice low and intense. "Would that get your attention?"

It did. Bowker sat straight up, like a schoolboy who has been told to stop slouching. For the first time Mallory knew he had hit a nerve.

"Ten?" Bowker said softly. "Where'd you get that number?"

"The same place I got your name."

Bowker's eyes squinted and he concentrated on lighting his cigar. "And where was that?"

"The NIH central computer files."

Again a nerve. Bowker looked truly startled. "The NIH? How did the government get involved in this?"

"They aren't involved. They know nothing about it. Yet! When my patient died, the one I told you about on the phone, I cross-referenced her medical facts with the NIH files and got ten other almost identical cases."

"And the doctors' names as well?"

"Yes."

Mallory let it hang. The death of all those doctors was his hole card. If anything would shake something loose from this pretentious old enigma, that would be it.

After a moment of puffing gently on his cigar Bowker looked up at Mallory. "And what do you make of this incredible mystery?" he asked sarcastically.

"I don't know what to make of it. Ten patients with the same low hematocrit? Nine dead doctors in as many years? And all within the first week of February every year since 1978? What would you make of it?"

Mallory watched Bowker's face carefully. Surprisingly, there wasn't a flicker of concern about the dead doctors. It seemed as if he already knew it. Old information, no surprise there.

But his face had gone white when he mentioned the dates.

That was a surprise.

Mallory saw it happen. Bowker was clearly shaken, but he quickly regained his composure and his expression went from surprise to anger. And, Mallory thought, a touch of fear flickered in his eyes.

"What do I make of it?" the old man asked, leaning forward. "Nothing. Nothing that any reasonable man would. You're indulging in magical thinking, Doctor."

He jabbed his cigar at Mallory. "You're like all young doctors nowadays, ready for any fanciful hypothesis."

Bowker sat back, his pale face calmer now. He was more in control when, after a moment, he said, "Why don't you get to the point. Tell me what your theory is, and what is it that you want from me?"

"I don't know what I believe at the moment. There are several possiblities. Some I don't even want to think about. But the most rational, and least magical, is that it's an unknown hematophagous disease that somehow has been transferred to the doctors. Perhaps like AIDS it is communicated through the blood. God knows why it hasn't been transferred to the children. With the children it may have a longer incubation period, but with adults it incubates for one year and then creates a rapid collapse of red blood cells and death."

Bowker smiled broadly for the first time. His teeth were obviously false, great yellow-ivory colored squares that resembled horse's teeth.

"Hematophagous," Bowker repeated. "A disease that *eats* red blood cells. What do we have here, little nasty PAC MEN chomping up all the healthy red cells?"

He leaned forward again, his cigar-laden breath pungent and penetrating. "Exactly one year?" he said incredulously.

The combination of spearmint false-teeth fixative and stale cigar breath made Mallory back away.

"You're being ridiculous, letting your imagination run away with you. No disease has such a precise, rigid incubation period. And to kill with such suddenness? No, Doctor, I'd suggest you go back to the drawing board. Ignore all these coincidences. Forget the doctors' deaths and the dates and concentrate on the pathology of the deceased patients. That's where the hard evidence is. That's where medicine can make some headway, not in grandiose theories about new virulent diseases killing doctors. That's coincidence, a statistical anomaly."

He doth protest too much, Mallory thought as he

waited for the diatribe to end. *He had the distinct impression that all this smoke and fire was simply to direct his attention elsewhere. His attitude had changed. The old man was clearly anxious about something. Underneath his acerbity he was more nervous, talking fast, like a salesman desperate for a sale.*

Ignoring Bowker's comments, Mallory said, "Just possibly this may be a disease that lies dormant and then attacks pregnant women in their last trimester, when their metabolism may be more susceptible to it. If that's so, the effect on pregnant women all over the country would be traumatic. Birth rates may even be affected."

Bowker threw his head back and laughed. It was a nasty, harsh laugh, closer to a smoker's hacking cough.

"That is the most absurd thing I've heard in years, which, in a world given to the fatuous and inane must be some sort of record."

He stared at Mallory. "You know, you are ridiculously romantic and sentimental in your view of medicine. I'll bet you have the same jejune attitude toward women and childbirth."

Mallory felt his face flush. Angry now, he said, "I don't consider it sentimental to be concerned about the health and welfare of pregnant women."

As he heard himself speak he flushed even more. He'd proven the old bastard's point by reeling off a witless cliche.

In control now, and on familiar ground, Bowker leaned back and puffed on his cigar. "Of course you don't. Look, you obviously know the biology of birth, but what of its ontology, its philosophical exegesis. Let me tell you what goes on from the moment of conception until the time the parasite leaves the sacristy to find a greater variety of succor.

"Years ago the English psychoanalyst D.W. Winnicott got it right. He labelled the infant, including the zygote *in vitro,* as a ruthless parasite sucking the lifeblood from the mother's body.

"Let me tell you a little story to illustrate my point. I was a young doctor in World War Two. My unit was one of the first American groups into Germany as the war ended. But the fighting was still going on and the Russians, who had preceded us by a day or two into what is now called East Germany, had *liberated* the people already. Mutilated bodies were scattered everywhere . . . sometimes it was only an arm, a leg, or a head . . . frozen in grotesque postures in the streets and gutters, hanging out of car doors, on park benches and in building doorways and windows.

"Men, women and children, the young and old, were all treated in the same brutal fashion. I don't know how this one child I saw survived. It was a cold, wet autumn and the child, a little girl maybe two years old, was squatting next to her mother. She had torn the mother's blouse open and was crying and suckling on the woman's flat, dead breast. The child was starving, to be sure, and didn't realize that its mother was dead. As I watched, it began to beat angrily on the woman's flaccid breasts. At first I was horrified and stood there stunned as the weeping child continued to pound and claw the dead flesh.

"It would stop the beating only long enough to throw itself on the woman and suck furiously until it realized it wasn't being satisfied. This went on for almost ten minutes until some other soldiers came by and took the child away.

"I was fascinated by this little scene. I had never witnessed such a clear expression of need, and such an uncompromising aggression toward a supposed love-object before."

Bowker smiled at Mallory, puffing on his cigar

furiously. Retelling the story had excited him.

"I needn't tell you how educational this miniature tableau of war was. It supported Winnicott's theory perfectly. Even from the first mytosis when the cell divides into two, the infant starts by malignantly using the mother. And after it's born it comes to see the parental role of serving it as its destiny. The parent rarely has a choice, and the child instinctively knows this. It relishes its power and begins an unrelenting manipulation within months of its birth. Its instinctive goal is survival at any cost and the complete capitulation of those around it."

Bowker had risen and was striding around the room; his tall, emaciated body, long thin neck and bobbing head made him seem like a mutant giraffe trapped in a pen.

"The mother's first role is, as Winnicott so brilliantly put it, simply as a 'transitional object,' a thing to be used by the infant, a role which eventually is transferred to all other living things that the parasite comes into contact with."

As Mallory listened in astonishment to the old man's cynical description of the beginnings of human life, he realized that the old fox had succeeded in changing the subject. He also realized that he was going to get nothing helpful from him. Bowker would drown him in words and tell him nothing. It had been a wasted trip.

Except . . . except that he was now sure Bowker was hiding something. The old man knew more than he was telling.

Bowker continued to talk, an endless stream of dismal opinion about people, human nature, and the meaning of life.

In the middle of a sentence Mallory stood up and put on his coat.

The old man stopped talking, surprised.

"Thank you for your time, Dr. Bowker. I'm sorry if I disrupted your evening," Mallory said as he started toward the door.

"But..." Bowker stammered.

Mallory turned and looked at the old man. The silence was heavy for a moment and Mallory understood. Bowker was a mean old curmudgeon who probably didn't get the opportunity to talk to another soul for days on end.

When he said nothing more, Mallory turned and walked out, leaving the old man puffing nervously on his cigar and standing alone in the middle of his large book-lined living room.

On the drive home Mallory reviewed everything he knew about the bizarre series of facts building up. He knew more now than during his confusing walk around Occam Pond the night of Betty Milner's death, but *what* he knew simply involved more facts. He surely didn't understand more. In fact, with Jeff's murder he began feeling submerged in a murky sea of violent and freakish energies that seemed to be closing in on him.

He had hoped that Bowker, the only doctor besides himself still living, would give him some insight into what was happening. But Bowker was scared of something. And Mallory couldn't blame him, for he himself had an icy lump of fear deep in his gut. He tried to ignore it, but it wouldn't go away. If Bowker did know something then he would be prudent to distrust a strange doctor knocking on his door late at night. But that scenario implied some kind of plot, a danger lurking somewhere in the background... watching.

Mallory shivered and snapped on the car's heater. A chill had just scrambled up his back like a terrified insect. *An unknown danger... a plot where people were murdered brutally with ritualistic precision.*

That was the only scenario that logically tied Jeff's murder to the bizarre series of February OB deaths.

But why? Why?

He had to figure out his next step. Find a connection between Jeff's murder and the low-hematocrit deaths. There was no evidence at all to connect them. Just his gut feeling. He would call the hospital and take a few days off. Devote all his time to finding out what was going on.

He wasn't sure where he should look next, but he would collect all the information on the low-crit patients he could from the medical library computer, call the families' homes, interview the surviving relatives. There must be other common factors that the patients and their families shared. If he could isolate what the families, or the patients, had in common, he might be able to see the beginning of a pattern.

It was a slim hope . . . but he had nothing else to go on. Bowker would not help him, at least not at the moment. He could count on Lili—and that was about it. He had never felt so alone, so utterly isolated in his life. The black, rain-soaked highway stretched before him, glistening in his headlights like the wet trail of some great evil beast he was unwittingly following.

Chapter Nine

For six hours the next day Mallory pored over computer records and medical files until his eyes burned and a monster headache began pounding inside his brain.

Lili had come over to his Hitchcock office for two hours during her lunch break. Together they had gone over the same territory again . . . and still come up with nothing.

His first break came late in the afternoon. Two of the children, one born in Chicago and one near Philadelphia, had been released from the hospital to the care of a nanny. *Both* nannies were from *the same agency*. Which may not be strange on the face of it, except that the children were born in different cities and the agency was based in New York.

Why would a child care agency with a New York City address pick up children in two distant cities? There was no record that the agency had Chicago or Philadelphia branches. Both times the agency address given to the hospital was in New York. Indeed, why would a nanny pick up a newborn child at all rather than the family? Especially after the tragedy of the mother's death? All good questions to which there might be reasonable answers. He would probably find out that the agency was huge, with branches all over the country but its billing offices and mailing address in New York.

It was a weak connection, but the only one he had after hours of back-breaking work. He called Lili and told her what he had found. She sounded pleased, and even a little amused at his *sotto voce* excitement. She suggested that they visit the agency. Check them out and see what they knew about the children. She had to first talk with the hospital and see when she could take time off. Hopefully tomorrow. Lili suggested that they meet that night for dinner and make plans.

Mallory was relieved. He had been feeling guilty that they had not seen much of each other during the last two days ... what with her work schedule and his being obsessed with Jeff's death and finding out what the hell was going on. He had been torn between calling her and pursuing the few tenuous leads he had, and every time he decided in favor of his investigation the guilt had ballooned.

Lili had not said a word. No recriminations, no subtle undercurrents of resentment, no snide double-entendres about whether he cared. She had simply waited patiently, and Mallory loved her for it.

Her skin was like living velvet. It seemed to pulsate and rise to his touch. Their lovemaking was frenetic, a great hungry feeding on each other. With her, he surprised himself in his ability to let go, to forget his constant sense of isolation, his feeling of being alone in an alien world. Only with Lili, and in the overwhelming heat of their lovemaking, did this happen. He had to fight believing it a kind of self-transcendence. For the heat of it burned into his mind a kind of wonderful lazy mist of forgetfulness. Nothing mattered when he was with her except the rush toward that blind fusing. And it wasn't just a selfish male-ego wanting to get off, for she pulled him along almost as if she had an invisible, enormously powerful cord with a hook embedded deep in his bowels. Sometimes he felt like a fish being reeled into a highly charged electric net that ensnared him and pulled him down into a deep sensual darkness.

At these moments he became disturbed at the sensation of losing touch with reality, and he had to remind himself of the real world. He would think about the biology of sex, the hormonal excitation, the self-perpetuating emotional needs that after being satisfied seemed to demand ever more. Just the hint of being loved gave rise in him a hunger for proof. And, as the feeling grew, the greater his need for more proof, more food for his hunger. Would there ever be enough for him? Maybe not. Constant hunger kept him on a pale diet. Only Lili seemed able to bring him to table and allow him to feast.

They lay in the rumpled bed, a cool, barely perceptible breeze danced over their sweating, flushed skins. They had not been able to finish their meal before a silent understanding, a magnetic, vibrant force drew them into the bedroom. The half-eaten dinner had been left on the table.

They didn't return to finish their meal until almost four in the morning. For most of the night they lay entangled, their bodies fused by a cool sheen of sweat and a fiery need to touch.

During the quiet moments when their minds cleared, they whispered their plans for tomorrow. Mallory confided his fears, his irrational, terrifying anxieties about preternatural forces lurking behind the scenery of their daily lives, manipulating them like puppets on a stage.

Several times she laughed softly at his intense imagery, whispering into his neck, kissing and biting the tender flesh curving into his shoulder, that he should have been a poet, not a doctor. She reassured him that the real world had real answers, that he was doing all the right things.

And he believed her. His experience and intelligence, the reasoning brain, was the only guide he had. "The heat of the mind," Keats called it, the light that illuminated the mysteries.

When they finally slept Mallory was at peace, lulled into the comforting vision of a world ordered by natural laws that were mysterious and frightening only until their rules were uncovered.

The drive to New York City took six hours. The agency was located downtown in Greenwich Village where the streets, unlike the logical grid pattern of the city, were a haphazard jumble laid down a century before. Like European cities, the Village streets not only lacked any pretense to being a part of modern city planning, but were aggressively illogical to strangers. The second time Mallory came to an intersection where West 11th Street crossed West 4th Street he pulled over next to a hydrant.

"This is impossible," Lili said. "We're lost. Why not ask directions?"

Across the street a man sat on a wooden bench in front of a pastry shop. "LANCIANI'S" was printed on both of the large glass windows in black letters. The man was drinking coffee from a paper cup and fingering through an issue of "The Antiquarian Bookman." He looked between sixty and seventy, wore a plaid shirt with a belt and suspenders holding up a pair of faded jeans. A chain ran from the side of his belt to his wallet in a back pocket. At least Mallory assumed it was his wallet. Obviously not a very trusting soul.

"I'll get some coffee," Lili said, "and ask where this place is."

Mallory watched in amusement as Lili, who was wearing a pair of tight slacks and a white see-through blouse, walked past the "Antiquarian Bookman." The phrase stuck in Mallory's mind. It seemed to fit the man. When Lili passed by, the Bookman's head came up like a beagle treeing a raccoon. In one glance his eyes did an intimate mental drawing of Lili's body. Sensing his appreciation, she glanced over and smiled. He beamed in response.

"Excuse me," Mallory said, leaning over to the passenger window. "Can you tell me where 105 Charles Street is?"

The Bookman glanced at Mallory, taking in everything with eyes full of humor and curiosity. He was apparently interested in what kind of man Lili would be traveling with.

"Since you seem to have good manners, sure," he said. "Take a left on West 11th, go one block and take another left. Two more blocks and that's Charles. 105 is to the right."

"Thanks," Mallory said as Lili came out of Lanciani's carrying two containers of coffee.

Again the old Bookman followed her fluid, graceful body with eyes that missed nothing.

Mallory pushed open the door, and as Lili slipped into her seat she motioned with her head toward the Bookman and smiled. "A lot of life still left there," she said as he drove off.

"Either that or he has a good memory," Mallory said.

The old Bookman's directions were perfect. They pulled up before the building in less than two minutes and looked the place over while sipping their coffee.

"Well, I couldn't have been more wrong," Mallory said, checking the address again.

"A big agency with offices all across the country?" he said sarcastically. "Look at that."

The building was an old three story brownstone. A small hand-painted plaque next to the front door read, "We Care, the Au Pair Agency for Children."

Another small notice was pasted over one of the dented, silver-painted mail boxes. "We Care" was printed over Apt 1B. Mallory pressed a red button and pushed open the door when the buzzer sounded.

The hallway was badly lit and, like the building as a whole, in desperate need of a washing or new paint job. It smelled of old newspapers, cockroaches and PineSol.

Another "We Care" sign hung on the door of the back apartment. Mallory knocked and tried the knob. It was unlocked so they walked in. A narrow hallway hung with childcare posters and flyers giving advice on nutrition and safety tips for kids extended twenty feet into the apartment. At the end of the hall a door opened to the right.

A pretty young woman in her mid-twenties sat at a desk directly in front of the door reading a Barbara Cartland novel. Her breasts were full and pushed up high by a bra that was too small and too tight and she wore too much makeup. She looked up at Mallory and smiled briefly. Her small, even teeth were a flash of opalescent white against pink lipstick.

"Can I help you?" she asked, her voice as tentative and lacking in animation as her expression. She placed her novel face down, preserving her place.

"My name is David Mallory. I'm a doctor. This is my nurse. We'd like to talk with someone about your agency placing nannies with children whose families are part of an investigation we're conducting."

The young woman's vapid expression didn't change. She stared at Mallory for a brief moment and then said, "I'm sorry, there's no one here that can talk with you. I'm alone today. And besides, it's company policy to not discuss any children or the families our people have been employed by."

This last was said by rote, as if memorized. She smiled again, her eyes glancing at Lili and then back to Mallory.

"Privacy," she said. "You understand. I'm sorry."

"Of course," Mallory said, smiling. His charm seemed to have as much impact as a cottonball thrown against a wall.

"But this is extremely important and involves the health of these children as well as the families."

"I'm sorry," she repeated. Again the smile that mimicked a rubber band being stretched and then going limp.

Outside Mallory silently cursed himself. It had been stupid to go in and immediately blurt out the truth. They left the car and walked to the corner of Hudson, a one-way street going uptown. They turned north, Mallory in an angry, self-recriminatory funk. Lili walked next to him, her arm loosely linked with his, enjoying looking in shop windows and watching people.

A few blocks up they crossed the street and went into a bar-restaurant that extended across the first floors of two adjoining brownstones. "The White Horse Tavern" had the bemused look of an old building that had been badly rebuilt and shorn up so many times over the ages that it didn't really have a clear identity. Dark original woodwork sat uncomfortably next to newly polished oak. Original 19th century posters hung beside glitzy neon signs flashing advertisements for Budweiser's and Miller's.

They made their way to a side room that had oak tables and a quiet atmosphere—in contrast to the front room that was rocked continually by a juke box with only one ear-shattering volume setting.

They ordered a sandwich, salad and coffees from a surly waiter who kept flipping his long blond hair back from over his eyes. He had a round sapphire in his left ear and a large turquoise and silver imitation Navajo bracelet that he twisted back and forth incessantly as if he were shaking flies from his hand.

When they were alone again Lili leaned over and patted Mallory's hand.

"It's all right, David. There's probably nothing there anyway. You were probably right. They do their billing from this address and probably hire freelance nannies who live in the cities where the jobs are."

"Maybe," he said, staring out the window. "But it's too odd to simply disregard. We've got to find out the facts here. Think about it for a minute. It's simply too incredible to accept that two nannies out of ten are from this hole in the wall outfit. The probabilities against that must be astronomical, And there may be more. What if other nannies connected to this place were involved with these ten cases?"

He shook his head, again cursing himself for not planning the whole thing better.

God damn it. He wished he was a better conman. Or more devious. Yes, a little more deviousness would have helped.

And then it hit him.

All right. Deviousness it is, if that's what it takes.

He turned to Lili. "Tonight we break in and look at their files."

Lili's eyes widened in surprise. Then she smiled.

"My, what a pirate you are underneath all the proper middle-class polish."

Mallory's face flushed. "I didn't believe her. Something funny's going on here," he said. "And I intend to find out why this funky little agency placed two women with the low-crit families."

They walked around the village for another few hours and just before ten o'clock they returned to Charles Street. The short, tree-lined block of brownstones was deserted, and they walked up the stoop and into the building as if they lived there. Checking on the off chance that someone was still inside, Mallory pressed the red button. He waited for a minute and pressed it again. When there was no response he took a pen knife from his pocket and pressed the blade between the door and the jam's trim. For twenty seconds he searched for the spring latch. He felt the knife point hit something hard. He pulled the door toward him slightly, releasing the pressure on the latch, and pressed the knife point hard into the metal. He worked the knife to the left so that the spring latch would be pushed back inside the door's plate. In less than a minute and a half he pushed the door open.

"My, my," Lili whispered. "Aren't you the professional. Where'd you learn to do that?"

"It isn't hard. When I was a kid we forgot our keys, and my uncle opened a door like this at our summer house in the Hamptons," he said quietly. They walked quickly down the hall, and he began the same procedure.

In even less time the agency's door swung open, its hinges complaining softly. He closed the door gently behind them, and they stood listening in the apartment's lightless hallway.

The building was silent. Even the hum of city traffic was so muted it seemed a throaty carnival whisper of machine sounds layered one upon another, each grating, each cancelling the other out until they all dissolved into an amorphous buzzing white noise.

Reassured after a moment that the place was empty, Mallory ran his hands blindly over the wall near the door, searching for the light switch. A weak yellow ceiling light suddenly lit up the narrow hall.

Mallory glanced over at Lili to see if she was as nervous as he was. She was grinning at him warmly, her face flushed with excitement.

"I haven't had this much fun for years," she whispered, clutching his arm.

Mallory grinned weakly, wishing he were relaxed enough to have fun. But he was scared spitless. His mouth was dry and tasted like he was sucking a rusty nail.

Lili snapped on a desk lamp, and they began opening drawers and files as quietly as they could. Mallory's hands were sweating, but Lili seemed to be enjoying herself.

Empty . . . Every damned drawer and file they opened was empty.

Mallory stopped and stared at the drawers, his mouth open, while Lili continued to search.

He felt his heart constrict in his chest. *Something was going on . . . there was a fucking plot . . . this place was a front.* "Bingo!" Lili cried.

Startled, he turned and saw Lili holding up a metal index card file. The lid was open and she was reading a 3 x 5 index card.

She handed the card to him. He read it and grabbed the box, fingering through the other cards. At the end he found a piece of typing paper folded up to fit into the file. He opened it and stared . . . dumbfounded.

It was a typed sheet of names and addresses, a duplicate of the index cards. The difference was that this list had his own name and address at the bottom, next to the name and birth date of the Milner baby.

Every doctor's name, and all the children and their addresses, from 1978 on, were listed. So were the names of the nannies—*all* of whom were supplied by this agency.

The eleventh name was one he hadn't seen before. It had not been listed in the NIH computer. Perhaps because it was so recent... 1988. An eleventh baby had been born at Alice Peck Day Hospital, in Lebanon, New Hampshire. Mallory was surprised. Two babies born so close to each other? Most of the others were scattered all across the country. Lebanon was only a few miles from Hanover.

But here was a break: The doctor who had delivered the baby, Walter Daley, still lived in New Hampshire.

Mallory's own name, and the Milners' name and address were the twelfth, at the bottom of the list.

But what made his heart skip a beat was a thick red line that crossed through every doctor's name on the list except three—Bowker's, the 1987 doctor of the tenth child; Daley's, who delivered the eleventh child; and his own.

All the others had been crossed out... A finger of blood had obliterated nine lives since 1978.

It was suddenly very close in the small room and Mallory had trouble breathing. A spasm ran through him and he trembled, internally, deep inside his gut, like a dog shaking rain from his coat. His hands shook as he read and reread the paper.

"Oh, my God..." he mumbled over and over.

"It's true," he said, his voice constricted and hoarse. He turned to Lili. "It's true. I didn't want to believe it, or even think it, but it's true."

He placed the paper flat on the desk. The heavy red lines turned bright orange in the yellow light of the desk lamp.

Lili was staring at him.

"Someone, for God knows what insane reason, has been killing these doctors. And they're the same people who murdered Jeff."

The only sound in the dusty suffocating room was his heart thudding in his chest.

"Not all," Lili said, her finger touching next to the last three names.

It took him a minute to filter her words through his fear and confusion.

"No, not all," he said. "But why? This is madness."

His finger touched the paper next to the dates of each doctor's death.

"Every doctor died within a week of the birth of the next child. What on earth can that mean?"

He stopped, then gasped. "My God, look at this."

His finger, the tip white, was pressed hard next to Daley's name.

"It will be a week tomorrow since the birth of the eleventh child. If the pattern holds, Daley will die within the next twenty-four hours."

Nibbling on her bottom lip, Lili studied the list of names and dates.

"Except Bowker," she said finally. "Why not Bowker? He delivered the tenth child two years ago."

"I don't know," Mallory said. "I was sure he was hiding something when we spoke. And now I know why he was so scared. He knew of the doctors' deaths . . . and that he was on the list. Whatever's kept him alive this long is obviously something he wants to keep secret. I'd do the same thing to stay alive."

Lili looked up at him sharply. "Would you really?" she asked, surprise in her voice. "You don't know what

104

he might have had to do."

For a second Mallory was puzzled by her question. Then he understood.

"Well, no, I'm not sure. But survival's a powerful incentive, and if Bowker could pay off the killers, and he had no alternative, then it'd probably be worth it."

"But pay off with what?" Lili asked, moving her finger down the list of names.

"Money? Information? And why couldn't the others have made the same arrangement?"

"I know, I know," Mallory said, running his hand through his hair. "It doesn't really make sense. But none of this does."

He snapped the lid closed on the metal file box and picked up the paper, refolded it and put it in his pocket.

"I only know one thing for sure right now," he said. "Daley is going to die by tomorrow night. And I have to try and stop it."

He looked at Lili, his eyes searching for understanding.

"I have a year to live . . . according to this," he said, tapping his jacket pocket where he had put the list. "Daley only has hours. God, how I wish this were a disease . . . then I'd have some idea of how to handle it. But this . . . I'm out of my depth."

He snapped off the desk lamp, took Lili's hand and walked into the hallway.

"C'mon," he said. "We have a long drive back to New Hampshire, and we don't have a hell of a lot of time."

On the drive back they talked about what to do next. Mallory was going to try and call Daley again as soon as they got home. He had tried in New York three times before leaving. It was now eleven o'clock, and he was already overwhelmed with fatigue. What he needed most was a good night of peaceful, uninterrupted sleep. But there was no alternative. He had to get back to see Daley right away.

The more they discussed what they had learned, the more nervous Mallory became. An alarm had gone off in his brain when he saw that list, and it had been ringing loudly ever since. For the first time he felt a real, palpable danger to himself. Before it had just been a sense of something wrong, of something deadly lingering just out of eyesight, something in the shadows. But now... *redlines... redlines...* glowed in his memory like neon on a dark night, like the trail of some bleeding, dangerous animal that would turn on him if he followed too closely.

But what worried him even more was Lili... and the danger to her if she stayed deeply involved in this mayhem. It would be better if she did not get any closer than she already was. In fact, the closer they got to New England and his making a connection with Daley, the more convinced he was that Lili must be kept out of it. Whoever was going to try to murder Daley would not hesitate to kill anyone else who got in their way.

"Their way..." he had said. *Why did he think it was a group? Probably because of the nannies, and the fact that the children... and doctors who had been killed ...had been scattered all over the country. That implied an organization. A group.*

A conspiracy? An insane, fanatical cult killing doctors who delivered babies on a specific day? Would the day have some occult significance? Some important meaning or connection with death... and blood? The image of Jeff's white body emptied of blood shimmered before him.

He wondered whether the nine doctors had been ritually murdered like Jeff. That would be one of the first things he would check out after he saw Daley.

Lili didn't like the idea of not going with him to see Daley, but Mallory prevailed in the end. She had to work at the hospital the next day. She had not scheduled any time off, and Hitchcock frowned on the staff taking off whenever they wanted. It was easier for Mallory; he was a staff doctor with weeks of vacation time built up over the last few years.

Besides, he argued, it may be dangerous and he didn't want Lili anywhere near it. Almost pouting, she finally agreed. But she made him promise to call her immediately after he had seen Daley. She wasn't about to be closed out of his life now.

The drive back took only four and a half hours. He had pushed himself to drive straight through, with only one quick stop for gas. As soon as he had dropped Lili off he called Daley again.

He sat on the bed, waiting impatiently as Daley's number rang. It was now almost four in the morning.

This time he was lucky.

"Hello," a sleep drugged voice said.

"Dr. Walter Daley?" he asked.

"Yes."

"My name is David Mallory. I'm a doctor at Mary Hitchcock. I'm sorry to be calling so late, but I have something extremely urgent to talk with you about."

"It'd better be, to wake me in the middle of the night," Daley said, a petulant tone in his voice.

Mallory was suddenly at a loss for words. He didn't know how to tell the man he was in danger, that someone was going to try to kill him before midnight tomorrow.

"Well?" Daley said after a moment, sounding more irritable.

"It's not something I can talk about over the phone,"

Mallory said in a rush. "I'd like to see you as soon as I can tomorrow morning."

"That's impossible. I have an extremely tight schedule."

Another long pause as Mallory tried to figure out what to say. He could hear the echo of their breathing feeding back through the phone lines.

"Dr. Mallory," Daley said. "If you cannot be more specific I'm going to hang up now. Write me a letter and I'll . . ."

"No," Mallory said, his voice low and urgent. "Don't hang up. It's vitally important for you . . . for your own well-being . . . that you don't hang up."

"What in heavens name are you talking about?" Daley shot back. "Is that a threat?" he asked, clearly angry now.

"No, no, I'm sorry it came out like that. I'm . . . Do you remember a patient by the name of . . ." Mallory was frantically trying to unfold the paper while holding the phone in the crook of his neck.

". . . Hilary Baker?" he blurted out.

Daley was silent for a long moment. When he spoke again his voice had changed. He sounded wary . . . and frightened.

Cautiously, Daley said, "Yes, what about her?"

"I have reason to believe she didn't die of natural causes . . . and that you might also . . ."

"Enough, enough," Daley whispered. "Don't say anything more."

After another long pause, Daley said, "I can't see you in the morning. In fact, I really will be tied up the whole day. Can we meet at six tomorrow?"

"Yes, no problem. Just tell me where."

"I'll be at Peter Christian's restaurant in Hanover at six. Do you know it?" Daley asked.

"Yes," Mallory said.

"If you get there first take one of the booths so we can talk privately," Daley said and abruptly hung up.

Mallory stared at the phone, listening to the grating buzz of the dial tone. It sounded like a tiny, angry insect caught in the lines, trapped and trying to get out.

He gently placed the receiver in the cradle.

Chapter Ten

Peter Christian's is a cellar restaurant underneath a travel agency and video store in the center of Hanover. A basketball player would hit his head on the low-beamed ceiling. Its decor is heavy dark-stained pine, high-backed booths along the wall and thick, shining polyurethaned tables down the center of a small room. An uncomfortable chest-level bar runs along the opposite wall.

But the food is fresh and well-prepared, and the atmosphere relaxed, so there are always people waiting—especially around six. Mallory arrived a few minutes early and waited impatiently in line, studying each lone male customer, trying to estimate if he was Daley. Fifteen minutes later he was still searching when he was escorted to a booth.

No lone males who fit Mallory's mental picture of Daley came in so he ordered coffee and a soup, which was served in an artsy heavy ceramic mug on a wooden paddle-board.

He finished his meal just before seven and still no Daley. He decided to phone him.

The public phone was in the back hall near the toilets. Mallory dialed and waited impatiently, his hopes sinking.

There was no answer.

For the next fifteen minutes he sipped his coffee, trying to control his too vivid imagination. Putting the best interpretation on it, Daley might simply be running late. A busy day can often get backed up. But then, this was not a normal day or a normal meeting. Daley knew that. It was clear from his voice before they hung up last night.

Under any reasonable circumstances he should be here. Or why couldn't he at least call the restaurant and leave a message?

No matter how he tried to handle his anxiety over Daley's being an hour late, a mist of fear seeped through the cracks. He went again to the back hallway and called Daley's number. Still nothing.

It was now almost seven-thirty. He couldn't stand it anymore. He paid his bill and left.

Daley's address on the "Redline Letter" was 96B Shaker Boulevard, Enfield. That was near the Shaker Village on Mascoma Lake. He checked a local map he had in the glove compartment.

Mascoma Lake was a mile off Route 89. It took him almost a half hour to find the turnoff and pick up Route 4, which passed the northern tip of the lake. Another local two lane tarmac, 4A, ran south along the western edge of the four mile long lake.

Mallory expected to find another of those pristine New Hampshire lakes, but instead he found an over-developed and over-populated middle-class resort. One house after another, sometimes no more than ten or twenty feet apart, squatted on the lakeside. Poor Mascoma, he thought. It must be struggling to keep its waters clean. Each side of the road was congested with cars and customized trucks pressed between the roadway and the houses. Pickups with spotlight racks on the roof and gunracks in the back window were everywhere. The pickups' metallic paint jobs, decorated with scroll work on the side panels, glowed eerily in his headlights as they flashed by. The lake seemed a silent black desert just beyond the cluster of houses and vehicles.

A couple of miles farther on the houses began to spread out and become more expensive. A La Salette Catholic Shrine appeared suddenly on the right. The "Shrine" was two large gray buildings and a theme park nestled at the bottom of a sloping hill. The whole place was lit up like a football stadium. Carefully trimmed hedge walkways with white statuary dotting the Shrine's park covered the slope.

Another, more quaint version of America's spiritual passion was a few hundred yards farther along on the left side of the road and backing onto the lake. A sign read "Shaker Village, founded 1761."

The village consisted of a Greek colonnaded graystone church, a large, four-story square building that looked like a monastery, and an assemblage of typical New England houses scattered closer to the lake's shore.

At least, Mallory thought, the Shaker Village wasn't surrounded by tarmac parking lots, neon lights and a manicured park with an army of bloodless saints in plaster-of-Paris robes standing mute and ghostlike in the shrubbery.

Mallory had been looking for it, but it still surprised him when it popped up in his headlights: An old and grubby, peeling, hand-painted billboard that read "Mascoma Lake Lodge and Resort." A fat arrow pointing left was bisected by the distance—1/4 of a mile. A later message had been plastered across the bottom of the billboard. "Sorry, we're temporarily closed."

This was it. He turned and passed by the southern tip of the lake, which was less than a quarter mile wide. From the looks of it the Mascoma Lake Lodge and Resort was more than "temporarily" closed. The three-story main building and barracks-like lodge were a ruin, windows either smashed out or boarded over with cracked, weathered plywood. There were holes in the roof, and the outside walls were covered with rotting shingles. It was hard to imagine families ever playing on the beach behind the deserted lodge or picnicking at the wooden tables scattered among the sparse pines along the beach.

As the road curved north on the eastern side of the lake, Mallory saw another arrow with a childishly hand-painted sign, "Shaker Blvd." There were no street lights, and practically all of the summer houses, even those that looked winterized, were empty. He was driving through a dead world, a desolate wind-rocked forest of trees and abandoned houses. The only living, moving things were the shadows. In his headlights the black shapes flipped past, racing alongside him, like fluid, emaciated creatures with bodies that bent into impossible shapes and scurried from tree to tree, always keeping just on the opposite side of the trunk.

A couple of miles along the winding, tree-lined lake road Mallory saw the sign, a simple wooden board hanging by picture wire from a nail in a tree. "The Daley's" it said.

A tire-rutted path on the left wound through the pines toward the lake's shore. Mallory turned into the drive. It was relatively smooth, covered with pine needles and only a few sudden holes to surprise the springs on his car. But for several hundred yards it twisted sharply among the trees.

When Mallory saw a dim light ahead he turned off the engine and sat for a moment, letting his eyes get used to the dark. The house, about twenty-five yards farther into the trees, was a darker square amongst the night shadows. He couldn't see well through the screen of trees, but it seemed only the single light was burning.

He opened the door and got out, shocked by the car's interior light suddenly illuminating the forest like an artificial dawn. He closed the door quickly, making as little noise as possible. But even his caution couldn't stop the loud click of the latch from echoing into the forest.

Every warning sense in his body was vibrating. He stood by the car door, his keys in his hand, listening. He had always enjoyed the night, standing quietly and feeling the dissonant harmonies of hidden forest voices. But tonight he felt only menace. The air seemed heavy with it.

He walked along the path slowly, cautiously, his ears straining for the smallest sounds. He stopped when he reached a clearing and stood next to a large pine tree, studying the house and grounds. The house was a bastardized two-story Cape Cod without any actual dormers, but a peaked roof shaped like a dormer. The lighted window was only about ten yards from the tree where he stood.

Mallory had approached from the northern side and could make out one end of a porch that was now enclosed in winter glass. The light came from the end window in the wall facing him. The other two ground floor windows on this side of the house were dark.

Silently, Mallory watched for almost five minutes. Nothing moved. And no sounds. Nothing. Not a voice, not a door closing, no footsteps. A screen of absolute stillness surrounded the house.

The flesh along his spine tingled, and the hair on the back of his neck bristled straight up.

The quiet was *too* complete. He couldn't even make

out any night sounds from the forest. It was as if an invisible blanket, one of those heavy mesh things they throw over bombs to muffle the explosion, had been spread over this part of the forest.

God, how he hated this. He didn't think of himself as a coward, but he was scared. As scared as he'd ever been in his life.

He *knew* something was wrong here. And the insane thing was that he had to go and see. He felt like he was approaching an accident: he knew it was bad, he knew there would be blood, and he knew he'd hate it. Yet he had to slow down and look at it.

But he wasn't being fair to himself. This was more than just a ghoulish interest in an accident. It was more than simply being relieved that someone else's misfortune had passed you by. This was his accident, or an accident waiting to happen to him around the next curve. His only hope to beat the awful odds building up around him was to see it all clearly, to understand what was going on and hope that he could avoid having it happen to him.

He walked slowly toward the house, feeling exposed as he moved away from the big pine. He kept to the left, out of the shaft of light coming from the window that illuminated an elongated patch of soggy brown grass.

A mist was suddenly rolling in from the lake. It rose up from the lake water, floating along the ground, caressing it like a lover.

It moved fast, so fast that he had the impression it was being blown toward him by giant fans.

The window was set high, about a foot above his eye-level. He picked up a fat rock and placed it in the soft soil beneath the window. Balancing himself on one foot he peered in.

The room was empty. A large pale blue couch was pressed against the right hand wall. A half dozen old clocks, none set to the right time, were scattered over the surface of an antique table.

A huge fireplace dominated the far wall and two stuffed easy chairs, their backs to Mallory, were placed in a half-circle in front of it. It was possible someone was sitting in one of them.

His foot and ankle began to ache so he stepped down. The ground sloped upward along this side of the house. Mallory moved quietly toward the other windows. They were dark, and he saw nothing moving.

He back-tracked and checked the windows on the other side of the house. Nothing. He hated the thought of it, but there was only one thing left to do. He had to go in.

The sense of dread that had been building within him surged up. He moved cautiously to the porch at the back of the house. He could hear the soft lapping of the lake behind him like a thirsty animal. The door was open, which in a way wasn't too surprising because people in this area were trusting and the burglary rate was extremely low. But something didn't seem right as he stepped inside.

He crept across the porch as quietly as he could, but the floors creaked. No matter how carefully he moved, the wooden floors groaned and snapped.

Damn it, he mumbled to himself. *Now that he wanted quiet the goddamn house wouldn't stop complaining.*

The porch opened onto a hallway that ran the length of the house. Mallory could see the open door of the lighted living room at the end of the hall's dark tunnel. He checked each side room as he tiptoed along the carpeted hall. Something in the air made him stop at the living room doorway. An odor. A dull yet penetrating smell with a slightly metallic quality. It reminded him of the smell of blood, yet he knew it wasn't. He had smelled blood too many times to mistake it. If a bruise had a smell, this would be it. But whatever it was, he didn't want to go into that room.

His heart thudding in his chest, he took a deep breath and stepped into the lighted room. It was empty . . . except for someone sitting in the fireplace easy chair closest to him. The chair was at an angle, facing partially away from him so he could only see a foot, the lower leg, and a man's light brown hightop Dunham work shoe.

He swallowed hard, a useless exercise since there was nothing there. His tongue felt like sandpaper.

Slowly, he walked over. The man was sitting with his head back, hands and arms on the armrests and his legs stretched toward the fireplace. Mallory assumed the man was Daley. His mouth was open, and you could imagine he had fallen asleep in front of a now-cold fire . . . except that the eyes were also open and his throat had been torn out. The expression in his eyes was one of pure terror.

Mallory stared, more shocked than he expected. The combination of Daley's open staring eyes and the terrible wound sickened him. He imagined Daley's fear and pain. . . .

Now he recognized it. The metallic odor. It was the smell of the raw open wound. For there was no blood, just a streak around the collar of his shirt and down the front of his chest. It was the fresh metal smell that hit you when you walked into a meat market as they were cutting up the morning's delivery.

He studied the wound, his training as a doctor taking over. It was not a normal cut throat. Mallory had seen that when he was an intern in Emergency. The throat wasn't just sliced horizontally, but literally torn out. The larynx itself and neck muscles on the right side of the neck were gone. The opening was large enough for him to put his fist in, and the flesh along the edge of the hole was jagged, as if it had been bitten by a powerful, hungry animal. A dog perhaps, or a large wildcat, would make such a horrible wound.

But what struck him most forcefully was the lack of blood. Just like Jeff. Daley's flesh glowed, as if the thin unnaturally white skin was nothing more than bleached parchment. Mallory was sure that, like Jeff's, the body had been drained of blood. But how? A wound like this would cause the place to look like a slaughter house. There would be blood everywhere.

He examined the body more closely. A slight stain of blood on the cuff of his shirt and on his wrist caught Mallory's eye. He gently pulled the cuff back. Two small puncture holes, like tiny black eyes, were etched into the skin, directly over the artery. He glanced over at the other arm and saw that a thin stream of blood had run down the inner arm of the chair. He lifted the cuff and found the same tiny cuts over the artery. But this time there were four holes, two sets about four inches apart.

He had seen enough horror movies in his time to immediately have visions of vampires sucking blood and tiny razor-teethed bats clinging to Daley's neck and arms. But that was ridiculous. More likely the blood-thirsty, insane cult responsible for this had put in needles and tubes to drain the blood from the arteries. The two sets of holes were probably just evidence of ineptness.

As he stared at Daley's pitiful, emaciated body the pressures of the whole insane week began to flash through his mind. He had seen many dead bodies, including the horrible desecration of Jeff Goldman, but now, standing in the room's glaring lights only three feet away from the dry-eyed staring corpse, he also felt the undeniable presence of an uncompromising evil, a cold and uncaring power that filled the night air like the chill winter mist outside. Whoever was responsible for these brutal, savage killings was truly insane. But it was madness with an icy resolve. Mallory sensed a kind of cold and implacable calculation in all this that left no room for pity, or indeed, any of the normal human feelings.

A shudder crackled through him, and he suddenly felt an immediate danger. As if the people who did this were returning, or already waiting for him outside in the darkness.

He moved out of the open light and into the shadows, not sure what to do. He didn't really think the killers were outside waiting for him. That was his nerves talking to him. If they wanted him the easiest way would be to come in the house and set him down in the other easy chair. But what should he do? Call the police? Did he want to report another killing . . . so similar to Jeff's? Two in the same week? He might never get free of the questions.

Get the hell out? That had a definite appeal. But maybe he could find something that would help? Daley seemed to know something was going on. Mallory could tell that from the way he had reacted when Hilary Baker's name came up.

He glanced around the room. No desk or files.

Carefully he began to search the house. There was nothing downstairs. Upstairs he checked each room carefully. He checked dresser drawers and the closets and found nothing of interest. When he opened the master bedroom he caught his breath and stared.

Oh, no. Goddamn it. He turned away and closed his eyes. His stomach gave a heave, bile flooding up into his throat.

When he looked back the old woman was still there. Stretched out on the bed, her eyes open and staring at the ceiling with the same expression, a mixture of horror and surprise. Her death had also been brutal. Five sets of tiny holes were scattered over her bruised, scrawny neck. Each hole was surrounded by a thin band of black and blue discoloration. He guessed that she was almost eighty and her circulation was probably poor.

"Had been poor," he corrected himself.

Mallory stood over the frail woman. She should have died peacefully in her sleep. Not like this, he thought. The old woman looked pitiful, a cast-off pale husk.

He put his fingers gently over her eyes and pressed the lids closed, but stiffening had already begun, and the dead flesh resisted. Cold and rigid, the stubborn lids stayed open so his fingers inadvertently scraped down over the dry glassine envelope of her eyeball.

Frozen gelatin. He jerked his hand away. The unblinking eyes stared up at him reproachfully, an old woman scolding an impetuous young man who intruded on her silence. He understood something at that moment, staring down at her sunken moon-white face, something that despite all the death and dying he had seen in the hospital, he had never really grasped before.

Leave the dead alone.

Tears welled up, choking him. He turned away and walked over to the window and looked outside. The dead are fixed in silence, space occupied but with no relationships, no contact with the world other than form. Everything is an intrusion to the dead . . . except silence. And we, the living, were always poking and prodding them. Cutting them open, pushing and pulling this part and that. Never respecting their silence. He would remember the lesson.

Leave the dead in peace.

Oh, Christ. Where was his objectivity now?

He stared out the window. The mist had turned into a full-blown, blinding fog. He could barely see the ground or the trees ten yards away. He turned and left the room, not looking back at the old woman. He had to finish his search and get out.

At the end of the hall he found what he was looking for. Daley's office. An old oak roll-top desk and a file cabinet were pressed against the far wall. The only other pieces of furniture in the small room were a couch and another chair.

He started with the files. There it was, "Hilary Baker." He took the file to the desk and snapped on the lamp. Disappointment flashed through him. The file was only a few pages long. It included her medical records, names of relatives, cause of death, which was listed as "heart failure," and other standard information. Her post mortem hematocrit was 250,000. Daley had underlined it and put a large question mark next to it.

Next to the question mark he had written *"Blood . . . Ask Father Paul???"*

"Ask Father Paul?" Mallory began rifling through the desk, searching for an address book. He found it next to the telephone.

Father Paul turned out to be a priest at the St. Simeon Catholic Church in Enfield. Mallory quickly jotted down his address and telephone number.

It was the only lead he had found after a half hour of searching. He wondered what Daley had talked over with his local priest. Why ask a priest about a hematocrit count?

Mallory was jolted from his reverie by the house beginning to talk again. A sharp squeal of wood on wood came from the attic. He felt a sudden urge to get out . . . now.

He put the file back and wiped his fingerprints off the drawer. The police were going to go over this house with a microscope, and he didn't want to be implicated in any way.

He carefully turned off the light. When he left he closed the door, cleaning the doorknob as he went. He did the same with each door knob and drawer he remembered touching.

When he left the house he returned the same way he had come, scuffling anyplace he saw soft sand. He stopped and covered over his footprints under the window. Then he wiped the rock and moved it back where he found it.

He paused at the large pine tree and went over everything in his mind. Had he forgotten anything? He didn't think so. He shivered and pulled his jacket closer around his throat. The fog had turned into a freezing sheet of icy particles, and he felt them collecting on his exposed skin.

When he reached the car he immediately locked the doors. A silly precaution, he thought, considering what he was facing, but still, it made him feel better. He started the car and turned on the heater. He shivered again, but this time not from the cold. What he had seen and felt in that house had shaken him to his core.

With his lights still off, he backed the car into a small opening between two trees and turned around. He drove slowly out the long drive with only his parking lights on. When he reached the lake drive he breathed a sigh of relief and snapped on his headlights. But as he drove the vision of Daley's terror-stricken eyes and his mangled throat kept coming back. And the old woman's face, the tight, strained facial muscles pulled into that nightmarish expression of horror . . .

He had held himself in check, calling upon every ounce of medical objectivity he could generate. But now it all rose up from somewhere deep in his gut. He pulled over to the side of the road and opened the car door just in time. His stomach shuddered violently, and all the raw fear and the horror of these slaughters exploded upward.

When it finally ended he was left in a cold sweat, his stomach queasy. He wiped his mouth with the back of his hand and put his head back on the car seat. He breathed deeply for several minutes, trying to control the nausea.

Still sickened, he closed the door. He had to get control of himself. He pressed down on the gas pedal and raced down the dark road, back the way he had come, almost happy to see the dilapidated Mascoma Lodge again. It no longer looked haunted, just tired and sick.

Daley's was haunted, he thought. It was a house that had had an indelible imprint burned into it from the acids of human violence. It had seen things take place within its walls that couldn't help but scar its history. It would never be the same. And neither would Mallory.

Chapter Eleven

St. Simeon's was a small white church at the base of a hill covered with tombstones. The graveyard behind the church, like the building itself, dated back to the 18th century.

Mallory had no trouble finding it. Directions from a gas station took him along Route 4A again, but a mile before the Shaker Village he turned off onto a rusted bridge that spanned a narrows, like the neck of an hour glass separating the two widest parts of Mascoma Lake. A single-lane brick underpass brought him to a mile-long gradual incline. The church was on the left as the road entered Enfield, a small village whose main buildings were a bank and post office. The police station, a few hundred yards past St. Simeon's, was part of the town library, and both were housed in a wooden-shingled family home converted to town use.

He had telephoned Father Paul an hour before. When he had mentioned that he was a doctor at Hitchcock and wanted to see him about a problem that Dr. Daley also had, the priest agreed to meet him immediately. Since he had appointments and a morning mass he couldn't leave, and Mallory would have to drive to Enfield.

Mallory parked his car in a vacant sand lot across the

street. The church was tiny by modern standards. A single large room for services, Mallory suspected.

As he mounted the few steps to the church the front door opened and a small, white-haired priest with a flushed round face put out his hand.

"I'm Father Paul," he said, smiling. His smile was warm and his handshake firm.

Before he could answer, Father Paul said, "And you're Dr. Mallory."

"Yes," Mallory said, "I'm pleased to meet you. Thank you for seeing me on such short notice."

"Well, I have a suspicion what it is you wish to speak to me about, and if I'm right, time is probably important."

The priest took him by the arm and led him inside. "Come, we'll be more comfortable in my office."

Mallory followed him to a door at the rear of the church, to the right of a simple triangular apse. An ancient oak lectern with a white linen cloth thrown over it dominated a two-step platform that ran the width of the church.

The room was tiny, no more than ten by ten. But two stuffed leather chairs had been squeezed in and were placed facing a small wooden desk. A four-drawer wood file cabinet was against the right hand wall. A cast-iron cross, with a crudely sculpted figure of the anguished Christ, hung behind Father Paul's desk. It must have sentimental value, Mallory thought. It surely didn't have much aesthetic value. It looked like it had been done by a talented child.

"Here, sit down," Father Paul said, motioning to one of the leather chairs. "I took the liberty of making us some tea. You do like tea, don't you?" he asked.

"Yes, of course," Mallory said, still studying the cross. It did have a certain primitive power.

Father Paul poured the tea from an electric hot-pot

that sat on top of the file cabinet into two gigantic white mugs. He noticed Mallory looking at the cross and smiled.

"That is a keepsake," he said, handing Mallory his tea and settling himself into his plain hardback office chair behind the desk. "It was carved and cast by an idiot savant. A beautiful child, or rather a man when he did this, with a seven or eight year old child's perception of the world."

"Was it a gift?" Mallory asked.

"Yes, specifically for me." Father Paul turned his head and looked up at the cross behind him. "Just before he died," he said.

"At the too young age of nineteen . . ." he added after a moment.

He turned to Mallory and smiled. "Well, I don't have much time, Dr. Mallory. I have mass in . . ." He glanced at a yellow Westclock on the top of the file cabinet, ". . . in less than an hour. So, what is it that I can do for you?"

Mallory liked the priest. He seemed an open and honest man. Full of Irish emotion, Mallory suspected, but that was all right with him. A little normal temperament at this time would be welcome. He decided to tell him the whole story and let the chips fall where they may. He would start with Betty Milner's death and the low hematocrit. If Daley had spoken to the priest about his patient's blood count, at least there would be some understanding. As for the rest . . . well, perhaps he would be lucky and at least have a sympathetic listener, if not a believer.

Beginning with the birth of the Milner child, Mallory told him everything. Except about last night. He had listened to the morning news and nothing had been reported. The bodies obviously hadn't been discovered yet, and he didn't want to tell him about

Daley's death until he saw his reaction to the rest.

He didn't embellish anything in the telling and left it as ugly as when he had experienced it. When he finished, Father Paul didn't say anything. He had his fingers laced before him on the desk. He was studying them, as if trying to figure out how to separate them.

Several minutes passed by and the two men sat silently. Mallory knew his story was difficult to digest and was prepared to give the priest all the time he needed.

Father Paul glanced up at Mallory, and his eyes stayed on the younger man's face. He fingered an obsidian or onyx rosary that hung over his heart. Mallory couldn't tell which of the shiny black stones it might be.

"I am going to be frank with you, Dr. Mallory." He sucked in his breath, a sigh of resolution. "I should preface what I'm going to tell you by assuring you that I am not crazy, or even borderline psychotic."

He smiled wryly. "Although I know some who would give you an argument on that little point."

The priest rose and began to slowly pace around the tiny room. "Also, let me assure you," he went on, "that I am not digressing by this little confession. It will all have a direct bearing on why Walter Daley came to me with his 'problem'."

Mallory noticed that Father Paul had used the word ironically. He was full of subtle little tones of voice; emotions and feelings not so much expressed overtly, but rather, Mallory suspected, as part of a code by which the priest tested the receptivity and intelligence of his listeners. He used these little vocal flags as a kind of emotional semaphore.

He stopped at his desk, took a sip of his tea and looked up at the crude iron cross. Then he turned and looked directly at Mallory. "I have been, during my checkered career as a servant of Christ, an exorcist."

The priest watched Mallory over the giant rim of his tea cup, which he had raised again to his lips. He held it there for so long that it began to seem a protective ceramic mask.

Mallory smiled inwardly. He couldn't dare show his pleasure openly. The priest would misinterpret him. But he smiled for several reasons. One, Mallory recognized that the good father was, even at the advanced age of his late sixties, still shy and vulnerable. Two, he knew he was really in it now . . . talking to an exorcist—*and accepting it!* And three, he was amused at his own reaction: He was relieved the man was an exorcist! He knew he was out of his depth with what he had come to call "this madness." He needed a specialist, someone who understood the peculiar insanity of these savage psychotics.

And here he is. Mallory smiled again.

"You find that amusing, Doctor?" the priest asked, his tone several degrees cooler than a few minutes ago.

"No, no," Mallory assured him quickly. "I was smiling because I had finally met someone who might be able to help me and clarify what the hell is going on."

"You may not feel the same way after I've told you the whole story . . . of why I got involved in the occult."

Father Paul plopped himself into the leather chair next to Mallory. He clasped his hands in his lap, put his head back and closed his eyes.

"I was a young priest just out of seminary, a passionate believer in everything I'd been taught. Uncritically, mind you. I never questioned the authority of my teachers. I accepted them and the church hierarchy as older, wiser, and far more able to deal with the world and its problems than I.

Father Paul smiled. "I had one passion, a single ideal

to which I wanted to devote my life. I wanted to serve Christ as the Master Himself had served the world. I worked like no other earnest young priest had ever worked. Until I met him. Jamie.

"Jamison Leo Kilpatrick. Another poor Irish from the lower east side of New York."

Father Paul looked at the iron cross, nostalgia in his eyes. "Jamie's mother was a waitress. A large-hipped, healthy Irish girl with startling red hair and equally red cheeks and lips. Her husband, Jamie's father, was killed in a construction accident the first day on his new job after arriving in this country.

"I met Jamie when his mother brought him to the church for counseling." Father Paul clasped and unclasped his hands several times as he sought for the right words.

"She was worried about the boy, for, you see, he was what they pejoratively called 'an idiot' or 'imbecile' in those days. Today I believe he'd be considered an idiot savant.

"He had an amazing talent to hear music once and immediately repeat the phrasing and notes exactly. With sculpting he had . . . a kind of . . . crude grace. Sometimes," Father Paul went on, "Jamie could create surprisingly powerful images. He said he had the pictures in his head, and he just copied what he saw. He also heard voices and saw things that would sometimes come true. But I didn't believe a breath of it at the time. In the Bible we are warned about soothsayers and those with strange powers. We were taught that such things were the work of the devil and to be avoided.

"When I learned of his strange talent I rejected it as either his febrile imagination or an aberration, an obscure part of his overall mental condition.

"What I didn't do is trust him, or accept what was happening to him as genuine and therefore worthy of being taken seriously. I ignored it even as I saw it tearing him apart. I was being true, you see, to the teachings of my church. And the church is, like most institutions, uncomfortable dealing with things they cannot control.

"But Jamie, that sweet boy, had none of our adult rational structures to hold onto. His childish mind believed every vision literally; every voice, every warning or dark image from his unconscious was to him as real as the clay under his flying fingers.

"The first day his mother brought the boy to me he had a great gash on his forehead. Twenty-four stitches it took to repair the damage from a fearful child's angry rock. You see, Jamie had been telling the other children about his voices and visions."

The priest sat back, his eyes raised to the ceiling. "Picture it. A big boy, nineteen years old and almost six feet tall and heavy in body and face, confiding to his mental peers, boys seven, nine and ten, describing in graphic detail that he had seen one of them dead alongside the road. His bloody head crushed and hanging over the curb.

"Well, within a few weeks one of the boys, the seven year old, was hit by a truck and his head crushed when it hit the cement curb. You can imagine the hysteria. Not only was Jamie ostracized, but they believed he had the evil eye, and the other children began chasing him and throwing stones at him.

"That is when I met him. In desperation his mother had brought him to me. She wanted me to convince him to stop telling people about his visions.

"I did my best. I talked and talked; I quoted scriptures. I appealed to his good nature to not frighten the other children. This was the most effective, for Jamie was a gentle soul.

"Well, all this fast talking on my part worked for a

while. Each time he'd come and talk with me he'd stay out of trouble for a few weeks. But then, bless him, he'd forget. His mother feared he was going mad, for the visions, and voices were coming more often. A climax came when Jamie had a vision of a neighborhood girl, a beautiful golden child of nine. He saw her dead, her body covered in blood.

"Jamie came to me, desperate. And for the first time I learned that strangers in the neighborhood, whom he called 'the shadow people,' were following him and asking him to come away with them. These shadow people only approached him from dark alleyways, from the shadows of darkened buildings and at night. They told him that his visions were real, and that he had a great talent that only they could appreciate and use.

"In the palm of his hand someone had scrawled a pentagram—in blood. He had run all the way to the church, his hand held far out in front of him. He came into my room clutching his wrist, holding the hand out to me, palm up, staring at the awful design.

"He was afraid of it, you see. He knew it was evil and dangerous. Which was wiser than me by far. I, in my confident theological training saw it only as a cruel joke, a nasty bit of vandalism."

Father Paul stopped now, his expression one of anguish. When he began speaking again his eyes were shining with tears.

"Sobbing, Jamie told me that the shadow people had pulled him into an abandoned building and one of them, a tall man with a very white face, had cut his own fingers with a white-handled barber's razor and made the sign in Jamie's palm as the others held him down.

"Jamie was especially terrified of the tall man because the night before he had a vision and saw him kill a little blond girl that Jamie knew from the neighborhood. He hadn't told anyone of this vision except me. I calmed him and reassured him as best I could, but I didn't . . . I didn't *believe* him.

"Two days later the little girl was missing. Gone all night. Parents frantic, angry mobs searching the streets. The police had no leads. Vigilante search parties scoured the neighborhood. She was nowhere to be found.

"And then Jamie, hearing the cries over the missing girl, came to me again. He trusted me, you see . . ."

Again, Father Paul paused. He wiped his hand across his face again, a gesture of despair Mallory was coming to recognize.

"Well . . . again I didn't believe him. I convinced him to go to the police and tell them all he knew. I explained to the police that the boy was simple—and he had these visions, but they didn't mean anything. He was a good boy and wouldn't hurt a fly.

"Of course they ignored me. They thought the 'big idiot,' that's what one of them called him, had killed the girl and hidden her body. So they began looking for the building Jamie had described.

"They found it . . . and the girl. Her body had been cut into five parts and each part placed in one of the five corners of a Satanic pentagram. Jamie was arrested, but too many people had seen him on the day and time that the pathologist placed the child's murder.

"He was released within thirty-eight hours. Then . . . oh, my God, I wish I had never lived through this . . . then, the very next day Jamie himself was missing.

"His body was found two days later by some children who were playing in an abandoned tenement.

"Jamie was nailed to the wall in a rubbish-filled room on the second floor. His body hung upside down in a satanic parody of the crucifixion. Big iron nails had been driven through his ankles and wrists."

Again, Father Paul passed his hand briefly over his eyes, as if physically trying to wipe away that terrible scene. "His throat had been cut to the bone," he said, his voice so hoarse it was little above a whisper.

The priest paused and closed his eyes. For a minute he said nothing. Then, in the same sad, quiet voice, he said, "I don't need to tell you the self-recrimination I put myself through. The fires of hell were too good for me. If suicide were not such a sin I would have joined the poor boy in death.

"I took leave of my duties, and for over a year I carried on an inquisition with my conscience far worse than Torquemada could ever have imagined. I fervently wished for time to go backwards so I could thrash the arrogance from my miserable being with thistle and thorns. Flagellation was, it seemed to me, the only punishment for my facile reliance on the smug theology of my church.

"Oh, yes, we admit to the existence of evil forces in theory, but the pastorals and advice we get from the church proper is really just theologically dressed-up 'Dear Abby.'

"As young priests we were advised to downplay the supernatural whenever the subject was brought up, which was rarely, and to guide the faithful toward a socially acceptable integration of their problems. In other words, to politely deny the existence of evil in our everyday lives and have parishioners seek psychological comfort and counseling. It was a 'keep-them-happy-and-ignorant' philosophy."

The old priest laughed, with more than a tinge of bitterness.

"Ah, yes, ironically, evil in world affairs was an acceptable part of the dialogue. We could say, for example, that the Nazis were evil, the communists were evil and working Satan's will. But when it came to personal problems, to the question of whether evil could actually exist in our daily lives, we relied, like Ann Landers and Dear Abby, on the psychologically convenient bromides.

"So, there I was, feeding bromides to a child-man who needed wisdom and honesty, who simply needed to be accepted, to be believed."

The old priest looked up at Mallory, his eyes scarlet with misery. "Even today I wonder what would have happened if I had simply said, 'Yes, I understand Jamie. I believe you.'

"When I returned to my church I was a changed man. I no longer was sure of the church's infallibility. I questioned everything as the creation of imperfect men ... no matter how high they were in the church hierarchy. I read everything I could find on Satan worship and occultism. And yes ... when people came to me, frightened by what they considered evil influences in their lives, I accepted them.

"You see, Jamie taught me to accept the existence of real evil in our world. I now know that evil exists ... not simply something to be used as a stick to frighten people into accepting God, but as a tangible, everyday reality in our lives. Something we must confront and overcome.

"I continued my work after I moved to New England. Dr. Daley knew of my involvement with these ... arcane religious beliefs ... and came to ask me for help."

He glanced up at Mallory and smiled. "You have the quality all good doctors should possess. You're a compassionate listener. But now you see why I could never deny you ... or anyone confronting these dark corners of life. I will help you in any way I can. What is it you wish of me?"

"First, the answers to a few questions."

He nodded his head, "Of course."

"Why did Dr. Daley consult you about his patient's hematocrit?"

"I'm sorry?" Father Paul said, looking puzzled.

"His patient's hematocrit, her red blood count?"

After a few seconds the priest grinned. "Oh, I see. No, he didn't ask me about that. He wanted to know about the religious significance of blood."

Mallory was stunned.

Had Daley known so much about what was going on? But why, then, hadn't he gone to the authorities?

A damned silly question, he thought. *Could he have gone to Dr. Pearce, or any of the Chiefs of Surgery, when he began to suspect something strange was going on? Not too likely. They'd shoot him full of thorazine and put him in a padded cell. And don't forget the moral behind Father Paul's little story about Jamie. Even someone as compassionate and open as Father Paul hadn't been convinced until it was too late. Look at the police's response to Jeff's death—especially when he hinted that something odd might be happening. Their only reaction was to suspect that Jeff might be mixed up with a weird cult. Charlie Manson loose in Norwich, Vermont? But then, wasn't that where he was heading now himself? How could he blame them? He had resisted the idea that this madness might involve anything beyond the ordinary insanity of modern life.*

"But haven't you talked about this with Dr. Daley?" Father Paul asked. "He could tell you more about his interest in blood sacraments . . . and his motives for asking . . . than I."

Mallory didn't know what to say. He wanted to tell the priest about Daley's death—but he would be putting himself in jeopardy if the police ever questioned the priest.

"Father Paul, could we talk in strict confidence? I

mean, could our conversation be under some sort of privilege, a 'vow of silence' perhaps?"

"If you mean the sacredness of confession, no, I'm sorry. We are having a normal conversation, and I can't interpret that as confession. Are you Catholic?"

Mallory shook his head.

"Then I am sorry. I can't offer the protection of the confessional."

For several moments the two men sat in silence. Then Father Paul said, "If it is important to you, I could give you my word that I will not speak of it to anyone without your permission . . . even under penalty of the law."

The priest's red-rimmed, piercing blue eyes were studying Mallory. "Unless, of course, you have committed some terrible crime. I could not offer my word under those conditions."

"Of course not. I understand," said Mallory. *He needed the priest. He needed him desperately. If anyone could help him, it was Father Paul.*

"I accept your word, Father Paul. And put your mind at ease, I haven't committed any crime. To answer your original question: I haven't talked with Dr. Daley because he's dead. Murdered."

The priest's face went white. "Oh, no. Sweet Jesus. What happened?"

Mallory told him the rest of the story. He omitted no detail of what he'd seen. When he'd finished Father Paul was shaking his head sadly as he poured himself another cup of tea.

"The old woman was Daley's mother," Father Paul finally said. "She'd been in failing health the last few years, and he'd taken her in so he could care for her until the end."

He sat down again in the leather chair next to

Mallory. For a moment he sipped his tea. Mallory could smell the tannin. The brew looked and smelled black now, for it had been steeping almost an hour.

"He was a good man," Father Paul finally said. "Kind and considerate of others. And I also now understand why he was so interested in the significance of blood in religious practices. At the time he didn't explain any of this. But it all clearly revolves around blood sacraments."

He paused and glanced at the clock, calculating how long he had until Mass.

"But apparently he wasn't as fully informed as you are. All his questions to me were general. He suspected something, I'm sure, but he was still searching.

"Blood," the priest said as he rose and walked to a small bookcase next to the file cabinet. He took down a book, *The Varieties of Religious Experience,* by William James, and flipped through its pages. He read for a moment, his lips moving slightly. Then he snapped the book closed, put it back on the shelf and opened another, a large black volume. Mallory could just make out the title, *The Encyclopedia of Black Magic.*

"Yes, yes," he murmured to himself as he walked back to his desk and sat down. After a moment he looked up at Mallory, his face grave.

"First, let me be clear. I don't understand what is going on any more than you do, but I can make a few educated guesses. I can't speculate about the mothers' deaths—that's a medical problem—but as for the doctors, a vicious cult could be involved or simply a lone madman, a religious fanatic obsessed with doctors, roaming the country killing them if they deliver a child on a certain day. But because of the apparent complexity of planning, the involvement of the child care agency in New York, and the deaths of the mothers, I'd have to agree with you that it is a group.

"The key is the blood. I didn't realize the full extent of what was going on when Dr. Daley came to me. Perhaps he didn't either."

Father Paul gently closed the book that lay open on the desk before him. He stared at the gold lettering on its cover.

"You should understand that blood has been one of the most significant parts of religious practice since the first pagans prayed to their stones and trees.

"In prehistoric times blood was used as a sacred drink to vitalize the warriors or chiefs, and to make barren women fertile. I'm sure you know that many primitive tribes hoped to absorb their enemy's spirit by drinking his blood or eating his flesh. Indeed, blood was used to bring forth any form of new life for it was believed to have enormous generative power. The priests of Baal cut great gashes in themselves so their blood would appease the gods and bring rain. The Aztecs, Mayans, and Incas cut their tongues, noses, and ears, and pushed giant agave thorns through their penises to honor their gods. They cut off the fingertips of captives so the blood could be used to communicate with the gods.

"In the Middle Ages most people believed leprosy could be cured by bathing in the blood of young children. Hans Andersen the writer witnessed an execution in 1823 and then watched as the parents of an epileptic child scooped the dead man's blood from between the cobblestones and gave it to their son as a cure.

"Witches traditionally signed pacts with the devil in their own blood. This is the origin of the idea when people consummate a friendship or vow by mingling their blood. And some even went so far as to drink each other's blood and call themselves 'blood brothers.'"

Mallory was becoming impatient, but he could tell that the lecture was coming to a close. "Blood is also used by satanic cults as a means of generating energy," the priest concluded, "to call forth spirits, or to solemnize their sacraments in the same way all religions have done for millennia."

"All right," Mallory said. "But what possible connection could all this have with mothers dying during childbirth . . . and doctors being slaughtered a year later? It's so damned frustrating. I know that blood is important, but I still don't know why."

"It seems to me you're dealing with two separate things here . . . the medical deaths of the mothers and the ritual murders of doctors. With the doctors' killings some things are clear. We're obviously dealing with a satanic cult, not only because of the blood, but because each doctor delivered a baby on a precise given date. February 2nd is a holy day, one of four major sabbats celebrated by wicca. In Christianity it's celebrated as Candlemas, the presentation of Christ to the temple. But in Satanism all that is turned on its head. In fact, in Satanism most rituals are foul versions of Christian sacraments. The terrible baptism of blood is a dark analogy of the Christian being 'washed in the blood of the lamb.' The Christian baptism produces salvation, the satanic is simply a dark parody, a washing in the blood of the hooved animal Satan. It's a vampire baptism. A blood exchange baptism. In fact, Dracula, and vampires generally, have been seen as anti-Christ figures."

"But what does all this mean? How does it help us?"

"I'm not sure yet. But I promise you I'll find out." The priest glanced at his yellow Westclock. "I must leave in a few minutes for Mass. You are welcome to stay and browse through my books."

Mallory could hear hushed voices coming from the church, the rustle of coats and the shuffling of feet as people entered and settled into the pews.

"Here," the priest said, pushing the large black book toward him. "Read this section on Satan worship and blood sacraments. We'll talk later."

He rose and walked to the door. His hand on the knob, he turned to Mallory. "Tell me, how did all the other doctors die?"

"I don't know yet. That was going to be my next step after talking with you."

"I wouldn't be surprised if you find they all died in the same fashion as Dr. Daley and Dr. Goldman ... killed ritually and their blood drained."

"For some reason, neither would I," Mallory said. "And each death will probably be listed as an unsolved murder."

"Yes," Father Paul said, his hand still on the doorknob. "And isolated. No connections between them ... except the ones you've discovered."

The old priest seemed suddenly tired. "You know Dr. Mallory, I don't want to frighten you, but I wouldn't rely too heavily on the pattern so far. Even though each doctor was not killed until a full year after he delivered a child, I think you may be in considerably more danger now than you realize."

Oh, I realize it ... I realize it, Mallory thought as Father Paul closed the door after him. *And it scares the shit out of me.*

Chapter Twelve

Mallory did not return home until late in the afternoon. He had read through a half dozen books in Father Paul's small but highly specialized library, growing more disgusted with each black revelation he stumbled upon. He had not realized the dark depths that the warped human mind could succumb to.

Mallory could hardly believe what he was reading. In one book on Christian tortures there was a detailed description of a young girl's painful death. The aim was to rid the unbelieving victim of demons, which, of course, meant freeing her from believing what the torturer disagreed with. The girl was sewn into the freshly gutted carcass of a large dog and left day after day in the sun until the growing multitude of maggots ate her alive. To make the process go faster the animal's intestines were often pushed back into the carcass and stuffed around the girl.

Mallory shook his head as he read of the incredible tortures devised by religious fanatics. The human imagination is surely wondrous and can, with genius, scale mysterious heights, he reasoned, but its power to ascend is equalled by its capacity to slide into a cool and calculated brutality that the hot violence of nature could never duplicate.

As much as madness tears apart the fabric of common humanity, so does it offend something deeper. Call it a communion of selves, a union of spirit, whatever it is that heals and fuses things. William James used the metaphor of each individual being a unique tree, yet the roots supporting each self go deep into a common ground and are nourished by a common stream.

Mallory agreed. Humans have an instinctual bond that excites all our communal efforts. It is a powerful force that spins the wheels of progress, that incites the individual to sacrifice one's self for others, and even drives the dynamo of impossible dreams... like organizing a trip to the moon.

The mad brutality of the black arts horrified him because of its senseless, systematic unraveling of the human fabric, of that wondrous tapestry that brought us up out of the dark pits of instinctual violence. Isolated madness cuts a single cord, perhaps a few threads, but the systematic madness of the holocaust, or the practice of the black arts, unravels whole sections of common evolution, for it excites an implacable, instinctual violence in masses of people.

Mallory despised the cold resolve that created such mass insanity because it shattered his world. It also scared him to death.

How, he thought as he left St. Simeon's, *how do you fight such madness?*

The martial solution would be to kill them. Medicine's solution would be to find them, isolate them and fill them with tranquilizers.

Tell that to Jeff Goldman and Walter Daley, he thought bitterly. *And to all the others over the last twelve years that have suffered at their hands.*

But still, Mallory was relieved. Father Paul had

agreed to do everything in his power to help. They had to be patient . . . and careful, Father Paul had said. Move slowly, cautiously, for these people would obviously not hesitate to kill them if they got in their way. Father Paul believed that there were many groups in America secretly practicing a wild variety of occultism, but this vicious group was not only secret, it was willing to kill anyone to keep it so. That, no doubt, was what had happened with Jeff Goldman.

Father Paul was going to call some people he knew who were involved with the occult underground and see what he could learn. After that they were at a loss about what to do. Wait and see what Father Paul could come up with . . . and then perhaps look up the families of the other dead women. But that seemed to be grasping for straws. Or, perhaps they should go visit Bowker again. Father Paul thought that together they might be able to shake something loose. The priest was as curious as Mallory about why he was the only doctor who had survived beyond a year.

One thing was sure . . . Mallory didn't want to wait twelve months for his turn in order to discover the truth.

Mallory waited two days for Father Paul's call. And while he waited he talked with Lili, explaining what he had discovered at Daley's and about his conversations with Father Paul. Lili was fascinated by news of the priest and questioned Mallory about him. She thought the priest would be an invaluable ally. Mallory also spent many hours at Dartmouth's Baker Library reading about occultism and Satanism.

He had just returned from dinner at Lili's when he discovered that Father Paul had called. It was late, almost one in the morning, and he found two messages on his machine. Each had a tone of urgency. He was debating whether it was too late to return the calls when the phone rang.

"Thank God," Father Paul breathed when Mallory picked up. "I thought something had happened to you."

"No," Mallory laughed. "I just came in and was wondering whether it was too late to call you."

"My friend, when you hear what I've learned, you may wish we'd never met."

"I doubt that," Mallory said. "Nothing could turn me away now."

"When can we meet?" Father Paul asked. "I can't talk about this on the phone."

"Shall I come over now?"

"Yes, I'll be waiting for you in the church," the priest said. Then the line went dead.

Mallory pulled up in front of St. Simeon's a half hour later, that old sick feeling in the pit of his stomach. He had been anxiously waiting for something to happen, but now, when Father Paul obviously had important news, he found he wasn't ready. The priest's call had unsettled him. The warmth and feeling of comfort generated by his evening with Lili had disappeared quickly, drowned by his too vivid imagination.

The front door of the church was open, and Mallory let himself in. The church was dark except for a crack of light surrounding Father Paul's slightly open office door. The sharp spray of yellow light guided him down the dark aisle.

He pushed open the door quietly. Father Paul was sitting at his desk, a single lamp casting a soft light over his hands and the book he was reading.

The old priest looked up and smiled, relief shining in his eyes. "Ahh, thank God, you're here."

He got up and walked around the desk, motioning Mallory toward one of the leather chairs. "Here, sit . . . sit . . ." he said impatiently with a wave of his hand.

He settled heavily into the chair next to Mallory. He reached over and patted Mallory's arm several times with rapid, nervous touches of affection.

"I have both good and bad news. I'm sorry it's been so long in coming, but everyone I have approached . . . well, to say they didn't want to talk to me is an understatement. Whoever they are, this group is one of the most frightening and vicious I have ever come across. People I talked with were terrified! As soon as I asked about a 'blood-seed' cult that held Candlemas, February 2nd, as an especially holy sabbat, their expression changed. Fear! That's the only way I can describe it. I couldn't pry any information from them, even with a promise of heavenly dispensation.

"I finally found one little weasel . . . no, that's unkind of me . . . one lost soul who was particularly brave because he was high. He had already been communing with his own angels and demons, so I don't suppose he minded talking with a lowly priest of an opposing deity. Nothing bothered him . . . not even the possibility of being crucified and bled to death by his own kind. He was flying . . . an immortal, you see. He was regarding all things earthly from on high."

The priest had used "blood seed" several times in conversation, and Mallory took advantage of a brief pause in his breathless narrative to ask, "What's a blood seed cult?"

"It's hard to explain. In its simplest definition blood is used as a seed . . . as a catalyst. You could explain it in terms of modern chemistry where one chemical is used to change the characteristics of another. Like fitting a chemical key into a chemical lock. Blood is used in a similar way to open certain doors that have remained shut for great periods of time... until a powerful combination of ritual and blood stimulates the dark powers to open the door and bring forth still greater forces. Or, at least that's the theory.

"If the timing is right... if the right ritual is used in conjunction with the powers of nature... then almost anything can be accomplished. Any power can be brought forth."

"How do the powers of nature fit in?" Mallory asked, puzzled. "I thought the black arts used different forces that were beyond natural law?"

The priest smiled. "It's not so simple as natural law versus unnatural forces. You have to understand that these people believe that all power already exists in the universe and is ready to be used. Nature uses one aspect, the black arts another. At certain moments there are... for want of a better term... key intersections where these forces meet. Rituals performed at these high energy palimpsests generate enormous power. Blood seeded at this moment is like a match to a pyramid of dry wood, igniting the potential energy waiting trapped within."

"I see," Mallory said, not at all sure that he did. "Rituals as a cyclotron and blood seeds as particles in an atom smasher."

Father Paul grinned, his face flushed. "Despite your sarcasm, Doctor, I think you have it. Anyway, my outer-space informant couldn't tell me much about the group itself. No one seems to know more than a few whispers. They have no name and are fanatically secret. The good news is that it's rumored they meet in an abandoned church. The bad news is that no one knows where it is. Somewhere in New England is the best I could find out."

"Oh, that's wonderful," Mallory said. "That leaves us only several million square miles to search."

"There is a little more," Father Paul said. "My informant tells me that the church is very old, one of the first built after the pilgrims landed in New England. Most early churches were constructed in the 18th century and a few ruins from the 17th century still exist."

He pushed the large book he had been reading toward Mallory. "This is a list of early churches . . . and their locations. It also tells us whether the building is a ruin or still used for services.

"Here," he said, pointing his finger at three churches he had checked off. "These are all in New England, all still standing, and all abandoned."

Mallory glanced down the list. One south of Plymouth, Massachusetts, another in southern Maine, and the third in New Hampshire, near Exeter between Portsmouth and Salem, where the coast and the three states intersect.

"Which one do you want to try first?" Mallory asked.

"The closest," Father Paul said, pointing at the "First Congregational Church of New England."

Chapter Thirteen

As they drove south on Route 89 to the New Hampshire coast, a short strip of land only eighteen miles wide squeezed between Maine and Massachusetts, another February storm drifted unexpectedly across the high ridges of the White Mountains and obliterated the midday sun. There did not seem any immediate threat of rain, but the overcast sky darkened the day and colored their mood.

New England is a place of contrasts. When the weather is not sunny, or the vast blue sky and crystalline air not dominant, it will most likely be cold, wet, and dark. Today was the exception. It was miserable without being dramatic, a dull battleship gray day without stark contrasts. It entirely lacked that quality of change common to New England that was so sudden it took the breath away.

The First Congregational Church of New England had been built deep in the woods a few miles from Exeter, one of the first towns settled in New Hampshire in the 18th century. A stooped, thick-lensed old New Englander pumping gas knew where it was. The old man's eyes were a shining bright blue, and when they touched something they tended to hold on. He was staring at Mallory when he told them the old church was the first ever built in New Hampshire . . . and that it had a bad reputation. No local people ever went near the place. A witch named Heather Williams had been burned in the field near there in 1749 . . . and another witch called Goody Pritchard had been beaten to death in the cemetery. It was set off on an isolated two-lane, pot-holed tarmac in thick stands of pine and aspen. A hand-painted roadsign with an arrow would point them to "Exeter Church."

The deeper they drove into the forest, the more brooding the day became. Great bruised blue-black clouds swept over the vaulted dome of tree tops. Daylight shadows lost their definition and became an amorphous darkness spread over everything. Gloomy stands of pine and ash and birch seemed silent sentries to the slow progress through their domain. Mallory rolled his window down, hoping the fresh air would revive his flagging spirits. But a mist had risen from the woods. It filtered slowly across the road, giving the impression that they were driving through an ominous gray cloud that was determined to obscure their way.

Father Paul, who was leaning forward peering through the fog, grabbed Mallory's arm. "There . . ." he said, pointing. A wooden board hanging from one nail on an ancient pine, the arrow aimed at the earth, said "Exeter Chu. . . ."

Mallory turned into the single lane road. It was what he had come to call a "washboard road," for the cross-hatchings came rapidly, jangling the car so violently that the springs thudded and squealed. They travelled five more miles into the woods when they suddenly saw the church. It reared above them, off to the left on a steep hill, a gray fieldstone and wood structure surrounded by the brown dead grass of a rocky field.

They parked next to the road, and when they got out

of the car the silence struck them almost as a physical blow. Perhaps it was just the muting effect of the fog, but there wasn't a rustle of a leaf, not even the distant call of a bird. A stream ran quietly next to the road in a deep gully, its waters hushed by the sheer drop of ten feet before rising up the hill toward the church. The old man had told them to look for the stream, and that it eventually fed into the Exeter River six and a half miles away from the church.

The stream was about a dozen feet across. Two pine logs nailed together with weather-blackened, slimy pine boards served as a bridge. Mallory went first and waited for Father Paul, ready to grab him if he slipped on the wet spray-coated surface.

Like most early churches in New England the cemetery was on the church grounds. As they trudged up the steep incline, two irregular rows of a dozen moss-covered stone markers sprang up from the brown February grass like the dirty teeth of some gap-toothed giant sleeping open-mouthed on his back. All but the deepest chiseling had weathered away, and only a few names and dates were still decipherable.

The air seemed leaden, not just weighed down by the damp mist that hung sullenly over the stones, but by a brooding malevolence that lingered in the graveyard. The whole place gave out a feeling of resentment at having intruders tromp through. Mallory avoided the graves and carefully walked between the stones.

"God," Mallory said, "this place has a rotten feel to it."

"There is no God here," Father Paul said, his voice calm. He turned toward Mallory. "Did you ever read Increase Mather?" he asked. Without waiting for an answer he went on. "Mather believed that there are spiritually malefic places. Spaces that are noxious, abominations that curdle and destroy anything that touches them."

Father Paul looked around the cemetery, then up at the church. "This is such a place."

Mallory reached down and picked up a stone and arched it through the air. Tangible, hard reality . . . it felt good to throw the stone. He heard it impact in the grass with a distant thump somewhere close to the church.

The church was larger than they expected and was constructed mostly of gray, flat fieldstone. Its arched entrance and heavy wooden door indicated careful building. The old place had been well constructed, obviously meant to stand for a long time. But the years hadn't been kind to it. The carved wooden panels on the large front door were riddled with worm-holes and cracks from the decades of changing seasons. Vines and brown moss sprouted from the cracks between the stones. Both Mallory and Father Paul thought that the door was original, as was most of the other stone and woodwork.

To their surprise, the front door was open. A heavy wooden bar about a foot long that normally would have lain horizontally across the door and the jamb was missing. A metal bolt added in modern times was broken in half as if it had been forced. The heavy door swung open easily with no sound. Someone had oiled the hinges.

As soon as they stepped inside the smell of great age, of sturdy objects compromised by time and moisture, swept around them. Mallory felt as if he had just ducked his head into a bucket of old, wet rags. It wasn't a clean smell, but bordered between the fuzzy odor of wet mold and the sharp metal smell of rust.

The little light that filtered through the grime-darkened church windows was absorbed by the oak pews and the soiled, tattered carpet that ran down the center aisle to the nave. Mallory suddenly found himself disliking the place intensely. He didn't know why, but it seemed to be waiting. The tiny vestibule was windowless. And beyond it that black filthy carpet, rancid-smelling and dark, like a giant dead tongue running between the pews and through the tenebrous room to the altar.

The molding interior of the church seemed to be a great squatting animal . . . waiting. And they were standing within the wet acid mouth of the dark beast. The thought gave him a chill that spilled over his flesh, causing goosebumps to rise.

Their footsteps were muffled in the carpeting . . . and yet somehow echoed with a dull thudding in the big room. As they approached the altar, which was surprisingly like Father Paul's in St. Simeon's, another odor came to Mallory. Wax! Burnt wax! He looked for candles but there were none. The place had been wired for electricity, even though it wasn't working when Father Paul had tried the wall switch near the entrance.

The priest had also noticed the lingering odor of candle wax in the air. He touched Mallory's arm and pointed at the floor. Thick blotches of wax had collected in that peculiarly organic pyramid shape that cooling wax takes. But this had different colors mixed together . . . black, red, and yellow.

"These are the candle colors used in 'Black Masses'," Father Paul said softly.

"Then this is the church?" Mallory asked.

"Maybe," the priest said. "This place is so isolated any number of people could have used it. And these old New England churches are the favorite spots for secret or occult rituals. One time a group of high school students were discovered performing satanic rites using chicken guts on Halloween in an abandoned church near Thetford, Vermont. Most of it's just kids fooling around."

"You don't think that's the case here, do you?" Mallory asked.

"No, I don't. The feeling I get here is great age and . . . coldness . . . an uncaring icy watching."

Mallory knew what he meant, which was a dramatic change from how he had felt before. Even as recently as a week ago, he had relied almost exclusively on reason. But he had come to trust his instincts more in the last few days. It seemed as if he'd developed another voice that quickly isolated and expressed his anxiety or fear. No, it wasn't a voice, but rather an inner awareness that began as a vibration somewhere in his stomach and rose like a cold wave up his spine to his conscious mind. The *knowing* it imparted wasn't verbal; it was a vivid feeling, or a series of emotion-laden smoky images that flooded into his mind.

He got the same feeling from this place as Father Paul . . . one of cool indifference, of neutrality, similar to the feeling he sometimes had in a dark patch of woods where the powers of nature seemed such an implacable, overwhelming force that he knew he could be struck dead on the spot, and the earth would quietly absorb him, not caring that a living being had suddenly died. But in buildings it was different. The same feeling of coolness, almost expected in a natural setting, struck him as odd in a man-made place, for he tended to think of the history of a place as being written upon by events. Objects, especially old objects, seemed to have a record. The same was true of places, like Daley's house. There would always be a quality of violence permeating that place . . . no matter how much time passed.

He had no doubt that hot, powerful emotions had occurred in this old place. Births, deaths, and simply the frantic hopes of people gathering together on long-ago Sundays seeking comfort. All of that leaves a record, a feeling floating gently on living space, waiting to be read.

But here there was nothing . . . nothing except the smell of wet mold and wax and a cold, uncaring flatness. It was almost as if the place had been wiped clean of all feeling, of all human connections.

But that was impossible. Nothing is left untouched by its history.

They systematically covered the whole room and found nothing—except the wax—that was clear evidence of satanic rites.

"Well, if this is where they hold their bloody rituals they have a good housekeeper," Mallory said. "I don't see anything exceptional."

"No, neither do I," Father Paul said. He was poking around on the altar. The back wall of the nave was covered with a heavy brocaded tapestry whose design was completely washed away by time. Suddenly the priest looked up.

"Here, come here," he said.

Mallory hopped up onto the three step altar platform and walked over to Father Paul. The priest was pointing at the floor. He had pulled back the rotting carpet near the oaken pulpit. A small square wooden trap door with two large iron hinges had been cut into the floor. A flat iron ring was recessed into the wood.

The priest bent over and lifted the ring. The trap door rose easily, its hinges groaning softly. Both men backed away and Father Paul gagged, covering his nose and mouth. The smell was overwhelming . . . decay, rotting flesh and mold wafted up from the pit.

"God, what a stink," Mallory said.

Father Paul shook his head. "I don't relish the idea of going down there," he said. "But I don't suppose we have any choice."

"No," Mallory said. "Who goes first?"

The priest looked at him and smiled grimly. "Youth

sometimes has the privilege."

"I always thought that was the reverse . . ." Mallory said as he stepped into the opening.

Narrow stone steps descended sharply into the darkness. Mallory had to bend backward to avoid hitting his forehead on the edge of the trap door as he moved cautiously down the steps. He stopped at the bottom, moving his foot into the blackness before him. The floor was earthen, a black soil packed hard by the centuries. He put out his hands, and they disappeared as they left the shaft of pale gray light from above.

He heard Father Paul's feet shuffling on the stone steps behind him. Then the priest was at his elbow.

"I can't see a thing," he whispered. "It's worse than going into a movie on a sunny day."

"I've been waiting for my eyes to adjust . . . and it doesn't get much better," Mallory said. He took a step forward, moving his lead foot in a small semi-circle in front of him. It was a velvet darkness, but cold, the kind of complete eclipse of all light that automatically generated panic. And not only was the pit lightless, the chill of damp stone pierced their flesh with tiny needles of ice. Both men shivered, and Mallory rubbed his hands together and blew warm air over his fingers.

Suddenly a light flared. Mallory jumped, twisting half around. Father Paul's ghostly face was illuminated by a long flamed, flickering gas lighter he held in front of him.

He grinned sheepishly. "I have a secret vice. Cigars." He patted his vest pocket. "When I'm alone, outside the church, I sometimes sit and have a quiet smoke."

Mallory smiled and nodded. Joking, he said, "Better your lungs than this darkness."

Father Paul stepped in front of Mallory, holding his lighter at shoulder height. They moved forward several paces.

"This place is huge," Mallory said, trying to ignore the stench of decay that assailed them. The circle of light cast by the lighter ended about a dozen feet away, and still they could see nothing.

Father Paul moved farther ahead until he came to a wall. It was the same gray fieldstone as the rest of the church. But this was covered with a pale green and yellow moss that curled up tightly against the stone, like closely cropped curly hair.

Mallory reached out and touched it with his fingertips. It looked and felt spongy, like old Jell-o covered with that rainbowed rot-mold that grows on decayed food.

Father Paul began walking along the wall to his left. Mallory estimated they had covered ten or fifteen feet when a twisted, gray figure suddenly loomed before them at chest level. A statue, about two feet high, sat atop a flat stone altar.

They were both shocked by the strange, twisted figure's sudden appearance out of the darkness.

"This is odd," Father Paul said quietly. He stared at the figure. Mallory leaned forward and studied the thing. The top half was clearly a woman, the bottom half just as clearly a fish. The tail was curved gracefully underneath in a double spiral.

"Blood . . ." Father Paul said, touching his index finger to a dark pool of dried blood that had collected in the curves of the fishtail.

Reddish-brown streaks had rained down from the stone head, as if blood had been poured over it. A caul of black dried blood completely covered the top of the crown. The face, breasts and body were also streaked with the stain. From years of use the rough stone altar was smooth with the coagulated blood.

"What is it?" Mallory whispered, staring at the statue.

"I'm not sure," the priest said. "But I think it's the Syrian goddess *Atargatis*. Sometimes she's called *Derceto,* or *Dea Syria.*"

Father Paul ran his fingers over the statue, his hand shaking. The upper female body was voluptuous. The breasts were full with nipples erect, as if the goddess were in a constant state of arousal. The goddess's mouth was partially open in passion, and blood had collected there before it had run over the bottom lip and cascaded down the chin and slim neck. It covered the engorged breasts with tiny red rivers, like bulbous veins full of blood that had leaked through the skin. The dark stain continued down the rounded belly into the pubic area where the scales of the fish half of the creature began.

"She was basically a fertility goddess," Father Paul said. "Half-woman and half-fish, for centuries she was one of the most powerful deities of the ancient world."

"What's a Syrian goddess doing in the basement of a New England church?" Mallory asked.

"Your guess is as good as mine," Father Paul said, still staring at the statue, fascinated.

The statue was obviously very old. It had been hand-carved and had two large red gems embedded for eyes. Mallory wasn't sure whether they were precious stones, such as rubies, or simply some sort of bright red quartz. But they glowed brilliantly in the flickering yellow flame from Father Paul's lighter.

Mallory noticed two fat candles stuck into recesses in the wall behind the statue. He took them out and Father Paul touched them with his lighter.

With the greater light, Mallory and Father Paul moved around the statue and altar, studying them. Again, Father Paul gently reached out and placed his hand on the flat altar stone. It was a square about three feet by three feet with a deep groove four inches wide cut around the edges.

He was about to ask Father Paul what the design meant when it struck him. The priest seemed to sense his thoughts and said, "Yes. It's for blood. Drainage channels for sacrifices."

The priest ran his finger along the groove. "The blood drained along here, and down into a cup here in front."

He looked up at Mallory. "Then it was passed around and drunk by the worshippers."

Mallory suddenly felt he was back in Jeff Goldman's room staring at the pale bloodless body. And Daley's, with the white translucent empty skin and the feeling of evil all around him.

"My God," he whispered. "I don't think I'm even in the twentieth century anymore. This all belongs in another time. Blood-drinking pagans. Animism. I can't understand these people, they're beyond me."

"No," Father Paul said. "You understand. It's just that the knowledge is deep, covered over by millennia of civilization."

Sick to his stomach, Mallory turned away from the blood-stained altar.

"No..." Father Paul said. "Look at this."

He was pointing at the blood stains.

"I've seen it, thank you," Mallory said.

"Not really," Father Paul answered. "Did you notice that it's fresh?"

Mallory stared. The priest was right. It was dry... but undeniably recent. Perhaps a week or two old.

"Oh, shit..." Mallory breathed, not even noticing the hot wax cascading down the black candle onto his fingers.

"Come on," Father Paul said, taking him by the elbow. "Let's see what else there is in this black hole."

They worked their way along the wall to the left of the altar and statue of *Atargatis*.

The wall changed character abruptly. It went from rough stone covered with moss to square blocks of smooth stone. Several more paces and they encountered a demon's head in bas relief. The head was human-sized and had been carved by a very skilled artisan. The eyes were deep-set, the brows frowning. But the mouth on the gruesome broken face was twisted in a lecherous grin. Mallory wondered what it was that the creature lusted after. The face seemed to forcefully push out from the stone as if it were trapped and somehow during the struggle had only partially broken free.

Another grotesque face was visible in the dancing shadows of Mallory's candles. Mallory took a step toward the second face, and a third danced out of the darkness about four feet beyond it.

"Look at this," Mallory said, holding the candles out. He quickly walked along the wall as one demonic, grinning face after another struggled from the wall. Each sculpted head was in the center of a smoothly chiseled square block.

As Mallory moved down the wall, holding his candles high and studying each face, Father Paul called out.

"Here, David. Come here."

The priest was standing in front of the first demon face they had seen. His fingers were tracing the deep groove outlining the square block.

Mallory stopped and watched as he squeezed his fingers into both sides of the block and pulled it toward him. The square stone moved slightly. Mallory put down the candles and helped. He cupped his fingers under the protruding chin of the demon face, where there was a small finger-hold, and pulled. The block was heavy, but it slid forward easily. As the stone came loose the odor of rotting flesh that had hit them when they opened the trap door rushed out.

A goddamn charnel house, Mallory thought. *A primitive morgue.*

It smelled as if they had desecrated a fresh grave. They set the heavy stone gently on the ground. It must have weighed at least fifty pounds.

Mallory raised his two candles and brought them near the opening, which was about two feet square. A tiny shrunken bloody skull, uncannily like the crowning head of an infant being born, loomed out of the darkness. The stiff white infant body itself lay on a thin wooden slab of half inch plywood. A small clay figurine of *Atargatis,* also stained with dried blood, sat next to the baby's head. A broken crucifix hung upside down around the figurine's neck.

"Oh, my God," Mallory said softly as they both reached in and pulled the slab out.

The baby's heart had been taken. The tiny chest had been opened roughly, the incision was jagged and had almost torn rather than cut the skin open.

"Sweet Jesus," Father Paul whispered, crossing himself. "I can't believe this. How can anyone do such a thing in the name of religion?"

Mallory swallowed hard, for he felt the bile rising from his churning stomach. He moved around to the side of the infant and lifted the candles higher so he could examine the tiny body more carefully. He was sick at heart. But he also felt threatened. This all had to be part of the same terrifying madness.

Trying to distract himself from the horror of the infant's sacrifice, he concentrated on the wounds.

"The poor thing was only a few days old," he said. "And it's only been dead about a week."

Then it hit him like a hammer between his eyes. He glanced at Father Paul, who was staring at him.

Neither man spoke, the implications were too horrible.

After a moment Mallory said, "Do you think it's possible?"

"Yes," the priest said softly. "Unfortunately . . . yes. I've seen it before. It's not uncommon for children to be sacrificed at Black Masses and during important rituals."

"But what could it all mean? This child was killed about the same time as Betty Milner and Jeff Goldman."

"I don't know yet," Father Paul answered. "But the taking of the heart is the same as draining the blood. Both symbolize the life force and are needed to generate power during satanic ritual."

Mallory glanced over his shoulder at the other demon faces bulging from the stone blocks. *It wasn't possible,* he thought. *Or was it? Other bodies? Other sacrifices?*

He stood and walked over to the next face and tried to pull the stone block loose. It scraped forward slightly.

Father Paul, his face ghastly white, joined him. His lighter was getting too hot to hold, and he snapped it off and put it back in his pocket. Together they removed the square block and placed it on the floor.

The hairless crown of another infant's head flickered in the candlelight. They pulled out the wooden slab. For a fleeting moment Mallory had the odd sensation that he was birthing a child from the underworld, pulling it out of a cold, gaping, inhuman vagina. The dead child slid fully into the candlelight, and he saw that it had the same ugly wound. The heart was gone, leaving only the tiny dark cavity of dried flesh.

"This one's been dead much longer," Mallory said. "I'd estimate at least a year or two."

"Yes, I'm not surprised," Father Paul said quietly.

"And I would bet it was killed on February second."

Mallory's face was grim as he stood and moved to the next face. The priest followed him, rubbing his hands together absently.

"I don't want to look," Mallory said.

"Neither do I," Father Paul answered, "but we don't have much choice, do we?"

Mallory's answer was to squeeze his fingers into the cracks of the slab and begin to pull.

They moved down the wall, removing the stone slabs one after the other. Behind each demon's face they found a crypt with a dead infant. There were twelve tiny corpses in all. Each had been sacrificed in an identical fashion. The heart had been removed. Each had a small sculpture of *Atargatis* and a broken crucifix next to the body.

The last few bodies were badly decomposed. When they opened the final crypt the infant's body almost crumbled into pieces when they pulled the wooden slab out. The rib cage collapsed inwardly, and the head rolled onto its cheek, the empty grape-sized eyesockets staring balefully at Mallory. A tiny skeletal arm shook loose and fell over the side as they lowered it to the ground. The joints at the shoulder, elbow and wrist shattered, and the frail miniature bones bounced dully on the earth floor like a grotesque game of pick-up-sticks. They put the one-armed body down, and Mallory gently replaced the bones in a patch-work pattern alongside the skeleton.

Stunned beyond speech, the two men stared silently at the ragged line of twelve corpses.

"What can it mean?" Mallory murmured, his mind a fog of swirling emotions and fear.

He looked over at Father Paul.

The priest shrugged. "It's too early to tell what kind of insane logic these people work by. We can only be sure that they are evil scum...."

Father Paul leaned against the wall and ran his hand across his eyes, rubbing them vigorously with his fingers, as if he had been reading for too long. He had grasped the rosary around his neck with his other hand. His face was the color of gravestones.

His red-rimmed eyes stared at the corpses and then Mallory.

"It is very strange, though," he said quietly, his voice hoarse. He squatted down and touched the forehead of one of the infants. He closed his eyes for a moment, as if he were seeing the baby alive, full of life.

In another moment he stood up, his face indescribably sad. He shook his head. "These poor babies. I really don't understand it. Most satanic rituals, especially these kind of sacrifices, are practiced for short term goals, quick benefits. They want immediate gratification. Power, vengeance, riches, love. The list is as long as human desire, and most of it reflects quick fixes for dissatisfied lives."

His eyes ran down the line of bodies. "But this is different. The ugliness of spirit runs deeper. And it's been going on for twelve years. Whatever it is they're after, they want it badly."

"What does it all mean?" Mallory asked. "That they have to renew their power once a year? Make new requests each year?"

"Possibly," Father Paul said. "But I suspect it's something longer term. There's a much larger purpose here. The same ritual each year."

"How long will it go on?" Mallory asked, still unable to absorb all the violence and death he'd experienced in the last week. "More sacrifices of newborn infants?"

Father Paul looked at him, the black candle flickering under his chin, giving it a grotesque-comic look, like a child's luminescent Halloween mask. He had a sick smile on his face.

"Until they get what they want," he said simply, his voice echoing hollowly in the silent stone chamber.

Both men felt drained. They stood as if hypnotized, staring at the small white corpses, trying to understand the reality of those who had murdered these children. The priest's eyes were glistening.

"C'mon," Mallory said, "let's get out of here."

"In a moment," he said, wiping his eyes. "There's a prayer for the dead." The priest knelt in front of the small bodies, one hand grasped his crucifix, the fingers of the other touched his forehead lightly.

"God, our Father,
We believe that your Son died and rose to life,
We pray for these innocents,
Who have died in Christ.
Raise them at the last
To share the glory of the Risen Christ.
Eternal rest give to them, O Lord,
And let perpetual light shine upon them."

Father Paul made the sign of the cross, stood up and turned to Mallory and nodded. They started toward the steps when a shuffling noise, a heavy sudden scraping sound came from above.

Mallory grasped Father Paul's arm and they stopped, holding their breath. The air seemed to throb as they listened.

There it was again. A footstep. Then another.

"Jesus," Mallory whispered. "Someone's in the church."

"Shh," Father Paul hissed. "The trap door's still open." He blew out the candle he was holding and Mallory followed suit.

They stood silently in the blackness, the infant

corpses scattered at their feet. The only light was a soft yellow glow filtering down from the trap door twenty feet away. The shaft of light shifted slightly as the figure upstairs slowly moved about. Whoever it was had a flashlight and was obviously searching the building.

The footsteps, which weren't trying to be quiet, stopped near the trap door. The shaft of light brightened, shifted, and then the full strength of the flashlight beam struck into the basement room. The beam roamed around the bottom of the steps for several seconds and then, abruptly, the trap door slammed shut.

The sharp thud of the heavy wooden trap door and sudden, total, breathtaking blackness struck at them like a blast of air. Too startled to move, they waited as the shuffling footsteps continued to echo softly overhead.

Mallory couldn't shake the uncomfortable feeling that the trap door had been locked. He tried to remember whether there had been a bolt or bar lock along the edge. He cursed himself silently for not having paid more attention.

The thought of being trapped in this charnel pit made his stomach twist and his mouth suddenly dry.

After a few moments the footsteps receded toward the front of the church. They waited until they heard the distant thud of the front door closing.

Father Paul let out a long sigh. In a second his lighter flashed. They lit the two candles and moved quietly to the steps.

Mallory went up first and pressed his free hand against the trap door. It rose easily and Mallory turned to Father Paul and grinned. He set the trap door back gently on the floor as Father Paul's head appeared.

Mallory glanced at his watch. It was after six o'clock and the church was dark. The only light came from their candles. As impossible as it seemed, they had been in the pit for almost two hours.

"Can we get out of here now?" Mallory said.

"I'd like nothing better," the priest said. He was still holding the crucifix tightly in his fist. His knuckles were white.

They left the church, walking quickly through the cemetery and down the hill, stumbling occasionally in the moonless night. They did not look back until they crossed the planks over the stream. And then there was nothing left to see. The black shrouds of night had obscured everything. But the sights and feelings of that charnel house lingered.

Chapter Fourteen

They were both silent on the drive home. The sights and smells from the charnel pit lingered. Mallory could still smell the stink of decayed flesh on their clothes. He opened the car's vent and cracked a window. It did no good. The smell remained. Perhaps it was just the memory? It wouldn't surprise him.

Many questions fluttered through their minds, like hornets threatening to land, and they were too emotionally drained to deal with them.

Father Paul glanced at the phosphorescent green digital clock on the dash. "It's almost nine o'clock. I haven't eaten all day and I'm starved. How about a rest stop?"

They exited and pulled into a Howard Johnson parking lot. But Father Paul ignored the orange-roofed restaurant and pulled Mallory by the arm into the "Kuala Inn's 'Aloha Room'" next door.

"I need a drink," he said unapologetically.

Exhausted and depressed as he was, Mallory couldn't help but smile. Cigars, and now alcohol. For an exorcist priest, Father Paul was destroying some stereotypes and turning out to be a pleasant surprise. But still, Mallory felt jolted by the sudden changes.

An hour ago he'd been in a pit under a two hundred year old church graveyard. Now they were walking into a glitzy, neon and plastic restaurant. He hated places like this—always heavy on the decor. It was all they really had to offer. He had tried socializing in bars several times during college and had felt consistently uncomfortable. He always had the sensation that it was futile time. Time pissed away laughing at unfunny jokes and trying to pick up women you didn't really care about.

The walls were decorated with fish-netting that was so heavy and thickly knotted it would have immediately plunged to the bottom of the ocean. Dozens of large varnished coconut shells were attached to the fishnets. All the coconuts had painted faces.

A giant fifteen-foot Hawaiian totem dominated the center of the room; colored floodlights on the ceiling encircled it. Flashing neon lights designed in tight spirals cast a disconcerting strobe effect over the drinkers, who were sipping brightly colored concoctions through foot-long straws.

Father Paul went straight for the bar and ordered an Irish whiskey on the rocks. Mallory ordered a light beer. They drank in silence.

The strobe lights flashed *red...blue...yellow* over and over again. Father Paul's pale, tired face flushed, became sickly blue and then jaundice yellow in quick succession. Mallory was sure he looked just as ridiculous.

Clowns in neon makeup.

Mallory wanted to leave, but he was too tired to move. They had a long drive in front of them so he had another drink and ordered sandwiches. They ate at the bar.

"Twelve," Mallory said. "Twelve. It's been going through my head non-stop. Everything seems a multiple of twelve. Twelve mothers dead in twelve years, twelve infants slaughtered in a filthy church basement, and I have the sinking feeling that they want twelve doctors dead . . . even if Bowker is still alive."

He had recovered some of his energy with the food, but he couldn't shake his depression. He loved a mystery but hated answers that were too elusive. Especially if they were answers that could save his life.

"Don't forget twelve children have been born. And there's already been twelve dead doctors if you count Jeff Goldman," Father Paul said. "But I don't think he's part of the plan. He was an accident. Happened to be in the wrong place at the wrong time."

"But why? What's the significance of twelve?" Mallory asked.

"In occultism all numbers are considered significant, and many have a special sacred or magical power. Most of the magical aspect of numbers has derived from the Greek philosopher Pythagoras. But they've been used in the Cabala, in medieval Christian symbolism, and even during the Renaissance in trying to reconcile the chasm between the pagan and Christian worlds."

Father Paul took another deep pull on his drink. He wiped the corners of his mouth and took a handful of the potato chips that had come with his sandwich. He had no inhibition about speaking with his mouth full.

"Each number has a specific meaning. One, for example, not only looks like a phallus, but it also represents the creator, the first cause, God. Two is the number of evil, because it is the first number to break up the unitary principle of life that one symbolizes. In three the opposites are reunited, harmoniously reconciled, so God is manifested in that number. It is the term of the Trinity. It is also sexual, for the male genitals are threefold, and the opposition between the male and female sexes is united in the number three. And because the number signifies moving toward completeness, moving from the beginning to the middle and the end, it has appeared in many folktales. Recall the oft given three wishes? The three blind mice? The three bears? They were all symbolic of wholeness during the Middle Ages."

The old priest was beginning to relax. The horrors of the church basement had faded a little. The three drinks that he had had were obviously having an effect. He grinned crookedly at Mallory.

"There . . . have you learned more than you wanted to know?" he asked, chewing energetically on the potato chips.

"Not yet," Mallory said, patiently. "I'd like to know the significance of twelve to these people? Why does it keep reappearing?"

Father Paul held up his glass and stared into the dark amber liquid. He took a long swallow, draining it. "After three . . ." He held up three fingers before Mallory. "Twelve is the major number of wholeness. There are 12 gods on Olympus, 12 months in the year, 12 signs of the zodiac, 12 hours of the day and 12 of the night, 12 tribes of Israel, 12 prophets in the Old Testament, and twelve stones in Aaron's breastplate. And the fact that Jesus chose 12 apostles, not more and not less, confirmed the importance of that number to Christian numerologists. Early Christians used to say that Jesus chose twelve because it showed the four corners of the earth the significance of the Trinity."

"But why twelve now, in this weird series of deaths and sacrifices?" Mallory persisted.

The old man shrugged and finished his drink. "Who knows? Numbers often hide names of power. The Trinity, 3, conceals the Father, Son, and Holy Spirit. The number 666 conceals the identity of the Great Beast of Revelation, the Anti-Christ. These madmen could be using it for any number of reasons . . . but most likely it's a satanic parody of Christian use. The twelve murdered babies could have been blood seeds for some grand scheme. Or simply a means of gaining power. Or sacrifices to Satan for a specific reason, like revenge on an enemy. I'm sure this group would have at least a dozen enemies they'd want to eliminate. We'll have to wait and find out."

Father Paul took a bite of his sandwich and after a moment of reflective chewing he looked up at Mallory, his eyes serious. "I have an idea . . . about what's happening," he said. "But I don't want to say anything too soon."

"What do you mean too soon? We're both just speculating in the dark. We're just searching for answers, aren't we?"

"Yes," the priest said cautiously. "But there are so many possibilities, there's no reason to go into every crazy idea that pops into my head."

"Maybe not, but I'd still like to know what the alternatives are."

"Okay, when I have alternatives you'll be the first."

"That means nothing now?"

Father Paul reached over and patted his arm. "Let me follow my nose for awhile . . . alone. I have an idea I'd like to check out. It's probably not important, but if anything comes of it I'll call you immediately."

The bill came, and as Mallory was counting out the money, Father Paul asked, "Who do you think came into the church?"

"Probably a caretaker of some sort. Whoever he was, he was lazy. Otherwise he would've investigated why the trap door was open."

"Maybe," Father Paul said. They got up and walked back to the car in silence, both men wrapped in their thoughts.

As the priest slid into his seat, he said, "I had the

impression it was a warning."

"A warning?" Mallory said, startled. He hesitated before putting the key in the ignition and stared at the priest.

"Just a feeling. Look at it from their point of view. They probably don't want any more attention. Remember, three killings of people from one area creates a lot of attention. And if they knew we were here . . . and wanted us to back off, well, what would you do?"

Mallory smiled. "Maybe I'd stamp around the church, scare the hell out of the snoopers in the basement. And maybe even slam the trap door shut on them."

"So would I . . . especially if I wanted to avoid killing them. If that was at all possible."

"Meaning we have a grace period . . . at least until things cool down from Jeff's and Daley's killing," Mallory said. "Is that your point?"

"Yes. Generally, that's how I see it. I don't think they want another local doctor . . . and a priest . . . turning up dead. We do have a little time. But I don't think these people are long on patience."

"I have the feeling you're right," Mallory said as he started the car.

When Mallory got home it was after midnight. The signal light on his telephone answering machine was blinking. He had three messages. One from Lili and two from the young Norwich policeman, Officer Kelly. He wanted Mallory to call him as soon as possible.

Probably another grilling, Mallory thought. He'd call him in the morning.

Mallory spent the next morning at Baker Library, reading and taking notes on esoteria . . . the sacredness of numbers, the Mayan and Aztec ritual taking of hearts in sacrifice, the myths and legends about the dark god Tezcatlipoca, a blood-thirsty deity who had several nasty personalities. One of them was called Xipe, who liked to skin captives alive and then wear their flesh. He tied the loose strips of skin from the arms and legs around his own wrists and ankles.

By lunch time he was convinced he was on the wrong track. South American and Meso-American religions, even though they involved human sacrifice and cutting out the human heart and using blood power to influence the course of nature, were not what he was after.

The sacrifice of the infants had more the quality of medieval Satanism, or the brute force of the Middle Ages.

He had made a lunch date with Kelly so he put the books away and walked across the Dartmouth Square to Bentley's, a trendy restaurant with lots of wood, glass and plants. Any respectable New York yuppie would have been perfectly happy there. In fact, it reminded him of O'Neal's Balloon next to Lincoln Center in New York. But the food was passable, and you could have a quiet conversation.

As if to confirm his opinion about the place, Mallory passed his Hitchcock irritant, Dr. Jack Weston, and a pretty blond he recognized as a Hitchcock nurse at a table near the door. He nodded, smiled and waved, and kept on going toward Kelly, who was watching him arrive from a corner table across the room.

They shook hands, exchanged pleasantries and ordered, all within five minutes.

Mallory pushed aside a long, straggly rhododendron branch that brushed against the back of his head.

"This thing needs a haircut," Mallory exclaimed, turning around and snapping off the offending branch.

He flipped the branch into the pot hanging above him.

He turned to Kelly. "I assume this isn't official, otherwise we wouldn't be in a restaurant?"

"That's right. Your part is over for the moment. The investigation of your friend's death is moving along . . . slowly."

"I'm not surprised," Mallory said.

Kelly grinned. "Do I hear cynicism about the effectiveness of our police force?"

"No, I just believe his killers are smart and vicious. I doubt if they would leave something as obvious as an identifiable fingerprint."

Kelly laughed. "No, experienced killers are rarely that cooperative." He leaned slightly toward Mallory. "In fact, we've had another murder, or rather two murders, very similar to Dr. Goldman's. That's why I wanted to talk with you."

Mallory kept his face impassive and waited for Kelly to continue. He didn't think Kelly knew. If they really thought he had been in Daley's house, this was a strange way of questioning him.

"I wanted to talk with you because I remembered what you said about cults. None of us, including me, gave it much weight at the time. We all thought Dr. Goldman could have been killed by a lone psychopath. But all that's different now."

"What changed your mind?" Mallory asked.

Kelly concentrated on buttering a roll. "Do you know a Dr. Walter Daley. He worked at Alice Peck Day Hospital?"

"I've heard of him," Mallory said. "But we've never actually met."

Mallory kept his voice and face as neutral as he could, but visions of Daley and his mother kept floating to the surface. And the babies, the torn, pale bodies of the babies in that long row with the gaping black holes in their chests. If Kelly only knew.

"Do you know whether Dr. Goldman was acquainted with Daley?"

"No, I have no idea. But from your question I assume Dr. Daley is dead?"

"Yes," Kelly said. "Very similar to Dr. Goldman's. His body was also bloodless."

"And this isn't an interrogation? It sure seems like it to me."

Kelly grinned. For someone pushing thirty, he had a surprisingly boyish manner.

"No, it isn't. Perhaps I've been a cop too long. Can't carry on a normal conversation anymore," Kelly said, still grinning. "We don't even have jurisdiction. Daley's killing happened in New Hampshire, and I heard about it from a friend with the Hanover Police Department. You know how it is. In a small town environment, we get together and talk about our day at the office."

Kelly stretched and then started buttering a second roll. Mallory figured Kelly had to have a fast metabolism to stay slim and put away so many fats and carbohydrates.

"I got curious because Daley's blood, and his mother's, was drained from their bodies."

"Just like Goldman's," Mallory said.

It wasn't really a question. Mallory was simply remembering out loud. But Kelly took it as a question and said, "Yeah, and even Weidemeier now accepts the possibility of a blood-drinking cult."

Mallory remembered Father Paul's description in the church basement of the blood draining into a cup and the worshippers drinking it. He wondered what Kelly would say about that.

Kelly smiled broadly, "And you have no idea how hard that was for him. He argued every step of the way. But three bloodless corpses are very convincing."

Kelly was so open and relaxed that Mallory was tempted to tell him more, to bring him into his confidence, but nothing would be gained by involving Kelly now. Bringing the police into it might drive the cult farther underground. Take everything out of his and Father Paul's hands. But it would obviously be helpful to have someone official that he could turn to . . . when things got rough. And he had no doubt that they would.

"Weidemeier still hasn't given up entirely on the idea of a lone sicko running around New England. A kind of serial killer, black magic style. And I think my chief tends in that direction as well."

"And you?" Mallory asked.

"Me? I think a psychopath is possible, but there's a lot of evidence to the contrary."

"Like what?"

"Oh, the incision in Goldman's groin artery was neat. Done by an expert. That made me suspect you for a short time."

Kelly grinned broadly at Mallory and raised his wine glass in a mock toast. "The same is true of the punctures they found in Daley's arms . . . and his mother's body. The holes were made directly over major arteries. Whoever made them knew exactly what they were doing."

"You said, 'blood-drinking' cult? Why couldn't it just as easily be a blood-sacrificing cult?"

Kelly studied Mallory for a moment. "Of course. Anything's possible. You've obviously given this more thought than I have. But what's the difference we're talking about here? Aren't the two things the same? I mean, if someone's drinking blood it isn't done casually at dinnertime. I assume it has some religious importance to either a cult or a lone psychopath."

"But why did you say *blood-drinking* specifically?"

Mallory persisted.

Kelly did not answer immediately. He absently pushed food around on his plate. After a moment he said, "Look, let's stop playing games. How about a deal? I think you know more about what's going on than you're saying. We both may have information that may be helpful to the other. Why not trade?"

"I don't know what you're talking about," Mallory said. "I don't have any special . . ."

"Oh, shit," Kelly said, cutting him off. He put down his fork. "C'mon, Doctor. We found your name in Daley's appointment book. You were to meet him at just about the time he was killed."

Kelly held up his hand, palm toward Mallory. "No, don't worry. You're not a suspect in this one, either. Someone saw you in Peter Christian's about the time Daley and his mother were killed. Is that where you and Daley were to meet?"

"Yes, but he never showed up."

"What was your meeting about?"

"One of his patients . . . and a medical problem we had in common."

"Is that all?"

Mallory nodded.

Kelly wasn't sure whether he believed Mallory or not. The doctor wasn't a very good liar and was obviously holding things back. He pushed away from the table.

"Okay," he said. "I'm not sure I buy it, but I still want to make a deal. I can't get involved officially, I'm just a low-level cop from a small town . . . and this thing has now crossed state borders. It's out of my hands, but to be honest with you, it's the biggest thing that's happened to me after eight years on the force. It's why I became a policeman."

He grinned sheepishly. "That may sound corny, and

a little bit like a TV cop, but it's the fantasy I grew up with. Good guys versus the bad guys. Most small town police work is giving traffic tickets to people just like yourself. Or arresting drunk good-ole-boys you went to school with."

He paused and caught his breath. "But this . . . this is real police work. Once in a lifetime something like this comes along. And I don't want to be pushed out of the way just because the killings are separated by the Connecticut River and a state line . . . and the jurisdiction is split and the investigation is thrown up to a higher level."

Mallory liked Kelly. He was a little rough around the edges, and simple in his approach to problems, but he seemed honest and didn't hesitate to bend the rules when necessary.

"Okay," he said. "I've laid it on the line. You know my reasons. What do you say?"

"All right. Maybe we can work something out," Mallory said carefully. He still wasn't sure where this was leading. Or where the advantage lay.

"I asked you before about your choice of words . . . about the blood-drinking cult, and you mentioned the precision of the wounds over the arteries. What about them? Anybody with a rudimentary knowledge of anatomy could do the same thing."

"A test so soon," Kelly said lightly. "I thought we'd at least get to dessert first. Okay, two important things have come up."

He stopped and held up his hand again. "By the way, this is all confidential stuff. It isn't illegal, but it wouldn't look good for me to be discovered passing information to civilians. None of this is for public consumption. Right?"

"Sure," Mallory said, nodding.

"Okay. Point one. Goldman's car. We got lucky.

Goldman had an oil change two days before his death. The garage's sticker was on his car's door. We traced his path from the time of his death backward. He'd been at the hospital working and at home for practically all of those two days. The big exception is the time he spent with you and your lady friend. Now, here's the kicker. We clocked the mileage for those last two days. Everywhere he'd been. There's 30 to 35 miles unaccounted for on the odometer from when he left you and drove home. Wherever he drove later that night after he left you is probably where he was killed."

Kelly's eyes were crystalline brown agates, shining with excitement. He obviously loved the chase. Mallory thought he was a bit like an excited puppy after his first cat. "I know we've covered this ground," he said. "But do you have any idea where he went that night?"

"No, really, I don't. Believe me, if I knew I'd tell you. I'm sorry."

"Okay, fair enough. But if you get any thoughts, give me a call. Here's my home number, just in case."

He wrote his number on a piece of notebook paper, tore it off and slid it over to Mallory.

"Point two," he said. "There's no mystery about how Goldman's blood was drained. Two neat incisions in the groin arteries, and he'd be empty in minutes. The real puzzle here is . . . what does the killer, or killers, want with the blood? You suggested they used it in sacrificial rituals. And by the way, on the basis of that idea I've sent off a few wire requests to other police departments. I've heard rumors that these kind of ritualistic homicides have happened in other states . . . not just here in the northeast.

"With the Daleys the draining of blood was done differently. No incisions. There were five sets of neat puncture wounds. But the punctures were not made by needles. At first it was assumed that blood had been drained from the Daleys' bodies through needles. Nothing so simple. We don't know yet what caused the punctures, but the lab says it *definitely* wasn't normal hypodermic needles. We get a more complete pathologist's report sometime tomorrow."

Kelly was staring straight at Mallory, his eyes hooded, his face serious when he said, "But even worse... and this is just between the two of us... Daley's throat wasn't cut. It was torn apart. The medical examiner thinks probably by some sort of animal."

A wry smile crossed his tanned, boyish face. "And if you think that's weird... the puncture wounds that aren't needle marks? The medical examiner thinks that they're bites."

"Bites?" Mallory said, truly startled. He had seen the throat wounds and thought that they were probably animal bites... but the needle marks?

"How can you be sure that they're bites?" he asked.

"Two reasons. According to the m.e., the shape of the holes is inconsistent with needle marks, but consistent with holes made by fangs... animal fangs. Maybe snake type fangs. And the second reason is saliva. There was human saliva surrounding each of the holes."

"Jesus," Mallory breathed. This was getting too bizarre. He looked up at Kelly. "Vampires?" he said, his tone incredulous.

Kelly smiled wanly. "I don't know from vampires, Doctor. I can't get my head screwed into this supernatural stuff. But we have some real sickos here."

Kelly pulled a piece of folded paper from his jacket pocket. "This is really confidential, Doctor. It's a part of the preliminary m.e.'s report. It's not yet released to the public, and I can't let you read the whole thing. But listen to this: '... the bite marks, lacerations and the tearing of the throat area are not entirely consistent with canine bites. The teeth pattern and bite characteristics do not fit the dental profile of the average dog... or other animals known to be aggressive toward humans.'"

Kelly glanced up at Mallory. "And later in the same report the m.e. says specifically, referring to Dr. Daley's and his mother's deaths, that the wounds were 'performed by a *species unknown*'."

Kelly carefully refolded the paper and put it back into his pocket.

"My friend on the Hanover police thinks the m.e. has a hole in his head. He thinks the m.e. doesn't know what did it, so he calls it 'Species Unknown.' End of the story. But my friend is waiting for the pathologist's report. He has his own theories. He thinks that the blood was drained first with needles... and then the holes were bitten into. By a group of psychos. He thinks they were first taking the blood... and then mimicking vampire bites."

He shook his head. "If that's what happened... can you imagine it? The sick bastards... killing someone and then biting the flesh. Ugh..." Kelly shook his head again and opened his mouth, put his finger in and mimed vomiting.

"And Daley's throat wounds?" Mallory asked. "Was the animal that made them also human?"

Kelly nodded. "Probably. There were traces of saliva all around Daley's throat, in the wound itself, and even on his shirt collar and wrists. The bastards drooled all over him."

"Oh, God," Mallory sighed. "It gets worse every step of the way."

Mixed within the anxiety and fear for himself, he felt an overwhelming sadness. The whole thing was miserably, achingly sad. Mallory had been struggling for days to get closer to the heart of whatever was happening. But now he was more and more feeling that the knowledge was dangerous. That something was being created here . . . that knowing one thing affected other things. One step overtakes another, one event runs into the next like water from a brook flowing into a river. He once read that in physics just by observing certain sub-atomic particles it changed their behavior. Something about the light illuminating the atomic particles in the experiment *changed* everything. Just by watching something you changed the outcome. Jesus. By his being involved in this, he was helping to create the conclusion. He was helping to bring about something that he knew nothing about and didn't understand.

Everything seemed related. He remembered that little jingle of wisdom—*For want of a nail the shoe was lost, for want of a shoe the horse was lost, for want of a horse the battle was lost, for want of the battle the war was lost, for want of the war the nation was lost.*

Inexorable, that was the word that fit. Things kept moving inexorably. He felt a constant, gradual shifting toward disaster. How else could he label the sinister forces he felt collecting around him? And he was powerless to stop it. He was a goddamn magnet. A magnet for sick, vicious animals to feed on.

Kelly waited . . . and watched. He was waiting for Mallory to loosen up, to tell him what he knew. He didn't want to push. Some instinct told him to take it slowly, that Mallory was at the edge . . . and if he were pushed too far he would tighten up in self-defense. He basically read Mallory as running scared, a man isolated . . . and scared shitless! In some way he couldn't understand, he felt sure Mallory was in this up to his neck.

Mallory looked up at Kelly and made a decision. He

began to talk. He told him everything! From the death of Betty Milner to the pitiful dead babies in the church basement.

When he finished Kelly was staring at him.

They sat in silence for a long time. Kelly was the first to speak.

"Okay," he said quietly. "I appreciate your frankness. But I can't entirely buy any supernatural angle. All I know is that some very strange shit is happening here. And I don't really care whether you call these bastards vampires or blood-sucking psychotics, I'm going to get them."

Kelly said this with a confidence that almost made Mallory laugh.

Chapter Fifteen

After his lunch with Kelly, Mallory returned to Baker Library where he spent the afternoon. He had asked Kelly to use his police connections to check into the deaths of the other ten doctors and the status of any investigations. He was confident that Kelly would find that they had all been murdered and that their bodies were drained of blood.

At Baker he switched his research to medieval sorcery and witchcraft, digging for something . . . anything that rang true, any small thing that reflected the facts. He took copious notes and by five o'clock his fingers were sore and his eyes burning. When he got home he checked his machine, hoping that Father Paul had called. The priest had been frustratingly enigmatic the day before about what his plans were. He had just smiled and told Mallory that he would be the first to know.

Later that night, just after he had put down his book and snapped off the light, the phone rang. He was still awake. He had been lying in the dark thinking and listening to the wind outside his window. As it brushed through the forest, trees came alive and seemed to breathe heavily, growling with a raspy voice at being disturbed. The wind whispered by the house in short, tremulous sighs, never staying long, never lingering but never really ever leaving.

When he picked up the receiver an official sounding voice said, "Dr. David Mallory?"

"Yes," he said.

"This is Officer Parker from the Hanover Police Department, Doctor. Do you know a priest, Father Paul Kennedy?"

Mallory's heart dropped into the pit of his stomach. "Yes," he said, his throat constricting.

"I'm afraid there's been an accident, and Father Paul was seriously injured. He's been asking for you."

"How badly is he hurt?"

"I'm sorry, I don't have any medical details. I've only been told that it's serious. He's listed as critical."

"Where is he?" Mallory asked.

"At Hitchcock Medical Center, Room 621."

"I'll be there in twenty minutes."

Mallory jumped into his clothes and was out the door in less than five minutes. He arrived at Hitchcock ten minutes later. He pulled into the parking lot across the street and jogged into the hospital lobby.

A burly policeman with a pasta belly hanging over his belt was waiting at the Information Desk in the center of the lobby.

He stepped in front of Mallory. "Dr. Mallory?" he asked.

"Yes, c'mon. We can talk on the way up."

Mallory walked briskly into one of the four elevators and pressed the button for the sixth floor. He was breathing hard and consciously tried to calm himself by slowing his respiration rate.

"What happened?" Mallory asked.

"We don't know much yet," Parker said. He was a low-key, matter-of-fact type. Mallory knew he just wanted to get his report made out and finish his shift. "Just that it was a car accident on Route 120 near Lebanon and exit 18. Father Kennedy has been in and out of consciousness for most of the last two hours. That's when he was brought in. Since I spoke with you I've also talked with his doctor. He told me that he had a concussion, two broken ribs and lacerations and contusions on his scalp, shoulder and back and chest. But the concussion was the big thing. He was worried about internal bleeding."

"Yeah," Mallory said. "Who's his doctor?"

"A Dr. Weston," Parker said.

"Oh, shit. That's all I need," Mallory muttered.

The elevator doors hissed open. Room 621 was to the right of the elevators, halfway down the corridor. As Mallory and Parker approached the room there was a loud crash, a wailing scream of pain, and the door burst open about thirty feet in front of them. A tall figure dressed in black bolted from the room and ran down the hallway, his black raincoat flapping behind him like raven's wings. He broke through the swinging doors at the farther end of the hall before Parker had a chance to react. Parker pulled his gun and scrambled down the hall, yelling for him to stop.

Somewhere a woman was still screaming. The sound, which came in shuddering gasps, echoed through the hall, turning heads and jolting the staff out of their routines.

Mallory ran to the room and pushed open the door and stepped into a scene from a horror movie. He stopped, too stunned to move. Several other doctors and nurses collected at his back. He could hear them suck in their breaths. They were used to blood and sickness and death. But not like this . . . not this kind of violation.

Three bodies lay sprawled in a sea of blood. Jack Weston, his handsome face with a look of utter amazement on it, lay across the narrow hospital bed. His throat had been cut from ear to ear. Blood was still pumping from the carotid artery in his neck. It burst a foot out from the torn flesh, curving gracefully in a slow pulsing arc to land in a growing puddle on his chest.

A nurse, the pretty blond that Mallory had seen with Weston at Bentley's, lay in the middle of the floor on her back in a lake of blood. She had been disemboweled and her intestines had mushroomed from her body like fat, writhing blue and red snakes. Her limbs were still jerking as she died, heels tapping on the floor, a sound like the distant thudding of lightly running feet.

Carpenter, the chubby, smiling nurse who had helped him deliver the Milner baby, was wailing. She was sitting in the other nurse's blood, her legs straight out in front of her, the long black handle of a knife sticking out of her abdomen. Both her hands were wrapped around the knife; tears ran down her cheeks as she howled.

Suddenly everyone was moving. The room became a hive of activity. Weston and the nurse were checked for life signs, but it was clear that they were beyond help.

Mallory kneeled next to Carpenter. He put his left hand behind her head, and the other grasped her arm. He gently began to lower her onto her back. A nurse appeared on Carpenter's other side and helped lay her flat. She stopped screaming and began a spasmodic moaning, like a frightened child who can't yet frame the words for her pain. She was staring directly up at the ceiling, as if trying to read an explanation of what had happened to her on the plain white surface.

Mallory felt her pulse. It was rapid and strong. But her lips were turning blue and her face ghostly white.

She was going into shock.

He leaned close and whispered in her ear. "Carpenter . . . what happened? Where's the priest?"

She didn't respond, but continued to moan and stare at the ceiling, her eyes roaming now.

"Carpenter . . ." he whispered more urgently. "Who did this? Carpenter . . . Who was it?" Her glazed eyes shifted and stared up at Mallory. Dazed and frightened, she breathed, "Death . . . he looked like death."

"Where's the priest . . . the man with the concussion who was in this room?" he asked.

Her eyes didn't move. But her lips framed words, as if she were carrying on a silent conversation with an invisible partner. Mallory knew she was falling rapidly into shock. He shouldn't be doing this, but he had to know.

"The priest . . . where's the priest?"

"Death . . . he looked like death . . ." she mouthed.

Then another doctor was next to him and a second nurse on the other side.

The doctor next to him hissed, "You know better than this, Doctor." He elbowed Mallory away.

Carpenter was lifted onto a gurney and immediately wheeled out the door to surgery, the knife handle wobbling grotesquely with every shock of pain that made her gasp.

On the chance that Father Paul had hidden from the killer, Mallory checked the bathroom and then the single closet.

He wasn't here.

He walked quickly to the nurses' station and checked the records. Father Paul was definitely registered in Room 621. He hadn't been released or transferred.

As he was going through the files a nurse appeared and demanded to know what he was doing. He identified himself as a staff doctor and asked her what had happened to the priest in Room 621.

"You must be joking," she said, surprise written across her face. "How should I know in this chaos?"

"Are you assigned to this station?" Mallory asked, his voice cold. The name on her tag was M. Russel.

"Yes," the nurse said. She was a pleasant looking middle-aged redhead with wide gray eyes, nervous and skinny as a winter sapling.

"Then you damn well should know," Mallory said. "That's your job."

"But . . . he was there the last time I checked. He was just off the critical list, but we were keeping an eye on him. I checked his blood pressure only five minutes before . . . before. . . ."

She waved her hand vaguely over her shoulder, back toward Room 621.

". . . before all this happened," she finally said, tears welling up in her eyes.

"It's okay," Mallory said softly. He patted her shoulder. "Just start a search. I want him found. He can't be far in his condition."

The nurse turned and started away. Mallory called after her. "And get me his records. Especially his head X rays. I'll be in the doctor's lounge."

It was almost midnight when Mallory flopped into a chair in the doctor's lounge and took a sip of coffee. It had been a hell of a day. In fact, it had been a hell of a week and a headache was beginning to turn its generators and send sparks flying around in his skull. It was hard for him to believe that it was only a week ago when he had been moaning in the cafeteria that he was bored.

He was worried sick about Father Paul. What had he gotten himself into? *An accident?* Not too likely with one of them following him right into the hospital.

Mallory shivered, his skin trembling like the surface of a lake in a sudden violent wind.

He was trying to imagine what the priest had been doing. What had he discovered that had brought them down on him like that?

The skinny redheaded nurse appeared over his shoulder. She dropped a folder in front of him.

"Thanks," Mallory said. "I'm sorry I was hard on you earlier. I was worried about my friend."

"I understand," she said, standing next to him with her hands clasped over her pelvis. Her mouth was set into a tight little pucker.

He flipped through the charts. Nothing deadly. Father Paul's concussion, if it was one, was minor. He was probably in a lot of pain, but no life-threatening damage had been done.

"Did you find him?" he asked, looking up at Russel.

"No, Doctor, we've looked everywhere. Checked every place possible. I've had security searching. They say he's not in the hospital."

Mallory shook his head. He couldn't understand it. Father Paul wouldn't have been in any shape to run away from the killer. Hell, he wouldn't be in shape to walk to the toilet unattended.

"How's Carpenter?" he asked. He didn't mention Weston and the nurse. He didn't want to hear any of the details.

"She's just out of surgery. The knife missed everything important. Nicked her spleen, but she'll be all right."

"Good," Mallory said, handing the nurse Father Paul's charts. "Thanks for your help. Do me a favor, will you? Keep security looking. We can't simply have misplaced a seriously injured patient."

He stood up. "I'm going home. If anything comes up

please call me. No matter what time. I'll leave the same message at the desk downstairs, but I'd appreciate your following through personally."

She nodded, her gray eyes lusterless. "The police are here and want to talk to you . . . and everyone else who was in the room."

"I'll talk to them later. They don't need me. There were enough people in there to keep them busy."

"Yes, Doctor," she said, turned and walked out.

Mallory went up to ICU. If Carpenter was awake from sedation maybe he could find out something more.

By now the police were all over the hospital. To get into ICU where Carpenter was he had to show his hospital I.D. He nodded to the nurse on duty and read quickly over her chart. The operation had come off well. No major complications. She would make it.

He stood by the side of the bed watching her breathe. Her face was bloated, and the oxygen tube in her nose was rubbing against her nasal membranes. Her nostrils were already red with irritation. He touched a little gel to the irritated area. Her eyes opened. She stared up at him, her irises dilated.

"How're you feeling, Carpenter?" he said softly.

She wet her lips and mouthed, "Okay." She tried again and this time a dry croak came out, "I'm okay, I guess."

"Can you tell me what happened?" Mallory asked.

She closed her eyes. "It was all so fast," she said. "I've already told the police as much as I remember."

"What do you remember?" he asked.

"I was taking the patient in 621 a sedative. Dr. Weston had ordered it, and he and Ellis went in while I was getting the set-up. When I walked in a tall man with blond hair was holding Dr. Weston by his shirt collar. He had a knife at his throat. Ellis was standing next to them.

"The man ordered me to come in and close the door and don't make any noise, or he'd kill Dr. Weston. He made Ellis and me stand next to him, and he sat Dr. Weston on the edge of the bed."

Her eyes began to glisten with tears, and Mallory patted her arm.

"He asked us where the priest was, but none of us knew. He was in the room just a few minutes before . . . Russel and I both checked on him.

"He became angry and told us he'd kill Dr. Weston if we didn't tell him. When we said we didn't know again he slit his throat."

"Oh, God," Carpenter moaned and closed her eyes. After a moment she looked up at Mallory. "It was awful. Just like that. He slit his throat, and Dr. Weston fell back on the bed and I screamed."

Carpenter rocked her head back and forth, "I know I shouldn't have screamed. I think it panicked him, but I couldn't help it . . ."

She looked up at Mallory again, her eyes full of tears, pleading for understanding.

"I know," Mallory said. "It's all right. There is no right thing to do in those kinds of circumstances. You can't know. . . . You did your best, that's what counts."

She shook her head slightly. Mallory wasn't sure whether she was agreeing or not.

"He threw Dr. Weston back on the bed and grabbed Ellis. We heard voices yelling outside the room and he . . . he cut Ellis . . . bad . . . across her stomach."

Carpenter paused and caught her breath. "He grabbed me by the throat . . . and I think he was going to do the same to me, but people were running outside the door, and he just stabbed me and ran. The next thing I remember the door opened and you were there."

Mallory didn't say anything for a moment. She was

breathing heavily and rapidly. A thin wet trail ran from the corners of her closed eyes and down her cheeks. He wiped them away gently with his fingers.

"Thank you," Mallory said. "You rest now. I'll call in tomorrow."

She smiled slightly but didn't open her eyes. Mallory slipped out of the room.

He went to the pay phone at the end of the hall and called St. Simeon's in Enfield. He didn't expect an answer, but he had to check anyway. He let it ring a dozen times, then replaced the receiver. He would call Kelly tomorrow. Maybe he could help find Father Paul.

The elevator opened nearby, and he jumped in. He wanted to get out of the hospital before the police began questioning him. It was possible that Father Paul had called him at home. Maybe he had left a message. If anything had happened to the priest . . . if that ghoul in black found him first. . . .

The pictures of split open bodies, of babies' chests gouged out, of Daley's torn throat and of Jeff Goldman's terrified eyes and hollow, limp body hanging by the neck . . . and now Weston's cut throat and Ellis' ripped stomach. . . .

It all flooded back, a stark technicolor vision rushing over his inner eye like a wave of shining water on a moonlit beach. The pictures pounded at him, beating on the back of his eyes.

He rubbed his temples with his fingers, pressing hard. It did no good. He had the awful feeling that the pictures would stay with him forever, never leave him at peace, haunt him until he died.

He left the hospital and walked to his car. The night was bitter cold. He hadn't noticed it before. But now, the frigid damp air and the darkness encased him, making him feel trapped in a tomb. It wasn't unlike the feeling he had had in the church basement while waiting in the chill darkness for the steps overhead to leave.

He slipped into the driver's seat and shook his head, trying to rid himself of the depressing images. It was almost as if he had no control, and they were being projected onto the screen of his mind by some willpower stronger than his own. He started the car and turned toward Route 10. The smell of the charnel house had come back, and he opened the windows all the way.

Chapter Sixteen

That night Mallory slept like the dead. And the fact that he woke up, his senses immediately acute, trembling with anticipation, frightened him. It had never happened to him before. He lay in the dark listening, his eyes open and staring into the lightless room. Still the wind, always the wind here along the river. And the sing-song muted whimpering of the trees.

Then, a shuffling, unhurried step came from outside. Out of the corner of his eye he saw a long shadow flit past the window. He turned but there was nothing. A low, throaty rush of wind passed the house, and a bare winter tree shook outside the window. Mallory heard its skeletal branches brush across the rooftop. Another scraping sound came from against the side of the house. Then silence. That wasn't a tree branch. It was a different sound. A human sound. Nothing moved and Mallory found himself holding his breath.

The cry of a night bird floated through the window. An early loon, for the slightest graying of the morning sky had begun.

The thumping sound came again from somewhere near the corner of the house. He pulled back the covers and sat up. He waited until the sound came again—from the back of the house. A low guttural voice coughed and was muffled quickly.

Jesus, he whispered aloud, *someone's out there.*

The image of the tall man in black fleeing down the hospital corridor came to him, his blood-slurred red footprints weaving an irregular pattern as he ran. He went barefoot to the bedroom door, searching for something to defend himself with. He hated guns, but now he longed for one.

He heard nothing more and walked through the living room to the kitchen door, listening before he pushed it slowly open. The room was empty and almost alight with moonlight coming through the four windows.

He could feel his heart pounding, the vibration reaching throughout his body, the carotid thumping in his neck.

A scraping, the sound of fingernails, against the back door sent the hair on his scalp straight up. He lifted the curtain and peered outside. The moon reflected on the river through the trees, touches of silver light against the blackness.

A face suddenly slipped in front of him. One moment there was nothing; the next he was inches away from a face covered with blood. One eye was closed, a flap of skin hanging loosely on the cheek. The nose was swollen and purple, the lips puffed and split. The face was grinning, or at least the lips were pulled back from the teeth. A bloodshot eye stared at him.

My God . . . Father Paul . . .

Mallory pulled the door open. The priest stood there, swaying, one hand on the door jamb. He started to speak, but his mouth closed abruptly, as if all the muscles in his face had suddenly died, and he fell forward into Mallory's arms.

Mallory carried him inside, kicking the door closed with his foot. The old man was heavier than he expected, but he got him into the guest room and onto the bed. He grabbed his bag from his room and sat on the edge of the bed. First he took out his penlight and checked the priest's retina for any cerebral bleeding. The retina was clear, and he breathed a sigh of relief. Then he went over him carefully. He cleaned all the wounds that had opened and put clean dressings on.

When he was finished Mallory put his stethoscope back in his bag and went into the kitchen to make some tea. The old man was tough as leather. He was suffering from exhaustion and dehydration. Rest and plenty of liquids and he would be fine.

He would give him tea laced with a good shot of Irish whiskey when he woke up.

Three hours later, and after two cups of Irish tea, the priest was sitting up in bed.

He smiled as Mallory came back into the room. "Hello, young Doctor. How have you been?"

Mallory grinned back. "Social chit-chat? After what you've been through?"

"Ahh, yes. It has been interesting," he said, nursing his pungent tea.

"What happened?" Mallory asked.

The priest laughed, then clutched his side. "Ah, me, yes. I must remember laughter and broken ribs don't suit each other."

He took another shot of tea and handed the empty cup to Mallory. "What didn't happen?" he said. "Where do you want me to start?"

"How about the hospital? Where did you disappear to? And how did you manage to get away from that black butcher who was looking for you?"

The old priest's grin disappeared. "Yes . . . he was a nasty piece of work, wasn't he?

"You won't believe this, boyo, but I dreamed it." He grinned again at Mallory. "And I'll be glad to tell you all with another of those wonderful cups of tea you brew."

"Another of those and you won't be able to talk about anything," Mallory said. But he got up and made him another half and half.

"Ahh," Father Paul sighed, taking a long drag. He set the cup on the side table. "Well, to start with the last first. As I said, you might not believe me, but when I came to in the hospital I knew I was safe. Or at least I thought I was. They gave me a sedative, and I went to sleep."

His face had relaxed. Color had come back to his lips, and he spoke with less strain. The Irish tea was as good as any sedative he'd ever seen, Mallory thought.

"Let me tell you, that dream was something. Unlike anything I'd ever experienced before. And the strange thing was that I knew I was dreaming. It was as if I was watching myself have a dream . . . in full technicolor.

"The first I remember I was running down a long dark road. It was in the woods and I could hear animals, or something, crashing through the brush on each side of me. I couldn't see them; they kept to the forest shadows. I knew I was running for my life. They wanted to kill me.

"I saw a light through the trees so I left the road and made for it, stumbling and crashing through the brush and screaming for help. The animals were close; I could hear them panting behind me . . . and feel their hot, stinking breath on my back. I made it to the light, which came from the open doorway of a small church, not unlike my St. Simeon's.

"The creatures were snapping at my heels by now, and I fell through the doorway, leaving my pants' leg in one of their mouths."

The old man opened his eyes and glanced at Mallory. His smile was not pleasant. It was a mocking grin.

"And now, young doctor, you think the symbolism is too pat. How nice, chased by demons the old priest finds succor in a church. How neat. It even looks like his beloved St. Simeon's."

He laughed quietly, but again, it wasn't a happy sound.

"Oh, no. God's design is nothing so simple. The inside of the church was a replica of St. Simeon's, right down to a hole in the carpet I've been complaining about for six months. But the filth . . . oh the filth of the place. Webs, giant cobwebs in every corner that were decorated with limbs . . . human limbs. Fingers, hands, legs, heads, hanging eyes, all struggling to free themselves. The webs were almost singing with their frantic movement. I fancied I could hear the heads screaming. Calling my name, pleading for help.

"I started toward the closest web, thinking to cut the pieces of flesh free. In that peculiar dream logic, I thought that perhaps they could somehow come together, be made whole again once they were set free.

"But from behind the altar a tall blond man dressed in black . . . in fact, I think he was dressed in priest's clothing . . . put up his hand to stop me. He lifted a bible from the lectern and stepped down. Holding the bible before him with one hand, and flipping the pages with the other, he walked toward me. He stopped a step in front of me, looking down at the bible and grinned. It was closer to a grimace, I think, for when he smiled I saw his teeth. They were covered in blood . . . and pointed. Sawed off and sharpened, like Alistair Crowley's eye teeth that he filed to a point. I could even see the file marks.

"Anyway, he grinned at me, and nodded, as if he had finally found the passage in the bible he had been seeking. He tapped the open book with his fingers, but when his hand came up it held a stiletto. Not a normal knife, not a hunting knife, for example. It was long and curved, shaped like a kukri. The kind of knife the village slaughterer used in Ireland when I was a boy.

"'I will open your flesh, Priest,' he said. His voice was low and hoarse. Then his hand moved so swiftly that I couldn't see it. It disappeared in a blinding arch. But I felt it . . . the knife . . . as it went stinging across my throat. I felt it open the flesh, slice through the cartilage of my windpipe, cut the muscle holding my head erect and felt the blood, hot almost like acid, burn down my neck and onto my chest.

"I knew then that I was dead . . . and I tried to scream. I opened my mouth and screamed, my hand clutching my throat, trying to hold everything together. But no sound came out. I felt my severed vocal cords blubbering, flapping with the blast of air bellowing from my lungs. But no sound. No sound."

Father Paul passed his hand over his eyes. "Ahh, me. Yes, that was some dream. I woke up then, screaming, my mouth open but no sound coming out. I was in the hospital bed, both my hands clutching my throat."

He smiled grimly. "I didn't let go, you know. For several minutes I held on, sitting there in that bed, convinced that my throat had been cut and that if I took my hands away my life's blood would pour out.

"When I finally accepted that I was alive I took my hands away and looked at them, checking for blood. But it wasn't over then, boyo. I was still convinced, you see, that that blond mock-priest was going to kill me. I couldn't shake the feeling . . . and the more I tried to rationalize it, the more I put it all down to a foolish dream, the stronger the feeling became. After five minutes I was convinced that he was coming for me. That he was near and coming for me.

"I knew I had to get out. As pained as I was, for I hurt so bad that tears sprang to my eyes just by the simple act of walking to the closet and putting on a robe. Everything was burning, every muscle and bone in my body was on fire."

He lifted his cup and drank some of the tea. He didn't seem to mind that it was cold. "But I made it, didn't I?" he said, raising his cup high in a salute to Mallory.

"I almost didn't, you know," he said after a moment. "I was so weak that I couldn't go far. When I walked out of the room I felt a terrible sense of urgency, as if he was just around the corner . . . waiting. I was too weak to run, and I saw a supply closet across the hall. It was open so I went in. I left it open a crack, watching, sure that he was coming for me."

Mallory shook his head. "Don't tell me that you were right there . . . hiding in the closet across the hall from your room all the time."

Father Paul grinned. "Yes, shameful, wasn't it? But not for long. I saw the black priest go into my empty room. For a moment I felt enormous relief . . . and vindication, I had been right. My dream had been right. But then I saw the doctor and nurse go in. And then the other nurse."

He closed his eyes and lifted his head up, his face to the ceiling. "And then . . . then the screams started . . . and I knew he was slaughtering them with that butcher's knife. I started to cry out, to scream for help, but he bolted from the room. Somehow . . . I don't know by what magic insight he had . . . somehow his eyes stopped on the crack in the door . . . and our eyes met."

Father Paul held up his hand, as if swearing a vow. "I still don't understand it, but he saw me . . . I know it. Our eyes held for a split second. He almost came for me. I saw his muscles jerk . . . at first toward me

... and then there were shouts, and he turned away down the hall. All of this took only seconds ... and then he was gone and a policeman ran by. I saw a rush of people come to the door ... and then I passed out. I fell there by the door, I assume pushing it shut as I fell because when I woke up it was closed. I was in the dark. I pulled myself together and waited until the hall was relatively quiet ... which was quite a while, for there was a lot of activity. No police yet, though, so I don't think I was out for very long. And then I walked out the same way the black priest had gone. Through the door at the end of the hall, down the stairs and out the exit.

"I walked for as long as my strength held out, rested, walked again and rested. It took me almost four hours to get here ... in what I would guess is a twenty or thirty minute hike for a young lad like you."

Mallory was impressed. Most people he knew would never have the guts and stamina to pull off what the old man had even if they were healthy ... and not battered to within an inch of their lives.

"And where have you been for the last two days?" Mallory asked.

The old man put his head down and stared at the cold cup of tea in his gnarled hands. He looked like an embarrassed little boy caught at something naughty.

He smiled crookedly. "Do you recall the photocopies of the letter with the list of names that you gave me? And the copies of the NIH computer printouts?"

"Of course."

"Well, after seeing those sacrifices in the Exeter church basement I went home and studied them. I had an idea that we were missing something. And we were. We were missing the children ... the birth of the children themselves. We had been concentrating so hard on the deaths of the mothers and the murders of the doctors that we had forgotten the children.

"Those twelve pitiful little bodies gave me the idea. They were blood seeds, killed on February second, Candlemas, the day of regeneration when Christ was presented in the temple. I think this cult used Candlemas not only to have communion with Satan, but as a time to generate power, to offer blood seeds so their twelve children could be born into this world."

Mallory sat back, too stunned to think clearly. "Blood seeds . . . the children . . . but why?" he stammered. "Even if you're right, why?"

"Oh, I was right," Father Paul said, "I made sure of that. They killed the children in the church, took their hearts and drained blood from their bodies and used it to empower the birth of their own children on one of Satan's sacred days."

"Their children?" Mallory said, growing more confused with every moment.

"Their children . . ." the priest repeated, his face solemn. "Those twelve children have been born to the cult . . . for what reason I do not yet know. But God help me . . . I have a sinking in my heart . . . It's weighed down by a terrible premonition."

Mallory's mouth had fallen open. This was going too fast. It was moving into scenarios that were simply too incredible for him to accept.

The priest held up his hand, the palm toward Mallory. He smiled again, a quick, nervous grin. "I know you have questions. But let me tell you what happened and maybe some of them will be answered.

"I became sure that the twelve children were somehow involved in all this cult violence when I compared the NIH list with the child care agency list. The addresses for every one of the twelve children had changed. Within the last two years every one of the children had been moved . . . from all over the country . . . to the northeast."

The old man paused, his dark, bruised eyes quietly watching Mallory's face.

"They all moved to within an hour or two of here . . ." His bony finger thrust downward, toward the floor, as if Mallory's bedroom was the center of the world. ". . . here . . . to this part of New England."

Mallory was too surprised to speak. His mind was reeling from the patchwork of facts flooding over him. He had no idea that the children . . . the twelve children were a part of all this. He couldn't make any sense of it. It seemed significant, even important, but none of it had any meaning for him. It didn't compute. Why would a cult kill so many . . . to give birth to a few children? For what possible reason?

As if echoing his thoughts, Father Paul said, "At first I didn't understand. Why would all the children be moved to this area? Then it dawned on me . . . whatever it was that they had been waiting for all these years, for whatever reason they had murdered doctors and sacrificed those babies . . . and probably even killed the mothers in a way we don't yet understand . . . it was all now close at hand.

"You see," he said, waving his hand in the air, as if underlining the truth written there, "they were coming together now . . . gathering their forces for the final phase of their plan."

Father Paul took a long sip of his cold Irish tea, wetting his dry mouth before continuing.

"But I had to be sure. I had to see for myself if the children were actually involved . . . or if I just had a crazy coincidence on my hands. So I chose the eldest, a twelve year old boy who is now living in Thetford, Vermont, just north of here."

"I know," Mallory said. "I noticed that a few of the children on the red letter list lived nearby . . . but it didn't seem important then . . . what with the killings of the doctors and the deaths of the mothers."

"Of course," Father Paul said. "On the face of it you were right. It merely seems a coincidence... an anomaly... unless you place the children themselves in the middle of it all.

"Anyway, I drove up to Thetford yesterday... no, I guess that was two days ago... and found the child's home. It was an old, rebuilt farmhouse on Route 113 outside of Thetford proper.

"No one was home so I nosed about the place. There was nothing suspicious, and I sat in the car on a dirt road about fifty yards away, watching the house, for two hours.

"Nothing happened until after dark. I was freezing and had just put on the car's heater to keep warm when I saw the house lights coming on. I waited another hour until they were settled into their routine and then crept down the road, keeping to the brush.

"Fortunately it was a cloudy night, and only a little moonlight now and then cracked through the clouds. But I was unnerved, I don't mind telling you. Not a sound... except my own footsteps. Every dead winter branch under my feet sounded like breaking bones... and I imagined the crackling echo could be heard for miles.

"When I reached the house I peeked through the living room window..."

Father Paul grinned again, his eyes sparkling with the humor of it all. "I felt a bit like a peeping Tom... but then I knew I was right. The mock priest, the tall blond dressed in black, entered the room with the boy. They sat on the couch talking when something... I don't know what... warned the child. He turned and stared right at me. Almost at the exact moment the man looked up... right at the window."

The priest took another quick sip of his tea. By now his eyes had a whiskey glow about them. His face was flushed, and he grinned quickly . . . on and off. "I don't need to tell you I was startled. There we were . . . eyeball to eyeball. The boy's eyes were . . . how can I describe them . . . hollow and yellow like shining ivory . . . empty, yet with an icy glow that sent a chill racing through my old bones. His eyes had the same implacable look, the same evil blue fire as the man's.

"You may not believe this, for you are a modern man full of modern ideas. But I saw everything in that child's eyes. He was evil. A child of Satan."

The priest raised his hand. "No, don't smile. This is not peculiar to a weird old priest. In Matthew 6 it is written that 'If thine eye be evil, thy whole body shall be full of darkness . . . The light of the body is the eye. . . .'"

Father Paul shrugged. "Well, believe what you want. In any event I saw it, and the child knew I understood. The boy then began a low, hair-stiffening brool that sounded like the humming growl of a mad dog. Well, boyo, I began running. I'm an old man, I know, but I was suddenly a twenty year old, a grey-haired, decrepit old priest running in the Olympics of his life."

He giggled at his own silly image of panting down the road and covered his mouth with his hand. "I got to the car . . . and thank heavens the engine started right up. It was still warm, you see. Well, I could see them in a shaft of blue moonlight . . . the tall blond head and the boy's shining pale face running down the black road toward me.

"When I turned the car down the road, I could see them racing back to the house. I assumed they were going to get a car so I drove toward the highway like a madman.

"I flew onto 91 south before I even saw their lights behind me. At least I assumed it was their car. I surprised myself by going almost a hundred. Normally that kind of speed makes me nervous. But I made it to 89 south and all the way to Route 120 before they caught up to me. The last thing I remember was the blond man grinning at me as he drove into the side of my car, forcing me off the road and into a wooded hill. At that moment I thought it was my time to go to grass."

He glanced at Mallory. "But you know more about what happened after that than I do."

For a long moment they sat silently, Father Paul sipping his whiskey tea and Mallory mulling over what he'd heard.

Mallory stood and began pacing the room. The important thing was that he'd found them. Father Paul had found them.

"We have to go back," Mallory said abruptly. "This is the first solid lead to who they are . . . and where they are." He stopped and stared at the old priest. "That is, if you're right."

Father Paul didn't say anything; he simply looked up at Mallory and smiled.

"We can't go to the police yet. We have no real evidence," Mallory said, thinking out loud. "It'd be his word against yours . . . and what could you say, that you saw it in their eyes?"

He sat back down on the edge of the bed. "No, the police would nose around and get us nowhere . . . except to warn them and scare them into deeper hiding. But Kelly, maybe we could get Kelly to go out there with us. Unofficially."

Father Paul finished off the last of his tea and shakily set the cup on the night table. He lay back on the pillow and looked at Mallory dreamily. "My boy, you go out there with your policeman friend if you want, but I'll take along my bible and a few little tricks of my own."

The old man closed his eyes. "Just let me sleep a while and then we'll go . . ."

In a moment his breathing began a deep wheezing rhythm, and Mallory slipped out of the room.

Chapter Seventeen

Another damn dismal February, Kelly thought. He lay in his bed naked, his hands behind his head studying the three large cracks in the ceiling that he had avoided spackling all winter. He hated February more than any other month. Well, maybe March was worse when Vermont was one great mud pie.

Despite the drizzly afternoon he smiled, remembering when old man Keane went to help a neighbor get his car out of the mud on a back country road. First Keane's truck went down over its tires. Then he got his tractor and that slipped in up to its engine block. They called the police, who got their tow truck stuck and all four vehicles sat in the mud for two days before a state truck-lift rig could hoist them out.

Out of curiosity he and Keane had measured the mud hole . . . it was forty feet long, as wide as the roadway and, at the worst spots, over four feet deep.

Kelly stretched his long body, feeling good. His kids were at school, and his wife was at the Four Aces Restaurant, no doubt walking her feet off. He was off for the day and already bored. In fact, he had been growing more bored for the past two or three years.

He ground out his cigarette in the small ashtray next

to the bed lamp. Pam hated him smoking. She said it was because she was worried about his health, but he knew it was because the smoke stank up the house. So he never smoked when she was home, and always opened the windows and aired the place out afterwards.

But nothing had changed the boring sameness of his life these last few years.

And police work, especially over the last two years, had turned out to be mostly bullshitting at headquarters. And waiting. Always on your duff somewhere... waiting. Sitting around in a patrol car. Sitting in restaurants. Sitting in the squad room. The only time he got off his ass was when he had to hand out a ticket.

And then along came David Mallory... *Damn, that whole thing was exciting. What a case.*

He had sent out a request on all of the doctors on Mallory's list yesterday but didn't expect to hear anything until the end of the week... if then. Computers made questions and answers move at electric speed but in between you could die of old age.

But he had much more interesting things for Mallory today. He checked his watch. It was almost time to meet. He sat up and rubbed his face. The rough carpet of stubble reminded him it was over a day's growth.

He got up, dressed, shaved, and packed the papers he had prepared last night in a manila envelope. He checked his watch again. It was time to meet Mallory.

When Mallory entered Peter Christian's, Kelly was already there, sitting in one of the high-backed booths, nervously twirling a beer in front of him. He looked anxious.

"Well, you look like you've had a bad night,"

Mallory said as he slid into the booth.

"No, just a sleepless one. Wait 'til you see what I have," he said.

Mallory ordered a mint tea and a vegetarian lasagna, remembering the many times he and Goldman had eaten here and how his friend's obsession with herb teas and health foods had amused him.

A manila folder lay on the shiny polyurethaned pine table. Kelly opened it and pulled out a sheaf of papers. Mallory could see they were computer printouts.

"Right after Goldman's murder I began doing some research. I've just received some answers to wires I sent out last week. And one thing I've learned is that we're not alone."

He shoved a paper across the table to Mallory.

"There's a new wave of occult crime all across the country. Police have been coming up against brutal murders where the evidence was different from anything they'd ever experienced before. None of the normal motives . . . anger, revenge, spur of the moment killings . . . seemed to fit. Even a new type of cop, 'cult cops,' is being trained."

He nodded towards the papers in Mallory's hands. "I've dug up some old police reports that knocked my socks off. They're from all over the country and describe 'cult' crimes."

Mallory was still trying to get a sense of the reports he was reading when Kelly grabbed another paper from the pile in front of him.

"Listen to this. Here's a homicide where the victim is decapitated. The body is found surrounded by colored beads, coins, and chicken feathers."

Kelly flipped the paper over to Mallory.

"Here's another, two of them, in fact, where there's evidence of the mutilation of animals and ritual sacrifices on crude altars found in wooded areas."

He pushed the two sheets of paper across the table.

"And here's some that involve satanic rituals and the sacrifices of children. And another listing homicides where the corpses are drained of blood and pentagrams or inverted crosses were carved into the victim's chests."

He flipped the papers to Mallory. One was a morgue photo of a victim's body. His face intense, he said, "Does that sound familiar to you . . . bodies drained of blood?

"I even found an old police bulletin sent out from the San Francisco PD. Listen."

Kelly read in a rapid monotone, his voice tight.

"Request for Nationwide Broadcast, San Francisco PD/CA.

Attention: Intelligence and Homicide Divisions. This department is currently conducting investigations into satanic cults which may be involved in animal mutilations and ritualistic homicides of human beings wherein internal organs are removed from the victims and used in church baptisms and rituals.

"Any information forward to . . . etcetera . . ."

He handed the paper to Mallory. "I'm about five years too late on this one, but I sent a wire to SFPD describing both the Goldman and Daley murders this morning."

The waitress arrived with their lunch, and Kelly sat back. He began spinning the nearly empty bottle of beer again, impatient for them to be alone.

When she'd gone, he said, "Did you read that stuff?" His finger jabbed at the papers scattered in front of Mallory.

"No," Mallory said, still scanning the dozen or so pages Kelly had shoved at him. "I'm not a speed reader."

Mallory ignored his food and began reading the photocopies of the police reports.

Memorandum
San Francisco Police Department
TO: Captain John R. Davenport
FROM: Officer Peter Tucca
DATE: January 10, 1987
SUBJ: Ritualistic Sexual Abuse and Homicide.

Sir:

Attached is my synopsis of cases of sexual abuse and ritualistic homicide that have surfaced during my research over the last five months in the State of California and elsewhere. I have interviewed most of the victims or assisted other agencies in their inquiries. I am convinced that the testimony noted herein is true. I hope this will clarify my point that the department must take cases involving satanic rituals far more seriously than in the past.

During my investigation of cult activity over the past several years, information has continually come forth that traditional witchcraft and satanic rituals were veering off into areas of criminal activity involving mutilation of animals, drinking of blood, and excising specific organs of the victims' bodies for ritualistic purposes. These brief synopses of the cases prove the point. The complete reports are appended in Appendices A through G.

HUNTINGTON, CALIFORNIA
DATE: 1986-87
VICTIMS: WMJ, WFJ
AGES: 14, 9 YEARS

Documentation: Police Reports; Child Protective Services Reports
Victims were abused sexually. Black candles

were used during rituals. Satanic chanting, mutilation of animals, and black robes worn by adults. These two children were injected with drugs and photographed during sexual activity with adults. They both claim, during separate interviews, that they observed the murder of a child (around 2 years of age). The victim was stabbed, arms, hands, and fingers cut off prior to the child being thrown into a ritual fire.

COSTA VERDE, CALIFORNIA
DATE: 1986
VICTIM: WF
AGE: 16

Documentation: Police Reports
The victim forced to drink blood, forced in S & M sexual activity with father and friends. Photographed during sexual acts. Observed animal mutilations. Observed homicide of WM, 27 yrs. WM subject suffocated, knifed repeatedly.

Victim's legs, heart, and penis removed during satanic ritual.

QUEENSVILLE, TEXAS
DATE: Unknown
VICTIMS: 5 Juveniles, 2 WMJ, 3WFJ
AGES: 3-13 years

Documentation: Police Reports; Medical Reports
Victims observed skeletons, skulls, ropes, knives and other satanic items used during rituals. All victims, including the 3 yr old, were sexually molested. Most were photographed dur-

ing sexual activity. All victims, at one time or another, were forced to devour body parts, both animal and human. All forced to observe homicides of a child and an adult.

Mallory's stomach was churning. He put down the reports. The smell of the tomato sauce in the lasagna was making him sick. He pushed the plate away.

He picked up another report and the morgue photo. The picture was of a young man, probably in his midtwenties. His nude body was stretched out on a stainless steel table. The sheet was clumped around his ankles. The body was covered with black holes, scarred gouges apparently from cigarettes or matches or even a hot metal probe of some sort. Mallory couldn't be sure. All the fingers on the left hand had been cut off at the middle joint. A large pentagram was jaggedly cut across the chest and stomach. The crude cutting was almost a quarter inch deep, and the flesh lay open in a white trough right down to the bone.

The report was of a homicide of a child, a nine year old girl, who had been killed while being raped. One of the suspects was quoted as saying: "This involves ultimate power . . . power both for Satan and ultimate pleasure for his worshipper. The child is killed with a knife in the heart exactly at the point where sexual climax and death come together. Sexual climax at the point of death. The kid has to be raped because that's where the power comes in. Ultimate control, pure power directly from Satan."

Mallory put the paper down. He covered his eyes with his hand. Then he began to rub them until he saw white spots leaping in the blackness.

God, what had he become involved in? What mad thing was mauling his life . . . sending it into this hellish mess?

"I know," Kelly said softly. "I felt the same way when I first read them. It's hard to believe."

"What I don't understand," Mallory said, shaking his head, "is the merging of sex and murder. Brutality and violence have always been just under the surface, but it somehow seems that sex is more and more getting mixed up in it all."

"Yeah," Kelly said, "it runs all through these reports on satanic homicides. The psycho-Satanists seem to get all excited sexually during periods of violence. I did a little checking into sex crimes and mass murders. A book by Colin Wilson, an English expert on this stuff, said that there was a definite connection between the violent energies of mass murderers and their frustrated sex lives. Peter Kurten, the Dusseldorf monster who killed dozens of people, would keep stabbing his victims until he had an orgasm. Can you believe that?

"In all the police reports I've read no one has come up with an explanation . . . except maybe Wilson. But most of it is a lot of Freudian psycho-babble."

Mallory didn't answer. He was feeling nauseous . . . almost to the point of vomiting. Sometimes he thought the only answer to this insanity was to throw it up, let the sickness he felt constantly inside him explode out. But he couldn't. He was torn between letting go and maintaining control. And holding on . . . a closed fist around his own destiny was his only salvation. If he let go he might lose it all. He would end up hiding under his bed or squatting in a fetal position in the closet. He had to hang on any way he could. So he swallowed the stomach acids that had already foamed up into his throat and tried to ignore the bilious aftertaste.

Kelly saw Mallory go green, and he let it rest. He knew how shocking this stuff was the first time you saw it.

After a moment he tried to change the subject. "I telephoned Officer Tucca, the guy who's done most of the work on these cases, and he said no one believed him at first. But he's beginning to make progress now . . . and he's collecting evidence from all over the country."

Mallory looked up at Kelly, his eyes bloodshot and raw from the rubbing. "Well, I believe him," he said.

"Look, I appreciate all you're doing, Kelly. And I appreciate your showing me these reports. But they don't mean a damn thing to me. I already know we're dealing with a crazy satanic cult. I already know they're brutal and that they kill people. And it doesn't give me any comfort at all to know that we're not alone . . . that simply depresses me, for all it means is that there are many more madmen running around than I thought."

Mallory pushed away his tea. He took out a five dollar bill and threw it on the table. "Thanks for the thought, but I've lost my appetite. And I have some things I have to do."

He stood up and slipped on his raincoat as Kelly collected his reports and shoved them back into the envelope.

"Call me if you hear about how the doctors were killed? Okay?"

"Sure," Kelly said. He was staring at his beer.

Mallory walked out. For once he was glad it was still winter. The crisp, cold air was antagonistic. The biting wind cut at his exposed, warm skin. He breathed deeply and the icy, prickly stab of it surged into his lungs. As he stood on the sidewalk outside the restaurant he began to feel a little better. Alive. Yes, at least still alive. Untouched by the dark, ravaging—he almost said "evil"—passions at work around him. But he wasn't sure he even believed in evil. Father Paul was convinced that a pure, unadulterated and personified evil existed. To Mallory that had the quality of a myth, an early Christian fairy tale. Violence, madness, brutality and hatefulness. Oh, yes, they were real. But motivated by insane human emotions. Not by some demon rising from Hades and hiding in the shadows.

He had to get back to the house and see how Father Paul was. Even though the old man was as tough as leather he had been badly hurt.

"Oh, shit," he mumbled. He'd forgotten to tell Kelly about Father Paul's discovery of the farm with the blond killer.

He turned to go back in . . . but the thought of descending those narrow brick stairs back into the cellar restaurant depressed the hell out of him. It could wait. It was more important to see how Father Paul was doing. He could call Kelly later that afternoon, or even tonight, and tell him about it.

Father Paul was still sleeping when Mallory arrived home. He went into his bedroom and closed the door to telephone Lili at the hospital. He was feeling guilty about having not seen her.

She had been patient. Every time he called her she reassured him that she understood. She knew how crazy his life had been.

God, was he falling in love? He wasn't sure. He had never been in love. He wasn't even sure he knew what love was. He sure as hell didn't have any of it from his parents. He knew he cared more for Lili than any woman he had ever known. But was it love?

When she finally answered he smiled to himself. Just the sound of her voice pleased him. He told her a little about what had been going on since they last spoke, and they made plans to have dinner.

But this time it would be special. While Father Paul

slept, Mallory showered and changed clothes. He left a note explaining where he was and placed it under a fresh cup of the priest's half-and-half Irish tea on the night table.

When he left just before five o'clock, Father Paul was still sleeping heavily. Good, Mallory thought. It was the best possible healing the old man could get at the moment.

Mallory drove into Lebanon and spent the next hour shopping at the Powerhouse Mall. He found a charming little shop, Artifactory, that was full of high-quality crafts and moderately expensive gifts. It had just what he wanted. He bought Lili a sapphire choke pendant and then went to a florist and got a dozen roses. It was corny, he knew, but he had to show his appreciation for her patience and understanding.

Lili lived in a two room apartment on South Main Street just outside Hanover. She had only been there for a few months but had already decorated the place. It was warm and full of earth colors. Browns, golds, and wine-colored furnishings gave the place a rich, sensual quality. African art—masks, wooden sculptures, robes, and headdresses—were scattered on the walls. It seemed appropriate, to fit that pagan core of her that he had sensed when they first made love. When he went there he always felt as if he had entered her inner sanctum.

She opened the door, her luminous almond eyes glowing. She was smiling, her lips untouched by rouge yet full with a glistening scarlet.

She put out her hand to touch his face and pull him in. But when he took the flowers from behind his back and handed them to her, she gasped and stepped back. A choked mewling sound came from her throat. Her eyes were horrified . . . that was the only word Mallory could find to describe it.

"Take them away . . ." she whispered, coughing deep in her chest. Her hands covered her nose and mouth. Her eyes were still stricken. "Please," she gasped, her voice hoarse. "Take them away."

Shocked, Mallory stood in the doorway staring at her. He finally found his voice. "What is it? What's wrong?"

She had backed all the way into the center of her living room. One hand extended toward Mallory, the palm outward, she said, "Nothing . . . nothing. I'm . . . allergic to them. That's all. They make me desperately sick. Please, take them away."

"Of course," Mallory said, backing down the hall toward the trash bin. Christ, he felt like a fool.

When he returned Lili was composed again. Her eyes were still slightly red-rimmed. But she seemed completely her old self.

"I'm sorry," she said. She put her arms around him and kissed his neck, just beneath his ear. She nuzzled her face there, breathing into the soft curve between his shoulder and neck.

"I feel so foolish," she murmured. Her wine-scented breath drifted up to him.

"Not half as foolish as I do. I'm so sorry. It was a stupid blunder."

"No, no. Not at all," she said, looking up at him. "How could you know? I've been violently allergic to roses all my life. I can't even be in the same house with them."

She stepped back and smiled. "Let's forget it. I've made an incredible meal . . . even if I do say so myself. And I'm starved, so let's eat and say nothing more about it."

"Sounds good to me," Mallory said as he let himself

be led to the table.

Dinner was delicious, just as Lili had promised. A salmon mousse, wild rice in a butter sauce touched with curry, salad with Belgian endives, and yellow wax beans sauteed in garlic and olive oil. Lili had already opened a moderately dry chablis, and Mallory poured himself a glass.

As she was serving he began filling her in on all the details of his visit to the Exeter church and on Father Paul's trip to the Thetford farm and his discovery that the children were involved. Lili had heard about the blond man dressed in black and the killings at the hospital. But she was shocked to hear that it was all connected with Father Paul and their trip to Exeter.

"Don't you think it's time for the police?" she asked.

"No, not officially. We have a Norwich policeman working with us, but we don't have any evidence of this group's involvement with the killings of Jeff and Daley. And we don't know who they are or where they are. If we bring in the police now, what do you think will happen? They'll dig up the bodies of the dead children in the church basement at Exeter. And so what? What connection does that have with Jeff's death? Or the Daleys? Or the killings at the hospital?

"The whole thing will become a media circus in twenty-four hours. Headlines about cults and ritual killings. We'll be swamped with reporters and television cameras from New York and Boston and everything will go underground.

"Maybe, just maybe, they might catch the man in black from Thetford. But I'll bet he's already in hiding. He's not going to hang around after what he did at the hospital . . . with witnesses, yet."

As good as the food was, Mallory's stomach was still sour. He sat back and sipped his wine. "No, we have a few cards left. If we can continue to work quietly, and find out who they are . . . and where they are hiding . . . then it will be time to call Kelly and bring in the police."

Lili reached over and touched the back of his hand. "No more," she said softly. "It's all we talk about anymore. And I have a few other things on my mind tonight."

Chapter Eighteen

After Mallory had gone, Kelly had ordered another beer and sat morosely in the booth. It took him a while to calm down. He was pissed at Mallory. He understood that Mallory was sickened by the police reports. So was he. But they had to be dealt with. Mallory was just a pussy. A clean-cut college type who couldn't really handle the stress of police work.

Kelly remembered how excited he had been when he had first discovered that he was on to something big. But maybe some of Mallory's panic was beginning to rub off on him. He was beginning to feel out of his depth. What did he know about Satanism and rituals? He was just a small town cop. Tucca had said that he had been a cop for almost twenty years, and the ritual killings were some of the worst he had ever seen.

And all that weird shit about vampires and human sacrifices. That had shaken him at first. He didn't believe a word of it even though the evidence seemed to be going in that direction . . . or at least toward a blood-thirsty, kill-crazy cult who used occult trappings. He couldn't take the occult stuff seriously. It was simply too unbelievable. It was like astrology, and all the rest of that bullshit. There was no way to confirm it.

At least not yet. And he didn't think there ever would be. He was becoming more convinced every day that they were dealing with a group of crazies. An insane satanic cult. Look at the madmen Tucca dug up. He'd like to get his hands on those bastards. What they needed was evidence . . . hard facts to follow up.

The idea hit him like a physical blow. He slapped his forehead.

The babies . . . Yeah, the murdered babies. If they were still in the church basement? Damn, why hadn't he thought of it before.

If he found those dead babies . . . and reported it . . . he'd be ten steps ahead of everyone else in the investigation. Especially if there was something there that would connect all the killings. Maybe fingerprints. He'd have to be careful so they could match prints with those in Daley's house and on Goldman's car.

He checked his watch. One-twenty. He could probably make Exeter by four o'clock if he hurried. He quickly paid the check and left Peter Christian's.

In February the sun set between four and five o'clock, and he didn't want to be stumbling around back roads in the dark looking for an old broken-down church. He made it to the Exeter turnoff a little after three and thought he'd have plenty of time. But it took him longer than he expected to find the place. He had to stop a half dozen times to ask directions. Two of the people he asked didn't know where the church was; two others sent him in the wrong direction. When he finally saw the old gray building squatting on the hill, the sky behind it was already a winter steel. But at least he'd made it before dark. It was after four, and he didn't think he could have found it in another half hour. The nighttime forest gloom was spreading fast, and shadows were becoming long and deep.

He snapped open the glove compartment and took

his flashlight. He started to get out of the car but paused, one leg already outside. There was something odd in the air, a hush, like the sudden silence when you're walking in the deep woods and the birds go quiet. The chill forest air, made heavy with a light mist, swirled in through the open car door, carrying with it a dank smell . . . like dead leaves, or the wet-rot wood smell of a tree covered with lichen that had been sucked lifeless.

"What the hell," he said aloud. He didn't think he'd need it, but if this was really the place where the cult did their thing . . . then some of them might be hanging around. He pressed the glove compartment latch and took out his snub-nosed Smith & Wesson .38 Chief's Special. He fingered open the chamber and checked its load, then slipped the gun back into the holster and hooked it onto his belt in the small of his back.

He looked over the terrain. The incline down to the stream was steep, and he searched for an easier path. He saw the jerry-rigged bridge and walked up the road to the narrow, worn path leading down to it. The stream was high with water, and the winter run-off was deep and fast. He noticed that the planks over the stream were slippery with water spray and slime, but with the confidence of a man raised in the woods he didn't give it much thought. As he crossed the planking his feet suddenly went out from under him, just as if somebody had lassoed his ankles and yanked his feet forward, landing him flat on his ass . . . one foot over the edge, dangling just above the water. Cursing, he got up and limped to the other side of the stream. His knee was scraped, and he rubbed it a minute before starting up the hill.

The cemetery was damned spooky . . . and even though he could still see well enough, he snapped on the flashlight. He ran its beam over the gray, molding stones. He'd always hated cemeteries at night. He didn't believe in ghosts or spooks . . . but he just didn't like the idea of walking on top of all those dead people. It seemed an insult. Something you'd never do if they were alive, so why do it when they're dead?

He made his way to the church, avoiding walking near the tombstones. His mouth was suddenly dry, and he fished out an orange-flavored Rolaids and popped it into his mouth.

Dead ivy and a dozen leafless rhododendron branches encircled the entrance archway. The thick, cast-iron handle on the church door was cold in his hand, already chilled by the night air. But the heavy wooden door swung open easily.

"Damn," he whispered. "What a stink." He swung the flashlight beam in an arc, getting a quick impression of the size and character of the place. His first impression was of darkness . . . a satiny film of shadow covered everything. And the smell . . . it reminded him of when he was a boy, and he had been trapped in a dismal, foul-smelling cave for two days with three of his friends. They had been on a hunting trip when a heavy winter storm hit them. They had no camping equipment because it had been a simple daylight hunt, and they had to wait in the lightless, stinking cave until the storm had played out. They were lucky to have found the cave, but it had been the home for every conceivable animal in the north woods. Piles of shit, both human and animal, had collected over the years, along with dozens of powder-dry animal corpses, half-eaten carcasses and chewed-up bones that were scattered all over the place.

There's a different smell to something that's died and dried up. It loses that wet, penetrating acid smell and becomes dull and heavy, a kind of shuffling, slow-moving smell that walks into your nose, and you think it'll never leave. That's what this place smelled like. As if something had been dead and dried up here for a long time. Only the wet smell of mold crawling over everything made it seem still part of the real world.

His dislike for the place was deep and immediate. This was a church with no god, a place of ancient dust, an eerie silence and spider webs. Cobwebs were stretched across the few dark windows, and the yellow flashlight beam illuminated the intricate mazes in golden lines, like weavings of shining golden thread.

Mallory had said that the trap door was on the altar. He swung the light toward the nave. The oaken pulpit perched stolidly on the platform, a mute square shadow against the waning light from the nave's windows. He walked down the aisle cautiously, feeling exposed and vulnerable, as if someone or something . . . was waiting crouched in the darkened pews. He knew none of it was true, but the feeling stuck to him, like sweat on his skin. Shadows seemed to shift and move with purpose. A quick flitting movement seen from the corner of his eye. He shook himself and said *"Shit"* out loud. It was all in his head . . . and he knew it.

He felt like a kid again breaking into the Petersen place. It was the day after his thirteenth birthday. The whole Petersen family had died three years before . . . mother, father, and the four kids . . . all dead, asphyxiated in their sleep when the gas furnace had malfunctioned. The bodies weren't found for three days, and the summer heat had done its job. The mailman reported it when he tried to deliver a package . . . a birthday gift for little Mikey, the youngest who was four at the time.

Everyone in town had stood outside and watched the six bodies, all covered with the morgue's black plastic body bag, carried to the county van. Even then the smell made the men light up their pipes and cigars and the women turn away.

After that no one wanted to go near the old house and the more run-down it got, the more its reputation grew. Growling, animal sounds were heard from inside as kids walked by. Sometimes even voices could be heard murmuring from behind the dark windows, sort of sorrowful like, as if the ghosts were talking over what to do next.

When he and Ernie Chapman broke in they had lasted about five minutes. The house creaked and groaned as if it hated the intruders. Ernie swore he saw a ghost open the cellar door. They had screamed and knocked the rotted back door right off its hinges breaking out. They had never gone back.

Didn't Mallory say he thought the place had a kind of cool neutrality? Hell, it felt to him like the goddamn place was really haunted. His skin was curdling up on his bones, and he had goosebumps fighting for space all up and down his back and neck.

The damp, mildewed carpet squished beneath his feet. *Disgusting*. It was like walking in wet marsh grass, never quite feeling sure that the ground was solid and that it might not suddenly sink beneath you.

The whole damn place pressed in on him, making it hard to breathe. The smells and dim light and sullen creaking and gasping of the floor boards all seemed to whisper *get out . . . get out . . . get out. . . .*

He found the trap door under the rug. He had to pull back half the damn thing before he saw the iron ring. Now his hands smelled of the old rug. He wiped them on the sides of his jeans. His knee still twinged painfully when he bent it so he moved down the steep stone stairs slowly, swinging the flashlight beam along each step. He wouldn't be surprised if a few rats jumped out at him from the black cellar below.

Shit. This wasn't turning out to be such a good idea. He hated rats. Always had. Even when he was only ten or eleven he and his friends used to spend hours at the West Lebanon dump shooting the little gray bastards with their .22s.

Pink eyes . . . that's what he'd hated the most. Their goddamn unwavering, shining pink eyes. You could be aiming right at them, your finger on the trigger, and the dumb fuckers would stare right at you . . . daring you to kill them. He never knew whether they had incredible courage or were just plain mean and stupid.

The stink was worse in the cellar. It was thick and penetrating, a damp, rotting smell.

He swung the beam in a slow arc. The room was huge. It seemed to go on forever. Only the wall facing him was visible. In every other direction his flashlight beam widened into infinity, illuminating only empty space, opening until it dissolved into a black wall of nothingness.

He turned the beam on the stone wall in front of him. It was made of flat gray field rock. The kind you see on old buildings all over New England. About twenty feet to his left he saw what must be the altar . . . carved out of a giant rock that jutted four or five feet from the wall. Whoever built this place didn't even bother trying to move the big rock; they just chiseled a flat basin out of it and left it where they found it. That meant that the altar was built at the same time as the church. Is that possible? Did that mean that the early Christians who built this place put in the altar at the beginning? Christ, that didn't sound very Puritan to him. What were they doing putting an altar in a church cellar? Had the Devil worship bullshit been going on here since then?

As he moved closer to the altar he noticed the statue sitting on top of the stone basin.

Jesus, it was ugly. About the size of a dwarf, the

thing's mouth was open, and the hard stone eyes, heavy-lidded and all covered with blackened, dried blood, were staring straight ahead into his flashlight beam.

He wished he could close its mouth. It seemed to be waiting to be fed . . . like an idiot chained to the wall and hungry, its mouth open, waiting for someone to come along and shove something in and feed it.

He turned away and played the light over the floor. According to what Mallory had said there should be babies' corpses scattered all over. But there was nothing. You couldn't call it clean by any stretch of the imagination, but the dark earthen floor looked swept. He could even see the straw marks from the broom.

As he searched the area around the altar his light touched one of the demon heads protruding from the stone blocks in the wall. Mallory had described it . . . but he hadn't done it justice. It was *repulsive*. Like one of those heads he'd seen in pictures of cathedrals in Europe. Heavy eyebrows, a flat, porcine nose, fat, protruding lips that hung open with a slack idiot expression. And the deepset eyes that seemed to follow him as he approached, his light steady on the face. It reminded him of those weird 3-D pictures of Jesus where the eyes follow you as you passed by. Though Jesus's eyes were always sentimental and sad . . . and these were angry, mean eyes.

"*Fuck you . . .*" he said out loud to the demon face.

He tucked the flashlight under his arm and pressed his fingers under the chin and on top of the demon's head and pulled. The stone came loose easily . . . but it was heavy and he quickly lowered it to the ground.

"*Jesus . . .*" he mumbled, and stepped back.

The tiny yellow skull of a newborn infant glowed in the circle of light. Flaps of dried skin curled away from the bony scalp. Patches of scraggly, thin white hair still hung onto the loose flesh.

Kelly was stunned. He had come here looking to find this . . . to get evidence that these sick bastards had actually done such a thing. But this was too much. He couldn't believe it was actually true. To kill a baby . . . Standing here and looking at it made him sick to his stomach.

He didn't want to look any closer. But he had to find out if there were more. Then he'd go report it. He went to the next demon head and pulled it loose. Another newborn in its dark cave, all white powdery skin and its body twisted up . . . as if all its muscles and ligaments had tightened and squeezed the bones together after it had died.

Kelly had a strong stomach—and he thought he'd seen it all—drunks splattered all over the road, farmers with their heads blown off by shotguns they were handling too casually after a few beers. But this . . . he had to fight to keep from vomiting.

He didn't know what it was . . . but something, a sixth sense, that old prickly feeling along the back of his neck when he knew someone's eyes were on him. . . .

He turned and swung his light toward the stairs. At the same instant his right hand went behind him, under his jacket and grabbed the butt of his .38 Special. He didn't pull it, but quietly unsnapped the holding-strap and stood silently looking at the tall, lean man at the bottom of the stone stairs. He was framed in the beam of the flashlight, and it would be an easy shot so Kelly wasn't nervous. In fact, if this was one of those sick bastards who'd killed the babies he'd enjoy shooting him.

The man was very pale, his skin almost a translucent cream-yellow ivory. His white-blond hair gave the impression that he was an albino . . . especially since his eyebrows and long lashes were also white-blond. His skin was satiny smooth, and his whole face seemed to glow softly. His eyes glittered in the beam of light, shining back toward Kelly with a bright glistening amber, like cat's eyes when you throw a light on them.

The albino was extremely tall, several inches over six feet. His hands hung down along his sides, relaxed. He was very handsome, in an effeminate way, with large eyes, an aquiline nose and a well-rounded, perfectly shaped mouth. He was smiling at Kelly.

Kelly returned the albino's stare and smiled back. There was something menacing about him that Kelly couldn't put his finger on. An aura of energy radiated from him, a kind of unnatural vitality came out in waves. Even with his pretty face there was a quality of danger, as if he was capable of sudden violence. Over his years as a policeman Kelly had felt the same way toward perhaps a dozen men he had confronted. He was often right. Instinctively, Kelly wasn't going to give this guy an inch.

Still smiling pleasantly, the albino stepped toward Kelly. He was about thirty feet away, and Kelly slowly took his gun out and leveled it toward him.

"That's far enough," he said quietly, his voice low and steady. "I'm a police officer, and I'm on an official investigation here."

The albino stopped, his eyes flickered down at the gun. When he looked back up at Kelly he was still smiling. But it was no longer a pleasant, relaxed grin; it had turned sardonic, as if a nasty joke had just occurred to him.

He started toward Kelly again, slowly, his step confident and easy.

"Stop . . ." Kelly said, raising the barrel of his gun. It was now aimed directly at the man's chest. "I'm warning you . . ."

The albino ignored him and kept walking toward him with that easy stride confident tall men have.

A surge of fear rose up from Kelly's gut. His mouth became suddenly dry, and he wet his lips. This guy wasn't acting normal . . . he was really out of his mind to walk into a gun this way.

The air in the cellar was sulfuric and dust-laden, as if opening the small crypts had disturbed the centuries of dirt and dust. Everything stank of ashes and old fires, mixed with the pungent death smell from the tiny crypts.

"Are you deaf?" Kelly called out, his voice rising. "Stop where you are. Don't come any closer."

He was about fifteen feet away, and Kelly took a step back. "I'm warning you."

He pulled back the hammer with his thumb. The hard clack of metal moving was reassuring to Kelly.

But the albino kept moving toward him, not even slowing down. His smile seemed to broaden slightly as he got closer. Kelly could see the peculiar amber flakes in the iris of his eye reflecting in the flashlight beam. Like glow-in-the-dark paint, his eyes were cold and luminous. Not angry or aggressive, they held on Kelly with an incurious alertness similar to the intensity of a stalking animal.

"Listen, man," Kelly said, nervously. "I don't want to shoot you . . . but if you keep coming that way I'll have no choice."

The man was only about six or seven feet away when, almost without realizing it, Kelly pulled the trigger. The gun exploded, kicking back in his hand to a full right angle. The blast was deafening in the enclosed space of the cellar, and the flash momentarily blinded him.

The cordite cloud billowed into a milky screen and for a moment Kelly wasn't even sure he'd hit him. But when it cleared, the albino was still standing a few feet in front of him, looking down at a tomato-sized shock of red on his chest. He seemed surprised and was staring at the hole with curiosity.

After a few seconds he looked up at Kelly, his eyes quizzical. He didn't say anything ... but simply raised his right hand toward Kelly, almost as if offering a handshake.

Shit, Kelly thought. *He's smiling again. This guy's got a hole in his chest, he's already half dead and doesn't know it yet ... and he's still smiling.*

Blood was pulsing out of the hole and dribbling down the albino's white shirt. For a moment Kelly was mesmerized, and he couldn't take his eyes off the bubbling hole.

Then the man stepped forward and seemed to reach for Kelly's shoulder. At first Kelly thought he was reaching for support, that he was going to keel over. But he grabbed the base of his neck, where the shoulder and throat meet. Kelly was shocked at the speed and strength behind the move.

Kelly wasn't really a slow man mentally, but it took him a moment to realize that this man was still as strong as a bull and that the cold hand around his throat was squeezing ... and hurting.

The white-haired bastard should be dead ... he should be on his back staring up at the ceiling and here he is grabbing at him ... attacking him.

A flash of panic exploded in his gut, and Kelly struck at the forearm with his left hand. The flashlight smashed into the bone at the wrist. But it didn't loosen the man's grip at all. The albino's amber eyes were staring directly into Kelly's. The pretty mouth was grinning now, the bow lips pulled back to reveal even white teeth all filed to a point. It was the mouth of a predator ... and the mad son-of-a-bitch was salivating.

Kelly began screaming at the top of his voice, cursing and shaking his head back and forth. He squeezed the trigger again and the man bolted backwards, his belly first, just like he'd been punched in the stomach. But the hand squeezed harder, and then both hands were on his throat, and he pulled the trigger again and again. The explosions echoed in the cellar until Kelly's ears were ringing. But still the powerful grip didn't loosen. He continued to pull the trigger even after the gun was empty, and the only sound was the heavy metal *click . . . click* of the hammer dropping.

Kelly was weakening. He was gasping for air and had to get free. He kicked up with his knee, reaching for the man's groin. He hit something solid, but the man didn't move. He used his knee again and then kicked out with his foot, aiming for an ankle . . . anything that would release the pressure. A sudden uncontrollable urge to gag swelled up in his throat, but he couldn't, his windpipe was completely closed off by the powerful hands. His lungs shrieking for oxygen, he violently tried to suck in some air . . . his throat spasming as the oxygen-starved muscles ceased functioning. In desperation he smashed the empty gun repeatedly against the albino's ribs.

Then, incredibly, he felt himself being lifted off the ground. His feet spastically kicked the empty air under him, and the gruesome picture of his dying by being hanged flashed before him. He saw Goldman's body, the purple twisted neck and dry, staring eyes.

His head suddenly began to spin wildly. He felt himself swirling around the dark edges of a whirlpool that drew him closer and closer to its black center.

He opened his eyes, and the man's face was only inches away. The cold amber eyes were still staring at him. Kelly tried to speak, to curse, to cry out . . . but nothing came. And then he fell deeper into the swirling blackness. The white-hot fire burning in his throat and the pounding in his head faded. His last thought before consciousness left him was that he was a dead man . . . and he didn't want to die. *Too soon . . . too soon . . . too soon.*

When Kelly awoke his head was thudding with a sharp, penetrating ache. He was surprised to be alive. But the pain convinced him. His whole body hurt with a fiery, burning pain. Especially his throat. The fire pulsed, burning more intensely with every beat of his heart. The albino had obviously bruised his neck and throat so badly that he couldn't even swallow.

He was wracked with pain, and a strange tingling sensation was scampering up and down his nerves. His body seemed numb, and he tried to find the parts. He lifted a hand, then a foot slightly . . . but he was too weak to do more.

When he tried to lift his head, his neck muscles wouldn't obey the command. He managed to raise up an inch or two, and then the sheer weight was too much and his head dropped back.

The simple effort of moving exhausted him so he lay quietly. He was vaguely aware that he was nude, lying on a narrow bed in the dark.

His eyes were open . . . but he couldn't see anything. It wasn't the church basement. It was warmer, and had a different feel. And the odors were different. This room smelled of warm soil and stone . . . a pleasant farm smell like earth freshly turned in spring plowing. There was also a hazy odor of incense, wild and pungent, like the bags of herbs and flowers his wife dried in their attic.

In the daze of his pain and the utter blackness, he lost any sense of time. He seemed weightless, floating in the darkness that was neither hot nor cold. He almost felt comfortable . . . if it weren't for the throbbing in his head and throat and the sharp, stabbing pains that sometimes shot through his body. A few minutes, an hour, ten hours could have passed before he heard the footsteps . . . and he wouldn't have known the difference.

When the door opened a pale yellow light slashed across the room. He couldn't see much, but it looked like the place was a large square cave. He was underground somewhere. And the walls were all covered with black paint or cloth. He was in a cot near the door. Four huge black candles as thick around as his arm were placed at the four corners of his cot. They were held in elaborate, ornamental cast-iron candleholders as tall as a man.

The albino stood in the doorway, a Coleman lantern in his hand. He walked toward the cot and set the lantern down next to it. His hand reached out and touched Kelly's brow. A gentle touch, almost loving. The fingertips skittered over his forehead, a soothing, calming stroke that Kelly's mother had used to comfort him whenever he was sick.

The albino's face hung over Kelly, only inches away. His eyes, a darker, burnished-brass color now in the shaded, indirect light, stared at Kelly's face. He lowered his head further, almost cheek to cheek, and for one panicked minute Kelly thought that he was going to kiss him. Kelly could hear the man's breathing, fast and light. And his breath . . . it was rank with the foul stench of the church and the dead children.

Kelly tried to raise up, to push him away, but he was so weak the slightest movement almost caused him to faint.

With a swift but fluid movement, too fast for Kelly's dazed senses to catch, the albino lowered his lips to

Kelly's throat. At first his lips lingered, nibbling, brushing against Kelly's neck. Then the sudden pain was so electrifying that Kelly groaned. An excruciating spasm flashed through him as the albino bit into the already bruised, aching flesh.

Kelly was helpless, unable to move a muscle, paralyzed with a lassitude that left him teetering on the border of consciousness. He could do nothing but cry out. But his cry was pitiful. He heard the soft, wretched whine as if it were coming from someone else. It sounded like the whimper of a puppy that's just been pulled from its mother's tit.

The albino sucked on his throat, moaning gently, his cool, thin hand still on Kelly's forehead. The pain was not as bad now. The sharp aching jolt was gone. A dull, almost warm ache remained in its place.

Kelly didn't know how long it went on. He floated in the sensual dream. The blackness was like a darkened movie theater the minute before the show starts. Memories of his youth, free and filled with wildness skipped through his mind. Technicolor adventures floated past . . . the first time he saw his wife, the birth of his children. The intense moment his father died in his arms, his open mouth limp and eyes frightened. They all melded in a chimera of feeling . . . until suddenly, without knowing why, the theater's lights went out. The show over, Kelly slipped into unconsciousness.

He was awakened again, but crudely this time. A hand was shaking him. He still hurt, but now it was a distant pain, as if it had happened before and he was only remembering it.

The albino stood over him. His brass-colored eyes smiling. He looked down on Kelly as a father regards his child in the crib.

Several other figures stood next to the albino. He couldn't make out who they were, for they were all back-lit by the light from the open door. And their shadows told him little, for his eyes could barely focus. Their bodies were wavering, shimmering as if they were mirages standing on a hot desert blacktop.

A twinge of pain shot through his leg, up from the knee he had cut crossing the stream. That seemed so long ago, another age, another life. He could hear a soft lapping sound, like a cat drinking milk. As the pain in his leg receded he could feel the tongue, wet and cool, rolling over his wounded knee.

Oh, my God, someone's licking the blood from my knee, Kelly thought. The muscles in his leg spasmed, and the leg jerked up and off the cot for a second. The soft slurping sound stopped briefly . . . and then began again. Two of the figures glided closer. They were small creatures and Kelly could hear them giggling . . . like children. A third child moved next to him and touched his chest. The child's fingers crossed his shoulder and skittered down his arm. A quiet mewling sound came from it. All the children were now touching him, their fingers flying over his skin. It was so gentle, so soft and sensual, that it seemed butterfly wings were flitting over him, wings lightly kissing his fevered flesh. When they began to suck and lick his skin it tickled, sending thrills of goosebumps over his body. He didn't even mind when each of them bit into his flesh.

For several moments they sucked and licked at his open veins, the strange little mewling sounds each made creating a sweet chorus of pure childlike music. Kelly let himself sink into it. He couldn't have resisted even if he had wanted to. He had only enough strength left to lie there and feel . . . even a mental complaint was beyond him. In fact, he began to yearn for their touch . . . it gave him an exquisite pleasure, a sensual thrill that vibrated like electric heat throughout his body as they ate him.

The other figure standing next to the albino bent down next to Kelly. It was a woman. Kelly could tell from her perfume . . . and also from her touch. He opened his eyes and stared up into the beautiful face only inches from his. Her pale skin was shaded by the dim light from the door, but it still had the glow of fine antique paper.

Her lips brushed over his cheek, then settled gently on his mouth. The kiss lingered and Kelly felt transported, his body flushed with heat, as if he were lying on a sun-drenched beach. She kissed his chin, the side of his face, and then lowered her lips to his throat. At the same moment her fingertips touched his chest, then his belly and finally brushed over his penis.

His erection was immediate, the muscles swelling so quickly and intensely that the sharp pain of her entering the open wound on his neck didn't even register. The sensations were incredible; violently hot streams of current coursed through him. Even the sounds of her sucking on his neck thrilled him. She moaned quietly as she ate him. She did not move her hand that held him, but an orgasm built in him anyway until he felt he would explode. When it finally happened his head was whirling, his mind a spinning, dizzying kaleidoscope of colors and sensations.

Vivid pictures of when he was a child riding his first carousel. A giant red horse pushing him . . . pushing up and down, pressing him up near the brilliant, glowing colored clouds of light circling giddily around his head, and then dropping him suddenly down to the floor, dangerously near the ground that was whirling around him, thrilling him beyond description.

He didn't know how long the feeding went on, but as

the woman sucked him, and the children continued their gentle butterfly nibbling, Kelly grew faint. In his mind the colored lights of the carousel dimmed, and the shadows began moving more slowly. First under the belly of the dancing, laughing horses, the shadows grew darker and wider, then they crawled up the animals' legs and the colored clouds circling overhead dimmed. The circus was closing, lights turning down . . . slowly, slowly Kelly came to a stop. He groaned. He didn't want to get off the pretty horse. He wanted to stay on it forever, listening to the music and his head spinning with the colored lights. But the lights dimmed and went out, and the horse limped to a halt and the music finally ended.

Chapter Nineteen

Mallory arrived back home just after nine o'clock the next morning. The house was quiet. Father Paul must still be sleeping, he thought. He moved quietly to the bedroom and glanced in.

It was empty. The bed was rumpled and the pajamas Father Paul had been wearing lay in a pile on the floor.

Mallory called, "Father Paul?"

He walked into the bathroom. Nothing. He began to worry. He had been living in a state of constant expectancy . . . in nervous anticipation of something else terrible happening. He had once read some research done by a neurologist in England, W. Grey Walter, who claimed to have discovered a new brain wave. He called it the "expectancy wave," and found it in EEG tracings of people who had what psychologists would call high anxiety experiences.

He was probably living proof of Walter's theory. Take his EEG anytime during the last week, and his "E" waves would have gone off the chart. He had begun to expect surprises, even disasters, at every unknown corner of his life.

"Father Paul," he called again, louder this time. He

began searching the house, his anxiety growing. If anything had happened to the priest, he would never forgive himself.

He probably shouldn't have spent the whole night at Lili's. He knew how dangerous it was to leave Father Paul alone. He had planned on returning early, but after they had made love he was so exhausted . . . and so wrapped up in the woman that everything else simply disappeared from his consciousness. When he was with Lili he felt comforted and relaxed. Which was rare for him during the last week. Hell, it was rare for him anytime. The simple truth was that he had fallen asleep and not woken up until morning.

He stopped at the sink and poured himself a glass of water, letting the tap run until the chilled well water rose up. What to do next? Where could he have gone? He was probably still too weak to have gone far on his own. Was he taken? Kidnapped? The idea came hard, curdling its way into his thoughts. Had the man in black figured out that the old man was here? Had he come to check out the possibility and found him?

Mallory shook his head, the thought too awful to consider. Stark, bloody images of what the man in black was capable of came to mind and made his imagination run wild.

A sudden flash of sunlight struck through the window, changing the Mexican counter tiles from a dull blue-gray to a deep metallic ocean blue. Momentarily blinded, he glanced outside at the golden morning light spraying across the rushing water.

There he was! The priest was sitting next to the river, his silhouetted back toward the house, staring out into space.

"I'll be damned," Mallory said and dashed out the back door.

"Father Paul," he called.

The priest turned and waved, a long, fat cigar in his hand.

"You had me worried," Mallory said, "when I didn't find you in the house."

The old man smiled up at Mallory and sucked on his cigar contentedly. He blew the blue smoke toward the water.

"Well, it's nice to know someone cares," he said, grinning. "But I slept longer than I can ever remember having done . . . and I woke up longing for a smoke."

He held up the cigar and rolled it in his fingers lovingly. "So, here we are, enjoying ourselves immensely."

The old man's round Irish face was pale and puffy. "How are you feeling?" Mallory asked, looking him over.

"Fine. My head still has a minor storm rolling around in it somewhere. Feels vaguely like a hangover. And my ribs ache when I laugh or try to breathe . . . but other than that . . ." He laughed lightly and waved his hand in dismissal, as if shooing away a fly.

"Your ribs will probably give you trouble for several days, but if you take it easy, you'll heal nicely."

Mallory squatted next to him, and for a long moment they silently watched the morning light brush over the surface of the river.

"I've been thinking about our dilemma," Father Paul said, affectionately mouthing the wet stub of his cigar.

"We can go three ways on this. One, we can go to the police and tell them everything we know. I'd advise against that because there's a very good chance we won't be believed . . . not about the satanic and occult parts of it anyway."

"Yes, I feel the same way," Mallory said. "They'd investigate, the press would get involved and we'd have a circus while the cult disappeared into the woodwork."

"Exactly," Father Paul said. "This group knows how to keep hidden. They've been doing it quite effectively for over a decade now. And I have no doubt that they would go to ground, and we would lose them forever. Just when I feel we're getting closer."

"And I don't think we'll ever have such an opportunity to find them again," Mallory said.

The priest frowned slightly, his pale long fingers caressing the crucifix hanging from his neck. "The second option is that we go back out to the farm. But this time we go prepared.

"The third is for both of us to visit your Dr. Bowker, press him about the cult. Even threaten him with exposure as a member of the group if he doesn't help us."

The old man glanced sideways at Mallory. "Since I assume Bowker is involved with these people in some way, that's more of a threat than maybe you realize. This cult would kill an apostate. And if we say that we'll claim he broke the cult's vows . . . and told us about them . . . why, he'd be as good as dead. And he knows it!"

A wicked gleam in his eyes, he tapped the side of his nose with his cigar-stained forefinger. "And for whatever reasons he has remained alive these last two years . . . that protection would suddenly evaporate. Oh, yes, I think he'll talk to us . . . he'll have no choice."

Mallory stared at the old man, a renewed respect for him. "You are a devious old Machiavelli under that Roman collar, aren't you?"

"I have no hesitation about manipulating one of these devil's disciples. In fact, I'd go to considerable lengths to destroy them."

The old man suddenly shivered. Despite the warming sun, the air was still chilly and damp.

"C'mon," Mallory said. "It's time for bed."

He took the priest's arm and helped him up.

"Hold on there, boyo," the old man said, pulling his arm free and standing on his own power. "No bed for me. I've had enough rest. Today we make a decision. Either the man in black or Dr. Bowker."

"You don't have the strength right now," Mallory said.

"Oh, yes I do, Doctor." The old man's face was set, his bottom lip protruding like an angry child. But his eyes were a hard crystalline blue. He stood facing Mallory. "And don't you be telling me how I feel.

"Either we go together . . . or I go alone. Now, which is it? The man in black or Bowker?"

Mallory studied the stubborn old man for a moment. He sure as hell couldn't do it alone . . . but given the chance he'd try. If he was that determined, it would be better to go along and watch over him.

"Look," Father Paul said. "It's probably already too late for the man in black. He's already gone to ground. But if we don't go to the Thetford farm today, we'll have no chance at all. Bowker can wait, I think. At least until tomorrow."

"All right," Mallory said. "But on one condition. You rest until we're ready to go."

The old man grinned like a mischievous child.

"You're on, boyo. But we must leave early. Get there in plenty of time before dark."

As the two men walked back to the house the full impact of what they were planning hit Mallory.

Before dark.

His night with Lili had almost washed away the savage week he'd just been through. But Father Paul's words, his fierce determination brought him back to the edge, back to the precipice where he had been teetering all week. He couldn't help but wonder if this time they weren't overreaching themselves, pushing too far and too fast without help?

He'd call Kelly right away and get him to go with them. At least Kelly had a gun ... and knew how to use it. He had some protection against these murdering bastards.

Kelly was gone. Vanished. According to Weidemeier he was off yesterday and was supposed to report to work this morning at eight. His car was gone, and his wife hadn't seen or heard from him since she left for work yesterday morning. She was worried sick and had been on the phone to Weidemeier every hour.

In fact, Mallory had been the last person to see him at Peter Christian's. Mallory couldn't help but hear the suspicion in Weidemeier's voice, as if Mallory were somehow responsible for Kelly's disappearance. But then, his attitude wasn't surprising. He and Weidemeier had not really taken to each other from the first.

Although Mallory would have liked to tell Father Paul about Kelly immediately, the priest had, despite his best efforts, fallen back to sleep, and Mallory didn't want to disturb him. He waited ... and wandered around the house. He tried to read, and finally took a walk along the river, his anxiety picking away at him like grubs burrowing and chewing away deep in his guts.

Kelly's sudden vanishing act bothered him deeply.

While standing at the river's edge and staring into the muddy water, trying to puzzle it all out, he suddenly decided that if they were going to confront the cult directly, they needed more defense than Father Paul's bible and his crucifix.

While Father Paul snored softly, Mallory drove to Lebanon. He pulled up in front of "Harry's Gun Shop" on Route 4, the main road leading into Lebanon. The gun shop was a small square building cluttered by the detritus of hunting. The glassy marble eyes of three stuffed deer heads stared at him reproachfully as he entered. Tufts of their moth-eaten hair seemed poised to leap off the creatures' stiff carcasses. Rifles and gun-cleaning supplies festooned the walls, which were covered with masonite pegboards displaying targets, decoy ducks and turkey calls, hunting knives, steel-tipped arrows, gloves, socks, boots, fishing poles . . . anything a hunter could dream of owning.

Mallory paused and stared at an elaborately constructed compound hunting bow that looked like it had been made by the inventor of that child's game, Cat's Cradle, where you weave strands of string around and through your fingers.

Shaking his head in wonder, he walked to the glass case filled with pistols that cordoned off the back of the shop.

The owner, who wore an army-style name tag with the inscription "Harry" on it, was reading "Gun and Ammo" magazine. He was heavy set, with a fat face and wearing a T-shirt that said "Don't Drink and Hunt, the Life You Save May be Your Puppy's." His bare arms were covered with tattoos. He was a caricature, a cartoon of what Mallory would have expected.

The whole transaction took ten minutes, and then only because Harry liked to talk. Mallory asked him to recommend a gun "for home protection," and Harry selected a Walther PK nine-millimeter handgun. He enthusiastically listed the gun's virtues. Then Mallory filled out a registration form where he swore that he wasn't a convict or insane, signed it, and wrote a check and walked out with the gun and a box of bullets awkwardly weighing down his jacket pocket.

When he got back, Father Paul was in the kitchen drinking coffee. Mallory poured himself a cup and sat down at the table and told Father Paul about Kelly.

The old man frowned. "Did he say anything about what he planned to do next?"

"No, nothing. But I got the impression he was going to continue collecting evidence about satanic cults. He wanted official back-up, credibility, when he moved against this group."

After a moment Father Paul said, "Well, there's nothing we can do about it right now. I pray he hasn't gone off and done something foolish by himself."

Mallory smiled despite his worry over Kelly. "Like someone I know did two nights ago?"

"That was a mistake, boyo, for which I've paid with my aching head and sore bones. And if you were a priest I'd confess to the sin of pride, but since you're just a friend I'll only ask for your understanding."

Suddenly he clapped his hands and stood up. "All right, now, give me a minute to collect a few special items from my bag of tricks and we'll be off."

The old man picked up his bible and stuffed a small vial of liquid in his pocket that Mallory assumed was holy water.

Tricks, indeed, Mallory thought.

In a way he was envious. He wished he had such simple solutions to complex issues. But when it came right down to it, he had the same problem as Kelly and the police. He couldn't bring himself to accept that there was anything supernatural here. It was man-made brutality. A viciousness of spirit, perhaps, but created by people and not fallen angels.

* * *

Thetford was another New England "hundred-yard" town. Like Norwich, which was fifteen miles to the south, it was an early settlement on the Vermont side of the Connecticut River. Along the hundred yard Main Street there was a general store, post office, gas station and a church, all constructed in white-washed clapboard.

The farm was two miles north of town. A large "L" shaped three-story house fifty yards off the road, it sat quietly against the forest tree line. A cultivated field, the weathered furrows now capped with a frozen Christmas tinsel of frost, ran east and north of the house and large red barn. There were perhaps twenty or thirty acres in all. Not a very imposing working farm. But it had about it the quality of conformity, a look that said everything is absolutely normal here. A look that Mallory knew was helpful to the owners.

Everything was quiet. No lights or signs of life. The driveway leading to the house was lined with small trees and shrubbery. But still too exposed to simply drive right up.

Mallory had stopped the car on the side of the road a few hundred yards back. He opened the trunk and the hood, as if they were having car trouble. Father Paul stayed in the car, and they both watched the buildings.

Nothing moved. No smoke or haze from the chimney, even though it had become a bitterly cold afternoon. The sun had completely disintegrated behind a pallid horizon-wide proscenium. A gusty wind inconsistently blasted down from the north in great blustery attacks. One moment all was calm, the next the car was rocked with a violent bellowing of arctic air, as if some anxious god of the North Wind was hyperventilating.

They watched the farm for almost an hour until it finally became clear that the place was deserted.

Maybe.

Not wanting to take a chance that someone was still in the house or barn, they drove back to a dirt road they had passed. It cut through the woods south of the farm, angling westward into the forest and mountains behind. Probably an old logging road, Mallory decided. The New England mountains were full of them.

They parked the car off the logging road in a small opening between some trees. Once in the woods the air became mist-laden, and the wind didn't reach them in the close growth. When Mallory opened the door a heavy silence greeted them. Soft under their feet, the forest floor was thick with the eternally present rotting carpet of blackened winter leaves and pine needles. The wet forest fragrance penetrated through the early rising night fog like a Cimmerian perfume.

The mute, shaded beauty and the walk through the steaming woods would have been a nourishment for the spirit except for their goal, which occupied both of their minds with a somber and melancholy alertness.

They walked through the snake-twisted tendrils of mist running along the moist earth in silence until the barn appeared abruptly between the trees. It had a single back door and two large carriage doors. They entered through the door, which was unlocked.

Like the house, the barn was normal in every respect . . . except that it was empty. And unused. Normal farm smells of animal sweat, dung, newly-stacked hay, were absent. The cavernous place even *smelled* empty. The air was heavy and gave the impression of being undisturbed for weeks, if not months. Tiny gray motes of dust floated leisurely in the great open center space, drifting slowly through the shafts of gray light from the four grimy windows.

The farmhouse was about fifty yards away from the

barn, and the idea of crossing that open space made Mallory nervous. He clutched the nine millimeter Walther in his pocket. Even though he had never shot it, and wasn't even sure that he could use it, the solid, cold authority of its presence calmed him.

Halfway to the house Mallory felt eyes were watching from every darkened window. A loud thud exploded behind them, and they both jumped half out of their skins. A sudden, powerful gust of wind had ricocheted past them and flung open the barn door. The report was almost as loud as a gunshot. They must have left it ajar, and it sprang open and slapped closed like an angry old lady's fan.

For a moment Mallory considered running back and closing the door, but if anyone was inside they had already heard it. Mallory took Father Paul's arm and trotted toward the side of the building where a few bushes would give them cover.

"I don't suppose we would look too suspicious if someone is watching?" Father Paul said sarcastically. He was panting slightly and holding his side.

Mallory checked his watch. It was now close to four, and the sky was rapidly darkening. Jagged crowns of spruce and hemlock were silhouetted against the sheet of gray sky behind them. Shadows from the mountains surrounding the valley where the farm lay fell upon the house and barn quickly . . . too quickly. Night seemed to be speeding toward them.

"Wait here, I'll explore," Mallory said, a little breathlessly.

"No way, boyo, we go together. C'mon, I'm all right."

To their surprise the back door was open. So far this did not seem a fortress or safe haven for a dangerous cult. Like many old-style New England farmhouses, the back door opened into a small mud-room-pantry, which in turn opened into the kitchen.

The kitchen was homey. A well-scrubbed wide-beam wooden floor, papered pale blue walls, and dark pine cabinets with white porcelain handles. There were the normal appliances, microwave oven, toaster, electric can opener, which surprised Mallory. For some reason he hadn't expected Satanists or killers to cook and eat like an average person. But then, these might be here simply to impress.

The house was solid and so did not creak or complain as they crept from room to room. Everything *was* absolutely normal. Nothing out of place. Even the furnishings, a blend of sturdy oak and plain upholstered chairs, was all you would expect.

They should get Andrew Wyeth to paint the goddamned place. It was perfect, homey Americana.

They canvassed the house and found nothing. Mallory came back into the kitchen where Father Paul was sitting and started to ask him if he was sure he had seen the man in black here.

But before he could say anything, Father Paul nodded his head toward a door opposite the oak counter where he was sitting.

"The cellar . . . try the cellar," he said, his pale, round Irish face a strange mask of exhaustion and excitement.

Mallory looked at him, puzzled. He was holding a flashlight in one hand. The other clasped his crucifix. A gossamer strand of cobwebs clung to his hair and the shoulder of his black priest's jacket.

Mallory took the flashlight and opened the door. A sickening odor of incense and wet earth wafted up. With Father Paul close behind him they descended the wooden stairs. He snapped on a wall switch and the sullen yellow glow of a single, low wattage light bulb appeared at the bottom of the stairwell.

Again, everything appeared normal. Boxes of glass jars for canning, brass lids, tools, a water heater wrapped in thick insulation held in place by two inch electrician's tape. Mallory turned to Father Paul, his face questioning.

"Over there," the priest said, pointing toward the dark right-hand extension of the cellar.

Mallory walked cautiously into the dark recess, rolling the flashlight's beam across the hard-packed mud floor and cinderblock walls. It was empty except for a few boxes of rusted fence wire, two partially-used gallon cans of dried-up house paint, and a half-dozen one-liter Coleman lanterns. A case of one-liter kerosene bottles, obviously fuel for the lanterns, was pressed against the wall.

"Why so many lanterns?" Mallory asked.

"I guess like most places lights are frequently knocked out by storms. Most farms have a good stock of storm supplies."

"But six of them?" Mallory said, shaking his head.

The cellar recess ended about twenty feet along, but a left hand depression contained a huge old oak door. A bar-latch held it closed.

"Did you open it?" Mallory asked, looking back at the priest.

"Yes, but not to go in. Just looked. And smelled."

Mallory lifted the latch and, even though it was badly rusted, it moved silently. The bolt hinges had been well oiled. The door also swung open easily with the weight of the heavy oak causing only a slight complaint from its hinges.

As the door opened Mallory immediately understood why Father Paul had seemed excited. A pungent burst of incense washed over them.

Inner Sanctum. That was the word that flashed in his mind. *They had found their ritual center, their black heart.*

A glance at Father Paul, who was making the sign of the cross over his head and heart, told him that the priest thought the same.

"Where do you think they are?" Mallory asked softly, his voice falling to a whisper.

"Either they've abandoned this place... I'm sure they have others... because they think they've been discovered, or they're busy somewhere and will be coming back."

"That second idea isn't a nice thought," Mallory said softly as he searched the walls near the door for a light switch. He found one and snapped it on.

Another single pale light bulb immediately in front of them lit up.

"They obviously don't like much light," Mallory said.

"Candlelight is probably all they need."

"Or maybe all those Colemans?"

"I've never heard of using Coleman lanterns in satanic rituals, but I guess anything's possible."

The stark yellow circle cast by the weak bulb only illuminated a few feet near the entrance. All beyond that was a curtain of black.

The silence in the room was almost total. The smooth hard-packed dirt floors muffled their footsteps. And the cinder blocks and low ceiling suppressed sound even more.

As they entered this "cellar-within-a-cellar" the cloying stench of incense became even stronger. Mallory almost covered his mouth and nose with his hand.

He flashed the beam on the walls nearest the doorway. No other light switches. He swung the light around the room. He couldn't see the full extent of it for it was a large room, hung dramatically with black curtains. An altar, also draped with black cloth, stood isolated in front of them like a coffin-shaped catafalque used at requiem masses after a burial. Two large candelabras holding giant black candles stood on either side of the catafalque.

Mallory and Father Paul approached the altar slowly, their senses alert to the unexpected.

But what they saw shook them both to the core.

Mallory's light flashed across a ghostly white form stretched on two steps leading up to the altar.

Kelly lay naked, his limp body on its back, his head hanging downward on the last of the steps. The angle of his body indicated that he might have tried to get down from the altar and fallen unconscious. His sunken eyes were open, black holes staring blankly into the flashlight beam.

Father Paul turned his head away and crossed himself. "Oh, sweet Jesus, how can this cruelty be?"

Kelly's flesh had the same thin parchment look as Jeff's and Daley's. Mallory could see the flat veins pulsing weakly under his white skin.

He's a dead man. . . .

Mallory knelt next to him, sick at heart. He stared at Kelly's ruined body.

Large puss-filled eruptions covered him. There must have been seventy or eighty, maybe as many as a hundred bites and cuts on every area of his body. Small pinpoints of dark, dried blood crusted at the peak of each purple-black sore. His desecrated, wounded, pallid body looked as if it had just been pulled from an open grave.

And his neck . . . his neck and shoulders were one mass of bites. A single, swollen, giant black sore. From his cheeks to his collarbone was a solid black-and-blue subcutaneous bleeding.

Mallory gently touched his wrist, which was puffed up to twice its normal size with edema. He could barely feel the pulse, which was rapid and weak. Mallory felt it begin to flutter, a spasmodic gasping of the bent muscle as it tried to continue functioning.

Kelly was already almost drained of blood. Even transfusions wouldn't help at this stage.

There was nothing he could do. Except make him a little more comfortable. He grasped his legs and hips and gently tried to turn him level. But with the touch of his hand Kelly groaned and turned his eyes toward Mallory.

"No..." he rasped, his voice unrecognizable. "Leave me..."

His eyelids fluttered, and a touch of bloodied saliva bubbled in the corner of his parched mouth.

He opened his eyes again and stared at Mallory. He raised his hand an inch or so off the floor. Mallory took the swollen blue hand and held it gently. Kelly winced.

Kelly's mouth moved, but he couldn't make out the hoarse, choked words. He lowered his head, his ear close to Kelly's mouth.

"Go...." Kelly groaned. "Be back... they'll be back...."

With what seemed a superhuman effort to Mallory, the dying man grasped his coat and pulled him closer. "You can't kill... can't kill them."

The effort too much for him, Kelly's hand fell away. His blood-caked lips trembled, and his eyelids fluttered again. His head rolled back, and he stared up into the lightless shadows, his eyes haunted.

By what memories Mallory didn't care to know.

He turned to Father Paul and shook his head.

"There's nothing we can do," he said softly.

"How long?" Father Paul asked. "Can we get him to a hospital?"

"Anytime now," Mallory said, standing. "He wouldn't survive the trip."

Father Paul kneeled down next to Kelly. He made a

sign of the cross over the dying man and began a soft, barely audible final sacrament in Latin. When he was done he crossed himself and stood up.

He turned to face Mallory. "We can't leave him here..." Father Paul began, looking around for something with which to make a litter.

"No," Mallory said sharply. His gut was telling him to get out. Kelly's warning had struck through his heart like an ice pick.

"We have to get out ... now ..." he said. "Kelly warned they'd be back. We can't fight them all ... not like this."

He took the reluctant priest by the arm. "Come on," he said, still staring at Kelly's limp form. "Now's the time for the police."

"But how can we leave him? The man deserves a decent burial."

"If we get the police he'll have a burial." Mallory was becoming panicked now.

"Don't you understand?" he said urgently. "If they come back now and catch us ... they'll get away with it all. We'll be dead. And no one knows about this but us..."

"No," the priest said, pulling his arm free. "I'm not leaving this man here for those swines to gouge and bloody more."

He bent over Kelly, whose eyes were glazed. "I'm sorry, boyo," he said gently. "This may smart a bit, but we've got to get you to the hospital."

He slipped his hands under Kelly's shoulders and legs and started to lift him. Kelly moaned, gasping in a great lungful of air. And then his head fell to the side. He was unconscious.

But even emaciated and sucked empty as he was, Kelly was still a heavy man and Father Paul couldn't lift him. He looked up at Mallory, his tired, lined face pleading.

Mallory shook his head. Poor Kelly would be dead in minutes. It hardly made any difference . . . except the pain moving would put him through. "All right. But let's hurry. You take his feet, they're lighter."

Mallory tucked the flashlight under his arm, and together they carried the unconscious Kelly out of the cellar and up the stairs.

The house was pitch black now, and the bouncing flashlight beam under his arm worried him. He was sure that the careening light could be seen easily from outside. When they reached the back door he whispered for Father Paul to stop. They laid Kelly gently on the kitchen floor. Mallory turned the flashlight off and put it in his pocket. He took off his overcoat and spread it over Kelly.

"Okay, let's go," he whispered.

Kelly's limp body became increasingly heavy as they walked across the frozen backyard. When they reached the barn they had to rest. They lowered him onto the floor. He had not regained consciousness, and Mallory wasn't even sure whether they were carrying a dead man or not. The barn was lightless, and Mallory searched for Kelly's wrist. Instead his hand touched the shoulder, and Mallory lightly rested his fingertips on the carotid artery. He felt nothing.

He snapped on the flashlight. Kelly's staring blind eyes were dry, the irises dilated. His mouth was slack, and blood-streaked mucus had gushed out and over his chin.

"He's dead," Mallory whispered, unable to take his eyes from the rictus on the man's face. "God, what a ugly way to die."

The flashlight's fat beam encircled the stone-white face. Kelly's frightened, haunted dark eyes stared up at him.

Father Paul knelt down and said a quiet prayer.

The sound of a car cut through the walls of the barn

like a knife. It was distant but coming fast. Mallory snapped off the flashlight and ran to the barn door. He peered through a crack. Headlights were moving along the road. He held his breath as the lights slowed at the driveway. The car turned in.

"Shit," Mallory cursed, his heart suddenly thumping wildly. "It's them."

He grabbed Father Paul's arm. "Let's get out of here."

"What about . . ."

"We can't," Mallory hissed. "There's no time."

Suddenly the car was outside. It stopped somewhere between the barn and the house.

The cough of the engine as it fell silent stopped their breathing. Mallory desperately searched in the dark for the bar-latch on the barn's back door. Car doors slamming and muted voices floated through the night.

He found the bar-latch and forced himself to slowly lift it, carefully avoiding even the slightest sound.

As they slipped out of the barn Mallory heard the back door of the farmhouse slam.

They had minutes, maybe seconds to get away. The barn would be one of the first places they would search . . . and when they found Kelly's body they would realize he had only been dead for a short while . . . and that someone had tried to help him get away.

Once in the trees, even though he could barely see Father Paul who was only five feet in front of him, Mallory began to feel better. He kept nudging the old man to go faster. But neither of them could see much in the tenebrous wood.

It was only a matter of minutes before they heard the voices. They were faint but clearly coming from behind them.

"Oh, Jesus," Mallory said, breaking out into a cold

sweat. They were already searching. He stumbled over a branch but recovered quickly and kept going.

They had come about a hundred yards into the trees. Mallory turned and looked back toward the farm. A few glimmering lights danced in the blackness.

Panting quietly, his breath rasping out of the darkness, Mallory followed close behind Father Paul as the old man crunched his way through the thick brush.

He hoped that the sounds of their own search might muffle the clamor he and Father Paul were making as they bashed their way blindly ahead like two panicked bull elephants.

They missed finding the car in the darkness but suddenly found themselves standing in the middle of the logging road. There was barely enough light to see their way, but they jogged down the road until the deep shadow of the car loomed out of the darkness.

Mallory clutched Father Paul's arm and whispered, "The car lights will go on when I open the door. So get in quickly. Don't slam the door. Just hold it closed until we get out of here."

The car's dome light struck the black forest around them like lightning. Mallory already had his keys out, and he slipped them into the ignition. He pumped the gas once and prayed that it would start.

The engine turned over, and to Mallory it sounded like the hallelujah chorus. The old man was panting heavily next to him. He was holding his ribs, his face a pained grimace.

Mallory backed out into the road and then switched on his parking lights, which, in the lightless forest illuminated the trees surrounding them like beacons.

He didn't drive fast. Controlling his panic, he carefully maneuvered down the rutted dirt road. All they needed now was to run into a tree or get stuck in the mud.

Even if they heard the car, or saw the lights, they were still on foot. There was a little lead time. It would take them a few moments to return and get their own car.

When they reached the blacktop Mallory was surprised to see no headlights racing their way. Could they have not heard them crashing through the woods? Or seen or heard the car?

As if answering his thoughts, Father Paul said, "Maybe we have too much of a head start, and they think we'll be back with the police?"

"Yes," Mallory said, still anxiously searching for lights in his rearview mirror. "What do you think they'll do now?"

Father Paul was quiet for a moment, thinking it over. He still held his hand on his ribs, and every few seconds he would take a shallow, careful breath. Mallory knew the old man was in pain. He'd give him a painkiller and make him rest when they got back.

"I don't know, but if I were them I'd pack up and move on. They must have other places around here. Other ritual centers. This group is simply too large and too well organized not to have safe places to hide. I'm sure they've probably planned for just such a thing happening."

"You're probably right."

He looked over at the priest. They stared at each other, both acknowledging the fact of their failure.

"We're not doing too well, are we?" Mallory said. "I guess it's time to call the police and bring in some help?"

After a moment Father Paul reached over and patted Mallory's arm. His eyes were sunken into black puffy circles, and his exhausted face was pasty white. "Don't fret, boyo. We're alive, and we know a lot more about them now. In fact, I think I even know what they're after."

They stopped in Thetford at the first phone they saw and Mallory telephoned Weidemeier. The burly Norwich cop was the only one Mallory knew personally, and since Kelly was involved he thought Weidemeier would be less skeptical and more likely to help them. Fortunately he was on duty.

Weidemeier listened quietly as Mallory rapidly told him that they had found Kelly and what they had seen.

"You've got to move fast," Mallory said. "Before they get away."

"Where are you now?" was the only question Weidemeier asked, his deep voice slow and measured.

"At a pay phone in Thetford."

"They go home and stay there. When this is all over I want to talk to you."

He hung up.

Chapter Twenty

The predicted rain had not started, but the wind was still just as capricious as during their visit to the farm that afternoon. It hummed past the house in short, violent bursts, and the full power of the storm that had been threatening all day was close. Mallory could feel it in the air. It had been a winter of such dismal evenings. Colorless drizzles and gray skies and weeks of troubled light eroding into black violent storms.

Sitting in front of the fire he felt protected, warm and safe, and was falling into a soporific haze. Except for Father Paul, who had been energized by the agitation and excitement at the farm.

"Evil," Father Paul was saying, "our society thinks evil is banal. Meaning trite? Ineffective?" He laughed once, harshly. "But I think those who say that are frightened people whistling through the cemetery."

He took a long drag on his cigar, exhaled, and stared at Mallory through the blue cloud of smoke.

They had been waiting three hours for Weidemeier to call and tell them what had happened at the farm. And Father Paul had been talking on his favorite subject for the whole time.

But Mallory had only himself to blame. He had

mentioned to Father Paul how he had felt a sense of malevolence, of real evil in the cult's cellar sanctum. That was enough to start him off on why our culture is paradoxically terrified and charmed by evil.

The old priest waved his cigar in the air, leaving a trail of smoke like a crippled airplane spinning out of control.

> "For all things turn to barrenness
> In the dim glass the demons hold.
> The glass of outer weariness,
> Made when God slept in times of old."

"That's Yeats on evil. At least he had a sense of proportion. He understood that this is a society of whim worshippers, a barren, shallow culture absorbed with trendiness. We're in a crisis of values and therefore evil, or anything arcane and different, is exciting and fascinating."

The old priest had worked himself up into an angry exhortation. "Look at the youngsters' hard metal rock records. Satanism set to electric guitars."

He waved the stub of his cigar again, but this time in a broken circle, like a smoky target framing his pale face.

"But they have no real conception of the power ... or the dangerous energy behind their fascinating little game played with evil. It can drive the innocent and bored children of our glitzy culture over the edge.

"Remember the California 'Night Stalker,' the psychotic Richard Ramirez, who butchered 13 people in 1985? He was a Satanist who was fascinated with evil. Clearly not anything you could call banal. Not only did he rape and kill his victims, but viciousness and brutality was beyond ordinary cruelty. He would enter unlocked houses at night, at random, and murder people in their beds. Senseless violence. In one case he gouged out the eyes of his victim . . . with his fingers! Is that ordinary? Banal? Some would say, oh, of course, he was simply mad.

"Hah, no sir, boyo," the old man said, leaning forward and jabbing the wet end of his cigar at Mallory. "Evil! He was absorbed by evil. Possessed. He had a savage commandment to kill. He drank blood. He dipped his hands in the blood of his victims and scrawled satanic symbols all over.

"When he was finally caught he came into court and raised his hand to the press, his palm covered with a pentagram and screamed, 'Hail, Satan.'

"Banal? No, I don't think so. When he was sentenced to die he flashed a two-fingered 'devil sign' to the photographers and cried out one word—'evil.'

"And when reporters asked him if he was afraid to die, he laughed and said, 'We all die. You don't understand . . . and you're not expected to. I am beyond your experience. Legions of the night will breed and kill. I will be avenged.'

"How's that for banal?" the old man asked. "No, he was not simply an abused child of a broken home gone wrong. The man was evil! Period!"

Father Paul paused and stubbed out his cigar. "Do you know what his last words in court were? They should be carved within the psyches of every preacher in the country." The old man's voice rose to a hoarse cry . . . "'Lucifer dwells within us all.'"

His eyes clouded with anger; he leaned over his cup and sipped loudly at his cold whiskey-tea. He was clearly a little drunk, and Mallory smiled at him affectionately. He was more interesting half-bombed than most people sober.

Mallory could hear him murmuring as he sat back against the cushioned chair and closed his eyes, "For all things turn to barrenness in the dim glass the demons hold."

The old man's crinkled face had turned to the color of moldy bread. His chin collapsed onto his chest. He quickly fell into a doze. It would do him good, Mallory thought. His wounded body still needed a great deal of repair.

Mallory had been waiting patiently, sipping his tea, waiting until the old man ran out of steam. His opinions had all the absolutism of youth. No room in this agile, aging mind for ambiguity or compromising grays. He wondered what Father Paul might have been like as a young man, full of energy and religious fire.

Mallory looked at his watch. Eight forty-five. What could have happened to Weidemeier? Had they been wrong? Perhaps the cult didn't leave the farm and had taken the burly cop just like they took Kelly?

He shivered, the image of Kelly's cadaverous, infected, naked body sprawled across the altar steps leaped unbidden before his eyes.

Thunder cracked, shaking the windows. He glanced toward the night-blackened windows and waited. Ten seconds later a lightning flash lit up the glass, striking brilliant blue-white shafts into the shadowed living room.

After the shocking white glow of the lightning, the room suddenly seemed gloomy, full of dark corners.

As Mallory stared into the fire and waited, he wondered what the future held. The cult had gone underground. Disappeared. Obviously, the cult wouldn't just go away. It remained a dark presence everywhere he turned, the evidence of their existence all around him like the ash of a consuming fire savaging the earth.

And so many dead. For what? What mad scheme or sick belief could justify such wanton killing? In his long diatribe Father Paul had said one thing that impressed him: "A madman with a great cause is more dangerous than a madman who is merely self-absorbed." And evil, or the belief that Satan is present in their lives, gave madmen their great causes.

And so with this cult.

Madmen with a great cause? Committed to evil and Satan ruling their lives? Or simply self-absorbed madmen?

A loud pounding shook him from his reverie. Father Paul's eyes snapped open, bleary and blood-rimmed.

"What's that?" he said hoarsely, his voice thick with whiskey.

"The front door?" Mallory said. He rose and moved quickly to the door and peered out the side window.

The bulky figure of Officer Weidemeier stood in the charmless glare of the porch light.

Mallory pulled the door open and without a word Weidemeier stalked in. He was not in uniform and didn't take off his overcoat. He scowled at Mallory, glanced over his shoulder and saw Father Paul in the living room.

"This concerns you both," he said and passed by Mallory into the room. He nodded his head at Father Paul and stood in front of the fireplace, warming his rear end. He stared at Mallory, then at the priest.

In the shadow-dancing firelight, Mallory noticed that his nose was bent, angling slightly to the left, as if it had been broken and not properly reset. Odd he hadn't noticed that before. It wasn't out of place in his meaty face. In fact, Mallory thought, if it hadn't already been broken it would have happened someday in the future to complete the man's image.

Weidemeier didn't say a word until he had lit a cigarette. Then he said, "What do you two think you're doing?"

Without waiting for an answer he went on. "Do you know what I think? I think you're a couple of nuts. Excited by weird cults and bizarre homicides. You maybe even chase police like arsonists chase fire engines."

A flash of irritation ran through Mallory. "Why don't you get to the point, Officer Weidemeier. We don't need to listen to this personal crap."

"Yes," Father Paul said, "your opinion of us isn't important. What did you find at the farm?"

Weidemeier's heavy face turned to the old man. "Nothing," he said quietly. "Absolutely zero. The whole place was clean."

Even though he was not too surprised, Mallory's heart sank. "Even the cellar?"

"Yeah, even the cellar. I spoke to the old man . . ."

Weidemeier pulled a small note book from his shirt pocket and flipped a few pages. "His name's Lederer, Harvey Lederer."

Weidemeier stared icily at Mallory. "He's lived there for twenty-three years. Nice old guy. Around seventy, no teeth and wire-rimmed granny glasses. Glad to show me around the place."

Father Paul and Mallory glanced at each other.

"Neat," Father Paul finally said.

"Yeah, beautiful," Mallory agreed. "God, are they smart and organized."

The heavy-set cop was watching them closely, his flesh-hooded eyes suspicious.

"And what's this shit about Kelly?" he asked. "You know his wife is hysterical? Where did you see him?"

Mallory sighed and detailed the whole story for him. Occasionally Father Paul would add a colorful comment that he overlooked. When he had finished Weidemeier did not say anything.

He took out another cigarette and lit it against the

stub. He flipped the stub into the fireplace. After a moment, he said, "You know, I wouldn't waste two minutes of my time with your crazy shit, except that we have an unsolved murder and a police officer who's missing, and I have to follow up every lead. Now I've stood here and listened patiently, and I haven't learned enough to pay for my gas. I still don't know what kind of game you're playing."

Weidemeier walked across the room and paused at Mallory's desk, his eyes running over a stack of unopened mail.

He turned back to the two men. "But I'll tell you one thing... and you better listen close. I don't care whether you're a priest and a doctor. If either of you bug me again with this crazy shit about satanic cults and send me off on a wild goose chase, I'll have both your asses up on charges of obstructing justice, malicious nuisance, and interfering in a police investigation."

He stopped at the door and buttoned his topcoat. He stood in the doorway, his huge body welded by the shadows into something monolithic, a dark, menacing authority. "And one last word. Stay out of it. Keep your nose out of things you don't understand. This is a police investigation, and I don't want to hear your names come up again... in any way. Understand?"

When Weidemeier had gone both Mallory and Father Paul were silent. They stared into the fire.

"Great," Mallory finally said. "We've killed the only cop who believed us, and alienated his partner."

"It doesn't matter," Father Paul said softly.

Mallory stood up and took the priest's empty cup. "Here, let me get you some warm tea."

After he'd brewed another whiskey tea, Mallory sat

opposite the priest. "On the drive back you said you thought you knew what the cult was after."

Father Paul sighed. He suddenly seemed deathly tired, and Mallory felt a twinge of guilt. He should put this man to bed and not be pumping him for information.

"I've dreaded this," Father Paul said. "For a long time I have suspected the worst. But today I became sure. It was the children . . . and a dream that gave me the idea . . . and the Black Mass of St. Secaire that the cult conducted at both the church in Exeter and in the farm basement."

The old man put his cup down and stretched his hands over his head, arching his back. He leaned back and rested his head against the chair. His face was a mixture of weariness and a quiet anguish.

"The Mass of St. Secaire is a blasphemous mass, an obscene parody of the Catholic mass. It's usually performed at night in a ruined church, its singular purpose is to kill a specific victim."

"Like Kelly?" Mallory asked.

"Yes, like Kelly."

"And the children?"

"I'll get to that. This may be hard for you to digest, so I must take it a step at a time.

"First, contrary to what I first believed, I don't think we're dealing with a normal group of Manson-type psychotics here. Or even a coven of blood thirsty Satanists like Richard Ramirez. They are more than that."

Father Paul paused, as if he were trying to find a word for something inexpressible.

"Something infinitely more dangerous."

He leaned back in his chair. "I had another dream . . . the morning before we went out to the farm. It was a strange dream. In it I was a child back in the classroom listening to my old seminary professor."

He paused and grinned, remembering. "Francis Andrew Wood. He was a strange man. A traditionalist, no . . . more of a fundamentalist. A brilliant man but a terrible pessimist. He was constantly haranguing us about Armageddon and the coming of the Anti-Christ. Warning us to be vigilant, and pointing out every event that he believed foretold the Anti-Christ's imminent approach.

"He would rise up on tiptoes, bouncing on his short legs, as he became excited.

"*'Look around you, children,'* he'd cry. *'Look at the false prophets. Jesus warned that many would go forth preaching that He was the Christ, yet deceiving the world about the gospel. He warned of the famine and pestilence we see all over the globe. He warned of Wars and plagues. Of the Great Tribulation.'*

"Dr. Doom! That was his nickname. Lovingly given. He would show us where all of this was prophecied in the Revelations of St. John. And now, as I get older and have watched the world gnawing at itself like a trapped animal, I think he might have been intuitively right. He felt it coming.

"In my dream he was a cross between wise teacher and fire-breathing Baptist preacher. He was screaming at us to wake up. Look around and be aware of the thief that would come in the night, for the Anti-Christ was knocking at the door, pushing it farther and farther open. And soon he would enter this world in full power.

"Oh, my, old Dr. Doom was a powerful speaker. And in my dream, just as the students were rising to cheer him, the door burst open and a fierce giant cat the size of a tiger stalked in. The creature had a mangy gray coat of fur that fell off in clumps as it padded toward the professor. When it leaped at him its full weight crushed him to the floor. It bit through his neck in one bloody crunch and began clawing wildly at the body, digging a hole in the corpse's belly."

Father Paul stopped and took a slow sip of his whiskey tea. "What it was after . . . was his heart. It ripped open the chest and took the heart in its teeth and tore it out. Then it loped from the room, the bloody prize in his mouth, the crimson tendrils of the heart waving behind, clinging to its flanks.

"At first I didn't know what to make of the dream. But when I thought of the twelve sacrificed babies . . . and the twelve newly born children . . . it all began to come clear."

The storm outside was now beating at the house, as if it were trying to get in, to break through the windows and tear down the doors. The whole house shook with the pounding.

The fire had dwindled to a limp red tongue, flickering, tasting the twisting air, but Mallory was too absorbed to get up and put more wood on.

Father Paul didn't seem to notice the fire or the hard percussion of the rain drumming overhead. He was completely absorbed in his memory. His eyes seemed dreamy, filled with a melancholy vision.

"And the final thing. The final connection between my dream and the twelve children and the cult was . . . the Great Tribulation.

"My professor based most of his apprehension about the Anti-Christ and the coming of the Great Tribulation on St. John's prophecies. And those prophecies are both wonderful and terrible. I have often envisioned old John in Patmos, sitting on that desolate island, his stone and mud shack nearby, a poor clay pot of gruel cooking over a smoking fire of dung chips. A hot, mouth-bleaching wind blowing around him like the breath of dragons. When the visions came they were furious, striking him from the heavens like divine lightning, smashing him to the ground, overwhelming his senses and plucking his consciousness away. What John saw was a great book and the seven locks holding it secret being opened. Each of the seven seals contained a prophecy of tribulations coming to the world.

"When the first seal had been cracked, John saw the beasts and the four horsemen of the Apocalpyse. 'And I saw when the Lamb opened one of the seals, and I heard, as it were the noise of thunder, one of the four beasts saying, Come and see . . .'

"After the first of the seven seals opened the book told of false prophets. The second seal told of wars. The third and fourth of famines and pestilence, the fifth and sixth of tribulations and heavenly signs. The seventh warned of injuries to the earth, sea, trees and rivers, and terrible plagues."

The old man closed his eyes, and intoned softly, as if reading from a scroll on his eyelids, "There shall be famines and pestilences and earthquakes in divers places. All these are the beginnings of the sorrows.

"After I remembered my professor's obsession with the *Time of the End,* with what theologians call eschatology, the final things, I tried to connect St. John's prophecies about the coming of the Anti-Christ with the world today.

"The more I thought about it, the more sense it made. All of the world's present turmoil was prophecied in the Revelations of St. John.

"Look at the rise of the television evangelists, false prophets corrupting the gospel in Jesus's name. Famines around the world, in Ethiopia and the Sahel, starvation of millions every year. And the spread of wars? We've had two world wars, and many believe this is only a lull before a third world war. Did you know that the UN estimated that there were over one hundred and fifty wars raging around the globe in one recent year? And plagues . . . new diseases, some even arising from our own technology . . . cancers from Agent Orange, AIDS, over thirty thousand chemicals released into our environment every year that create new and exotic health problems. And talk about injuries to our rivers and lands. Just look at how the earth is being abused."

Father Paul leaned toward Mallory, his face intense.

"It took me awhile to remember that these tribulations are not caused by the wrath of God. That is a mistaken reading of 'Revelation.' Many think the Great Tribulation means the wrath of God scorching the earth before Armageddon; oh, no, it is the opposite. It is the wrath of the Great Beast 666, the anger of Satan, visited upon the earth—that is the Great Tribulation. It is an unleashing of evil upon the world. It is the coming of the Anti-Christ. That is what the cult wants, it is what all the blood-letting, all the sacrifices and killing is about."

His eyes were acid-bright, crystalline blue pools rimmed in blood. A look had crossed the priest's face. There was regret in it, and something else Mallory saw. For the first time he saw fear in the old man, a terrible, aching fear.

Mallory was fascinated by the old man's passion, by his burning vision, but he couldn't believe it.

Father Paul must have seen the skepticism in Mallory's eyes, for he said, "Oh, yes, you may not believe it, but this cult is preparing the way for the coming of the Anti-Christ. The twelve children are an evil parody. They are the satanic apostles preparing the way for the Anti-Christ.

"Look," Father Paul said, his words tumbling out. "Each of the children has been born with a blood sacrifice. Blood sacrifices are used to summon demons. Which means that they are all filled with a demon spirit called up during the simultaneous death and birth of the twelve children. The death of human babies coinciding exactly with the birth of Satan's children, don't you see?"

When Mallory didn't respond, he went on. "But more importantly, it means that they are a direct parallel to each of Christ's twelve apostles. They are Satan's seeds, and just as the apostles prepared the way for the Christian religion, so will these twelve children prepare the way for the coming of the Anti-Christ."

For a moment Mallory couldn't speak. Everything during the last week had had a touch of madness about it. At times he seemed to be living in a great global insane asylum. But this was too much.

"I'm sorry," he finally said. "That's beyond me. The coming of the Anti-Christ?"

"But it is the only thing that fits," Father Paul said intensely. Small ribbons of white foam had collected in the corners of his mouth. "What other explanation is there?"

"Insanity! Madness!" Mallory said. "Good old human brutality. That's good enough for me."

"Then you're thinking with your head . . . and not feeling your way. You're reacting according to your conditioning. You're letting yourself fall into the same trap I did forty-five years ago with Jamie. My God, man. It's in the air around you, can't you feel it . . . this isn't a group of your everyday madmen, your run-of-the-mill sadists."

All the old man's verbal skills suddenly left him. His burning eyes seemed about to be extinguished by tears. He stumbled to speak, and Mallory could almost hear his mind chattering. But the words were spinning, stumbling over each other as they came out.

Finally the priest fell silent, worn out. He passed a frail hand over his eyes. His expression was morose, a granite gray face of despair. His mood had swung so dramatically during the last few hours—from confidence to reflection and now anguish, that for the first time Mallory wondered about his mental stability. Had he drunk too much? Did liquor depress him? Make him irrational? He debated giving him a tranquilizer, but the old boy had consumed too much alcohol, and it would be dangerous.

The old man's eyes were closed, and his face had settled into a limp acceptance. Perhaps he was asleep? Mallory thought. It'd be the best thing for him.

Yes, Mallory was frightened and fear had crawled up from his bowels more in the last week than at any time in his life. But he wasn't a supernaturalist, a religionist or a believer in the occult. Intuition, inspired leaps of insight, yes. Perhaps even some form of telepathy or ESP. But the devil incarnate? An actual Anti-Christ bringing the Great Tribulation? That was too much. Yes, the vast black vision of worldly destruction had shaken him. There was something creepy in its uncompromising global violence. And he didn't have to believe in the supernatural to see that the prophecies had shocking connections to modern events. Coincidences? Probably. But still, the dark visions touched something at the core of him, curdling his spirit. What frightened him the most was that it didn't have to be factually true for the insane and violent to accept it . . . and act on it. What was it Ramirez had said, "Legions of the night . . . breed and kill."

Now that scared him! Madmen with a great cause? That kind of madness scared him speechless.

To distract himself, he walked over to the large French windows looking out toward the river. The storm was at its peak, and rain fell with a depressing heaviness, a thundering cascade pounding on the back porch and obscuring his vision.

In the gloom and sparkling shower of rain slanting through the backyard's night lights, his eyes briefly lost focus, and in that instant a figure dislodged from the darker shadow of a tree trunk and crouched, shuffling like a wounded animal, across a few yards of open space and disappeared behind a large round bush. Two circles . . . *animal eyes?* . . . glowed in the velvet blackness, like two shining coins of tarnished brass.

Mallory blinked, and looked again. There was nothing. The hallucination had lasted for three heartbeats and then fluttered, dissolving. The beating silver rain, intermingled with wind-blown shifting shadows, made him unsure of his senses. He wasn't sure he had seen anything at all.

A shiver crackled over his skin like a charge of static electricity. An intuition of danger? Nerves? He wasn't sure. But he had a sense that he was being watched.

Christ, was it never going to end? What to do? It went on and on. Well, if they were out there watching he hoped they'd get their asses frozen off.

The talk of the children and how important they were to cult had intrigued him. An idea rose up, an idea on how to force them out of the woodwork. Flush them out. If they can't find the cult, perhaps he could bring them to him. If the children were so important he would take a child . . . the twelfth child. They would have to get it back. Make them come to him . . . on his own terms. And he would be waiting with his Walther PK.

But first he had to get Father Paul out of danger. Their adventure to the farm so soon after his car accident had exhausted him and set back his recovery. He was fainting with fatigue. His tired, wounded body needed a solid week in bed to recover. He expected an argument, but he would take him home and then follow his plan. The old man would be better out of it this time.

What was it Father Paul had said? "Perhaps we are the instruments of our own justice."

Chapter Twenty-One

It was as he expected. Father Paul had groused all the way to Enfield. He did not want to rest and insisted on being taken to St. Simeon's.

As he got out of the car, Mallory could see his legs weaken and begin to tremble. He grasped the partially-opened door and hung on for a moment, his pasty white face drawn into a painful rictus. The rain had not let up, and Father Paul sat back down and pulled the door closed, but not hard enough to latch. Chill drafts slipped into the car. His tired, skin-shrouded eyes fixed on the smoky window, streaks of rain colored by sodium light from the single street lamp ran a crazy, twisting pattern over his face.

"Aliena misericordia," he muttered. He smiled grimly at Mallory. "This is a strange mercy, young Dr. Mallory. What am I to make of it? Are you trying to be rid of me?"

"Not at all," Mallory lied. He did not like lying to him, but there was danger in what he was about to do . . . and Father Paul would be better out of it. And if anything happened to him, Father Paul would be left to carry on.

"I want you to have a complete rest . . . for as long as

you can stand it." The half-truth made him feel better.

"Humph," the old man sighed. "I have a feeling you're planning something and not telling me about it."

Mallory knew the priest well enough to simply wait him out.

The old man didn't pursue it. "Just remember, young doctor," he said, "these are not people to confront without elaborate care. Please, nothing until tomorrow. One night of sleep and I'll be fine."

"All right," Mallory said, avoiding his eyes. He adjusted the car's heater.

"Good night, then," the old man said and opened the door. He stepped into the sheets of rain, and, holding his jacket collar high around his neck, he hobbled as quickly as he could up the steps to the church.

Mallory waited to see him safely in, then turned the car toward Canaan.

The drive to Route 10 and then to Canaan on the New Hampshire side of the river was quick. It took him only ten minutes to find the house. It was larger than he had expected. He did not know why, but he had always thought of Betty Milner as a poor woman, or working class at best, even though her hospital records indicated she was married to a successful businessman.

The house was a large and expensive Cape Cod, surrounded by a stone wall as high as a tall man. There must have been at least nine or ten acres to the estate.

He drove past the house and parked off the road. The driveway gates were closed. But no guards. The gates were too high for him to climb. He would have to make his way through the woods and go over the wall closer to the house. He hoped they didn't have any dogs. He had planned this carefully... except it hadn't occurred to him during the drive that there might be dogs. He had no way to divert them. The rain had slowed from its earlier angry attack, as if the clouds were finally drained, but a thin drizzle persisted. He was thankful that he had worn a black anorak, and he snapped the throat catch closed. He pulled the hood over his head.

Soggy dead leaves squished underfoot. Rain-laden pine branches lashed out at him like wet towels snapping in a locker room. Before he had gone ten feet into the woods, his shoes, socks and lower pants' legs were heavy with the night-chilled rain water.

He had brought along a penlight, and its pitiful amber circle of light was next to useless. He snapped it off and waited until his eyes adjusted to the violet darkness. Twenty or so yards along the wall he found a section that had a cup-shaped depression. It was only about waist high at this point, and he clambered over, scraping the heel of his hand on stone chips as he let himself down on the other side.

Standing mute, his back against the wall and his muscles trembling with adrenaline overcharge, he listened. If he heard a single dog bark he would go back over the wall like a horse in a steeplechase.

Only the wet kissing sound of drizzling rain falling from the trees onto the moist earth.

The house, its windows coal-black sentries watching, was about fifty yards across a wide lawn dotted with shrubbery. He moved carefully, keeping in the shadows, darting from one black sanctuary to another, stopping often and listening for the slightest unnatural sound. The windblown drizzle of rain muted everything, even his own hard breathing. The cold mist collected on his skin as if he were in a sauna and dripped down into his eyes and over his mouth and chin.

It appeared no one was home. The house seemed

deserted. He pulled back the sleeve of his anorak and pressed the light button on his watch. A little after eleven o'clock. But just because there were no lights he wasn't going to get careless. He moved cautiously across the soggy lawn and tried the aluminum and glass back porch door. It was locked. With the thin blade of a small pocket knife he had brought along, he pressed back the latch. Porch doors were not meant for security but only to keep out flies and block winter chill. It swung open with a high, whining squeak of wet metal rubbing.

He crept across the porch. The door into the main house was open. Turning the knob slowly, he pushed the door open and stepped inside. He gently closed the door behind him and waited, listening. Only the bleeding of rain off the roof and down the gutters, muted now, sounded from outside. The inner house was mortuary quiet, except for the splattering of rain dripping off him onto the floor. He looked down. A dark puddle was spreading out around his feet in an uneven circle. He reached into his pocket and brought out the Walther. In the dark he clumsily felt for the safety and pushed it off.

The pistol swaying in front of him, he began a quiet, methodical search of the house. If no one was home he might be able to find something about the cult, maybe give him a lead to where they were now . . . or what their plans were.

His progress was slow, for he opened every door as if someone was waiting behind it. He had checked every room downstairs except the one at the end of the front hallway.

A sound, weak and unarticulated, suddenly floated to him. It seemed to come from the door at the end of the hall. He snapped off his penlight and for a moment let his eyes get used to the dark. He saw a purple, hazy light coming from under the door.

His palms had begun to sweat, and he put the penlight in his pocket. He walked the length of the hallway with the double thumping of his heart in his ears. He opened the door quietly and looked in. A night light burned dully in the baseboard across the room.

It was a baby's room. Toys scattered everywhere. But somehow the disarray seemed contrived. Organized, as if the toys had been placed on the floor and around the room by an adult to give the impression of child's play. He'd seen the havoc children created in a hospital playroom many times, and it was nothing like this.

A scrambling, mewing sound, like angry kittens fighting to reach their mother's breasts, suddenly impaled him. It came from the corner of the room, to his left. His wet feet squished on the carpet with each step across the room. As he got closer he realized the hulking shadow shape in the corner was a child's crib.

His eyes were accustomed to the dark now, and there was just enough glow from the night light for him to see. He heard the child's soft, even breathing before he reached the crib. The baby was sleeping on its back, one arm thrown above its head, the other across its chest.

It was a strikingly beautiful child, with an exquisitely formed mouth and delicate, dream-fluttering, long lashes. Wisps of light blond hair rested softly on the brow. It was impossible for him to believe Father Paul's theory. This child one of Satan's demons?

He smiled at the sleeping infant, regretting his plan now.

What madness! How did he let himself get into this? Kidnap a child because of an idea? Because of a theory that its parents were Satanists?

He was about to turn and leave when the infant's

eyes suddenly snapped open. They were startling eyes, large and flecked with brown-gold. For a heartbeat the eyes were sleep-drugged and puzzled, then they flickered wide, as if in recognition. But that was impossible.

Then the infant smiled, a bright, knowing smile. Its golden-brown eyes crinkling up, it reached its hand up toward Mallory, a baby's gesture of affection and recognition.

A tingling charge of excitement passed over his skin, and he abruptly became conscious that his jaws were aching from clenching his teeth. For some reason he had suddenly become anxious, fearful. With a shock, he realized that the child made him nervous.

There was something strange here. This baby had an odd energy about it. Its ability to focus, to respond intelligently, was phenomenal. It reacted with the maturity of a one year old rather than an infant only a couple of weeks old.

The baby giggled then, a soft, chortling sound. The sound was not pleasant. On another child, one that was not relaxed and smiling, Mallory would think it was choking or gagging on liquid. A sensation not unlike a fly scrambling across the back of his neck sent a thrill down his spine.

He put the gun in his pocket and reached into the crib. The child let out a scream that would wake the dead. But it wasn't panic; it was laughter. The baby was hysterically laughing with that wild, uncontrolled glee that children sometimes express.

Shit, Mallory blurted out. *The baby obviously wasn't here alone, and that screech would bring . . .*

Before he had finished the thought a penetrating, high-pitched wail filled the room, and Mallory was struck from behind. He fell forward against the crib and lurched to the right, onto his knees. He twisted around to see . . . which he knew was a mistake the instant he turned. The woman, a long-faced middle-aged fury, was snarling, her lips pulled back like an attacking dog's. She screeched and clawed at his face, her nails raking down his cheek and neck. He grabbed her wrists and pushed her away, but still screeching like a banshee she bit his hands, her teeth grinding down to the bone. Blood poured from around her mouth as she hung on, growling and tearing at his hand.

He struck the side of her head with his free hand, smashing his fist again and again into her cheek and face. She groaned and the piercing, sharp pain that stung his hand ran up his arm diminished. He ripped his hand from her teeth and pushed her away. She fell onto her back but bounced back up like a gymnast.

She crouched on her haunches, a snarling, spitting animal ready to attack. The tight bun of hair had come loose and scraggly gray strands hung down over her face. Her eyes glowed like tarnished silver.

Panting, Mallory reached into his pocket for the gun, but before he could pull it free she sprang toward him, knocking him against a wall of shelves. Toys of every description—dolls, miniature cars, balls, a Monopoly game, a puzzle and even a tiny playhouse filled with gaily dressed wooden people—showered down over them.

This time she bit into his shoulder, at the base of his neck. With a rush of panic he realized she was going for his throat. He yanked the gun from his pocket and smashed it against her head. She released her hold for a second, but then she snapped forward again, her open mouth and teeth bloodied, biting into the same spot.

Mallory let out a scream and began pounding her with the gun. The pain in his neck and shoulder was excruciating. Visions of Kelly's wounded black neck, and Daley's torn throat, skidded through his mind.

When her grip relaxed a second time he lurched forward, throwing her off-balance. He jumped up, squatting, holding the gun before him. Blood was pulsing from the torn flesh on his left hand. He pressed it under his right arm, hoping the pressure would slow the blood flow. The damn crazy woman might have torn some major veins.

She crouched again before him, ready to spring at him, alternately panting like a dog and keening like a woman in agony.

"Don't . . ." he said, his voice strangled and hoarse. "I don't want to shoot, but I will if I . . ."

She snarled again, her aged yellow teeth turned greenish in the blue night light, and leaped toward him, directly into the gun.

Startled by her mad disregard for the gun and its lethal consequences, Mallory backed away. But this time he was not caught off balance. He stepped to the side, grabbed her around the rib cage and spun, hard, throwing her against the wall. She crashed into the ancient cast-iron steam radiator. A sickening mushy thud, like a fist striking into an open wet palm, echoed in the room as her head struck the radiator.

Mallory knew she was dead before her limp body had slipped completely forward onto the floor. She lay with her back propped against the radiator, her bare open legs sprawled before her, her dress riding up on her white, scrawny, blue-veined thighs.

Gasping for air, Mallory stood up, his legs shaking. He knelt next to the woman and felt her pulse. It was a reflex, a thing of habit, but unnecessary. She was dead. Blood seeped in a crimson stream from behind her head, around her neck and flowed down her chest. The bloody front of her dress was already plastered to her bony breast.

God, what have I done? he murmured.

He stared down at the woman's still face. A purple bruise seeping a reddish stain had swollen her cheek and the side of her face. Her right eye was puffed closed, blood leaking from between the lashes. Her expression was not peaceful, but rather set in a grim, determined way, as if she had just told the devil that she was going to walk all the way to hell.

He sighed and stood up. Mallory was surprised at his reaction. He was not as affected by her death as he would have imagined. In fact, he felt dry. Empty. Used up. Such an unemotional reaction to having just killed someone shocked him . . . and scared him. Was he simply becoming desensitized to all the violence and brutality he'd seen in the last week? Was it fear, an overload of his nerves? He didn't know . . . and didn't have time to figure it out now.

He left the woman where she was and picked up the baby, who was now gurgling happily, and several blankets. He worked quickly. He didn't know if anyone else was in the house and had heard the commotion. The infant watched him as he wrapped the blankets around his tiny body. The golden flecked brown eyes were luminous, almost as if they were powered by some inner light. And unwavering. They focused on Mallory's face with a chilling fascination.

Mallory found himself becoming unnerved by the child's concentrated staring. It had a nasty quality to it. A normal infant his age was still adjusting to spatial relationships, and the eyes wandered in a curious open stare. But this child's eyes could speak.

He tried to ignore it but then flipped a corner of one of the blankets over the child's face, loose enough so it had plenty of air. But as soon as he did the child made a peculiarly sibilant sound, very similar to an angry cat hissing after it has been put in a box.

It cried out several times, spitting and mewling, as

Mallory carried it across the lawn and through the woods to the car. Mallory paused often to listen and scan the dark lawn and house. Nothing moved. No sounds.

Perhaps he'd get away with this, after all.

Fortunately the rain had all but stopped. Only a light mist remained . . . and the miserable cold breeze that pushed it about in mini tornadoes.

He strapped the child into the back seat with the seatbelt and pulled back the swaddling blanket to see if it was all right. The infant's golden eyes were wide open, glittering with a fury that shook him. He could clearly feel the child's loathing.

There was now no doubt in his mind that this child was abnormal, something very special. It possessed an enormously well-developed sense of self. It had sophisticated, concentrated emotions unknown in normal babies. Its eyes and skin seemed almost radiant, powered by that weird inner energy he had sensed. Again that fly was crawling over the tiny hairs on the back of his neck.

Perhaps Father Paul was right!

As he turned the ignition and the engine caught, a sudden prickly thrill of anxiety ran through him.

He stared out the steaming car window. Twisting swirls of fog were beginning to roll across the wet earth, clotting for a moment before shifting into another shape.

He sat quietly, trying to gather himself together. He felt he was unraveling. His guts were twisting into a gnawing Gordian knot of dread. His hands began to shake again, the palms damp. Somehow he felt like that churning fog . . . amorphous, scattered, unsure.

And fear! A pernicious, fermenting fear! He might as well admit it.

And his fear was directly related to that helpless

child in the backseat.

Or was it helpless? It seemed to be wrapped in an uncanny power.

For one panicky moment he felt he couldn't move. His sweating hands were glued to the steering wheel. His legs immobile, nerveless. His face and neck felt numb with a gelid flush. He tried to move but couldn't, and the more he failed the greater his panic became.

Then he abruptly stopped trying. Something within him told him to stop fighting it. He knew that the body incestuously feeds on its own energy. Panic breeds panic. Fear breeds fear.

He relaxed, went limp, tried to breathe slowly and deeply. But his mind was erratic, floating directionless. He couldn't focus or direct any single part of himself, his eclipsed consciousness threatening to wink out entirely.

The strange paralysis went on for several minutes, his mind flooded with conflicting feelings. It almost seemed as if the child's anger was communicating to him, reaching out with febrile tentacles, touching his mind and heart, sucking away his willpower, undermining his emotions, confusing him.

Suddenly he shook his head hard, violently, trying to throw off the confusion. "No, damnit," he said out loud, his voice harsh. His hands came free of the wheel, and he slammed his still bleeding hand against the dashboard.

He groaned and grabbed his wrist as a piercing electric pain shivered through his hand and arm.

But the pain cleared his head, shocking him back to reality.

The baby cried out, its cry still part anger, but now it seemed tinged with fear. It screamed louder, rising in pitch until it was screeching in a horrible, ululating wail.

It sounded as if the child was being murdered, and

Mallory twisted around, still holding his wrist, and looked back. It was fine. He had thrown off the blanket and was staring again at Mallory. His face flushed scarlet with the fury of its crying, but its lambent eyes were wide open and flashing like gold in a miner's pan on a moonlit night.

Mallory pressed on the accelerator, and the car bolted forward. His sense of power and control over the car an unexpected joy. He smiled at the feeling.

The child continued to scream and wail, and even though Mallory felt he once more had control over himself, he also had a terrible sense of urgency to get away from that house. To get the child away. To crawl away somewhere and hide. He glanced into the rear-view mirror. There was no one on the road behind him. Nerves again.

He shook his head, surprised at what he had done.

Kidnap a baby? And kill an irrational old woman trying to protect it? What had he become? What was happening to him?

Yet there was no turning back. The only way he could survive now was to go forward. Find the blood-thirsty group and vindicate his actions. Prove that what he had done was necessary.

But no matter how he tried, he couldn't escape the sensation of having crossed over a line; somehow he had passed beyond an invisible boundary. With the killing of the old woman, and the kidnapping of the child, he had done something unforgivable. And what made him jittery was—*he didn't know what the ultimate penalty for this transgression was! He wasn't concerned so much with legal punishment. He was now in immediate danger. No longer a year's reprieve. The cult would be after him like a pack of hungry dogs.*

The child slept, or at least Mallory thought he was

sleeping. When he had put the child on the couch it had continued to hiss and whine in that peculiar animal sound it had. Mallory ignored it and sat across the room in his easy chair. The cocked Walther in his lap. It held fourteen bullets in a single clip.

He had not moved from the chair, not to eat, drink, or go to the bathroom. The back door was open. All other doors and windows securely locked. His chair faced the entrance from the kitchen. They would have to come at him from that direction. He could hear the wind's guttural whispers outside. The rain had almost completely stopped, but the wind kept on.

He had been waiting in the dark room for over four hours, turning over his thoughts like stones and examining the stained underside, not ignoring even the most repellent insects that scurried away to hide. He had uncompromisingly examined his mistakes, his blindnesses—*especially not being more aware and warning Kelly to be more careful*—and had tried to forgive himself.

But he had beaten up on himself for long enough, and now he was getting restless.

The luminous dial on the mantle clock read 3:40 in the morning. He wasn't anxious, or even particularly nervous, simply restless and wanting to get on with it. Unusual for him, he knew, but since he had accepted the risk, and even made peace with himself over the death of the old woman, a kind of expectant calm had settled over him.

Fatalistic. That was the word that came to mind as he reflected on the last weeks since he had delivered the Milner baby. Yet this acceptance of the immutability of things, of their inevitability, did not compromise his sense of purpose. Yes, he had been shaken by the old woman's death. Disgusted, yet in an odd, twisted way, pleased. It indicated that they were vulnerable. That they could be beaten. He had begun to think of them as somehow superhuman, people with dangerous and mysterious powers to kill and then disappear. Kelly's death, the brutal slaughter of a tough, capable man, had created the largest crack in his armor. And then the cult's vanishing act. All accomplished in a few hours. Amazing.

And the child. Yes, he had also been shocked by the child's unique, even uncanny, qualities.

Mallory, however, still resisted the idea that there was anything like Father Paul's "incarnate evil" involved. In fact, even though he was growing slightly apprehensive during the long wait, he was also expectant, even eager for them to come for the child.

And now he had no doubt that he would use the Walther.

Another hour passed . . . but still he would not leave the room. His bladder was beginning to ache but for some reason he couldn't fathom, to leave the room, abandon his plan, smelled of weakness. He was no longer going to turn away from conflict, no longer bury himself in work.

The child slept on, apparently capable of following its normal sleep routine even in a strange environment. Mallory glanced at the clock for the hundredth time. 4:46. Dawn in little over an hour.

For the first time doubt began to seep in. Had he miscalculated?

Then he heard them. Footsteps outside the living room window. A moment later the handle on the front door rattled. The lightless room was still. All Mallory could hear for several minutes was his rapid breathing and the double thudding of his own heartbeat.

A dull, abrupt scraping sound from the side of the house told him what he wanted to know. They were moving around the house. Soon they would be at the back door.

He waited breathlessly. His palms starting to sweat again.

When the sound of the back door opening finally came Mallory couldn't help himself... a nervous shock shot through him and he jumped. He gripped the Walther tightly and turned its muzzle toward the doorway. He sucked in a great lungful of air and willed himself to calm down.

Soft footsteps, wet and slurried from the rain-coated earth, came from the kitchen.

It sounded like more than one, but Mallory couldn't be certain.

Then, an utter silence so complete that Mallory sensed they must be standing still in the kitchen. Listening? Sensing his presence? A clammy sweat broke out on his face and neck. The cool breeze from the back door having been opened brushed over his skin.

His eyes were welded to the kitchen doorway, its black square center outlined dimly by its white paint.

A lean figure of medium height suddenly appeared in the doorway. It stopped, and Mallory could vaguely see the head swing back and forth, surveying the room.

Somehow the baby must have sensed something, for it let out a mewling, sibilant cry from under its blanket. Soft, but clear. The shadowy figure walked directly to the couch. It moved past the furniture gracefully, confidently, as if it could see perfectly well in the dark.

It stopped in front of the couch, bent over and picked up the child. The figure murmured softly, lovingly, to the baby, who answered with a cooing, contented warble.

Then, to Mallory's surprise, the shadow sat down and cradled the child in its arms, whispering to it in a voice soft and dulcet.

Mallory's left hand had moved slowly toward the lamp on the end table next to him. But he paused, unsettled by the figure's movements. Clothes rustled and the two whispered and cooed to each other. If Mallory didn't know better he would think it was a mother and child being reunited. Then there was the incredible, unmistakable sound of a baby nursing.

His searching fingers found the switch, and he snapped the light on.

At first he couldn't register the surprise. It overwhelmed him.

He stared at her. She was smiling at him, the child suckling at her breast.

Lili! Oh, my God. Lili! It can't be!

He blinked, tears blurring his vision, his mind divided against itself. His eyes saw something that his mind rejected.

Her perfume suddenly reached him . . . mixed with the smell of his own stale sweat . . . and his heart ached.

He couldn't speak. A numbing tightness in his chest had taken his breath away.

She regarded him calmly as the infant sucked hungrily on her full, round breast.

"David, David," she said, her voice soft and musical. "Why did you have to go to this extreme? I realized that underneath your proper exterior you're impetuous, but I didn't think you'd be this foolish."

He still couldn't speak. His mouth was dry, his tongue sawdust, and a thickening in his throat made it hard for him to swallow.

She was still smiling at him, while gently stroking the baby's head.

"I wanted to save you, David. Like Bowker. I wanted to have you join us. Become one of us. But this . . ."

She nodded toward the infant with her head, her

long hair waving over her shoulder, motioning toward the child as well.

The impact of her presence was shattering. For a moment he couldn't take his eyes off the infant suckling. He remembered all their sensual moments together. The feel of her skin, the softness of her breast and the heat of her sex. The long hours together, of naked skin welded as they whispered confidences.

And the trust. The trust that he had confided in her.

Suddenly he was not only aching with hurt and shock, but a cold and implacable anger swept over him. For a fleeting beat of his heart he wanted to kill her. To pull the trigger and blow her head off.

"And all the others?" he asked, his voice small and dry. His head had started to throb. It felt like a tiny homunculus with a pick and hammer trying to get out of his skull, threatening at any moment to burst through the bone.

She looked at him quizzically. "All the others? What do you mean?"

"The other doctors. Did you make love to all the other doctors?"

She laughed, a full, throaty laugh that sent chilling memories up and down his nerve endings.

"Of course," she said, looking at him as if he were a jealous teenager.

And it was, he realized, uncomfortably close to what he did feel.

"It was necessary, you see." She started to gently rock the child as it sucked vigorously. He had never seen her so beautiful.

"I am the protector for each of the twelve. I had to assure their safety and be present at their births. And the simplest way to do that was to be close to the doctors who would deliver the child."

"Daley? And Bowker, too?" he asked.

She shook her head at him, grinning mischievously. "Now, David, I've already answered you. Why pursue this? We have more important things to talk about."

Her calm, conversational tone was driving him crazy.

"The only thing I want to talk about is . . . why? Why all the death? Why did all the doctors and mothers need to die? Why the sacrifice of the twelve babies? Why Jeff Goldman and Walter Daley?"

Lili sighed and looked down at the infant still hungrily sucking on her breast. When she spoke her voice was mildly impatient.

"Contrary to what you might think, David, we do not kill for the pleasure of it. Only when it is absolutely necessary . . . either to protect ourselves, or because our religion demands it.

"The doctors had to die because in every case they became suspicious of the low hematocrit. We, or rather I, diverted them long enough for us to hide and protect our children. They eventually had to die because, like the children in Exeter, their sacrifice gave more power to the birth of each of the twelve. The mothers died simply because the children needed their blood."

She regarded Mallory for a long moment, her face suddenly thoughtful. Her voice had again become soft and seductive. "Human blood is necessary for these children. They are nourished by blood. Their seeds are not of this world. I don't expect you to understand this, but blood creates a bond between the Master and humans . . . a bridge that allows Him to be a part of them, to be with them always."

"The Master?" Mallory said, his own voice sounding eerie and distant, as if he were speaking through a long tube.

Lili smiled and stopped stroking the child's head. She didn't answer.

The infant, disturbed by the abrupt change, pulled away from the nipple, its mouth tainted with a pink milk that dribbled down its chin. It stared at Mallory, its eyes full of curiosity.

Mallory found himself suddenly hating the child. All the insanity and violence came down to this . . . to a handful of weird children.

But still obsessed with her betrayal, he asked, "Why did you help me . . . give me so many leads?"

Lili pressed the child back onto the nipple and murmured to it, softly, in a language that Mallory didn't recognize.

She turned to Mallory. "I didn't tell you anything you weren't on the verge of discovering yourself. You would have thought of using the NIH central files yourself, and you were searching every drawer and file in the Au Pair Agency. Sooner or later you would have found the index cards and letter. It seemed wise to help you take the last step you were going to take anyway."

"To create trust?" Mallory asked, his stomach tied into a sickening knot.

Unconcerned with his obvious anguish, Lili nodded and turned her attention back to the child.

Of course, Mallory thought. *All of her suggestions were logical steps he was moving toward himself. And what better way to keep him in their control? They always knew exactly where he was . . . and every move that he was making.*

It had all been a game, a devious manipulation of him from the beginning.

What a fool he'd been! What an incredible fool!

Mallory felt his face flush. He was consumed with disgust for himself and hatred for her and her cult of sick killers.

"And when were you going to sacrifice me?" Mallory asked, his voice cold. "Some night after we'd made love?"

Ignoring his tone of hurt lover, she turned to him, her face expressionless. "No, in fact I was hoping that we could have you join us. Become one of us."

Mallory was so confused that it took him a minute to register what she was suggesting. Then he began laughing. "You're joking. You must know me better than that. I'm as far from being interested in cults . . . or anything religious . . . as anyone you've ever met."

"That saddens me, David." Her unreal autumn eyes were level, holding on his face. "You realize that you know too much about us?"

Mallory wasn't prepared for this type of casual, direct threat. But he wasn't frightened. She was underestimating him.

"You forget I have the gun," he said.

Her beautiful face remained calm. "David, for an educated, capable man you're really such a child."

Mallory suddenly felt a presence behind him. A tall, rail-thin man with snowblond hair stepped from the shadows. Mallory momentarily froze, watching the ghost-like figure move toward him. He glided across the room and stopped just behind his chair. The man's face was impassive, the deepset eyes curious as he looked down at Mallory.

It was Father Paul's black-priest. The slaughterer from the hospital. Fear impelling him, Mallory leaped up and spun, bringing the Walther around at chest height. He didn't have time to use it. The albino's hand snapped out and grasped his neck before he was all the way out of the chair. With his other hand he wrenched the gun from Mallory.

The albino's long white fingers were incredibly strong, but they didn't strangle; they merely held him captive, like a butterfly impaled on a pin. The man's eyes were like shards of golden ice, completely lacking in human feeling. But he watched Mallory's face with an avid, hungry concentration. As if his victim were a specimen to be studied. His fingers tightened around Mallory's throat, pressing on the carotid artery. Mallory's head was already spinning. Thirty seconds of no blood to his brain, and he would be dead. Panic overwhelmed him, and he tore at the hand and arm, digging his nails into the cool flesh.

The carotid was pulsing inside his skull, beating at the soft tissue of his brain. His starving brain screamed for oxygen, and the throbbing became unbearably painful. It thwacked away, hammering like an angry blacksmith shaping some recalcitrant blood-red metal.

He gagged, his stomach spasming, almost exploding upward in fear. He was going to die. Suddenly he could fight no more. Energy drained away from him, and he sank into oblivion, almost as if the blacksmith had thrust the sputtering hot metal into a bucket of cool black water.

Chapter Twenty-Two

When he awoke he was light-headed, and his mouth tasted like dirty straw, but there was little pain. Oddly enough, only his eyes ached. The circulation to his optic nerve must have been affected by the pressure on the carotid, he thought. He blinked his eyes several times, getting the circulation moving and looked around, trying to get his bearings. The first thing he saw was the altar, a shining black cloth draped over it, and he knew exactly where he was. The Thetford farm's cellar!

A large pentagram at least thirty feet in diameter had been painted across the floor. And now he understood one other thing—why all the Coleman lanterns and bottles of kerosene were stored in the farm's cellar. They were part of the cult's rituals. Five lanterns, their hard, garish light turned low, were placed at the head of each of the five points.

He was tied in a chair, his hands behind his back, just beyond the fifth point. He was facing the altar, which was at the head of the pentagram. He knew the doorway into this part of the cellar, where he and Father Paul had first entered, was behind him and off to the right.

His hands, and especially his fingers, were tingling and turning numb from the circulation being cut off. He methodically moved each of his swollen fingers and tried to get the blood moving. It did no good; his hands only started to ache.

He looked around again, diverting his attention from his throbbing fingers, and was surprised to see four other prisoners beside himself. They were sitting in the shadows, each of them so quiet that at first Mallory thought they might be dead. But no, they were probably either drugged or rendered unconscious as he was.

The dim, wavering glow from the lanterns made it hard to see across the pentagram's thirty-foot diameter, but Mallory could make out an overweight, puffy-faced man slumped over in the chair opposite him, nearest the altar. He looked like a lawyer or a banker, overfed and overindulged. Next to him was a woman, young and commonly pretty. Her head was thrown back, her mouth open as if she were sleeping. The third chair was occupied by a nondescript man of middle-age. Next to Mallory was a teenage boy, his face a carpet of pimples. His head, which was slung forward onto his chest, was shaved on the sides and topped by a four-inch Mohawk tinted a bright orange. He had a swastika tattooed on the side of his neck and a skull and crossbones drawn in red ink on his bicep.

The five chairs were scattered in a broken circle around the five points of the pentagram. They were all positioned a few feet outside the pentagram points, as if positioned for privileged spectators who were being given a full view of the proceedings. But Mallory knew better. From everything Father Paul had told him, he, and the others, were here for more bloodthirsty reasons.

Mallory remembered Father Paul's description of

the Black Mass and noticed that the three points of the pentagram were pointing down, away from the altar. A reversed pentagram. Everything a negation of the Catholic Mass, black candles were used instead of white, prayers were said backwards. Communion consisted of drinking blood and eating flesh instead of wine and the wafer.

The pentagram's five points symbolized the four elements of fire, water, earth and air, surmounted by spirit. By reversing it they negate the power of the Trinity because the three points now face down, toward the earth and Satan's domain.

Graceless light from the lanterns threw an unflattering glow over everything, creating heavy shadows and anemic highlights. Motes of dust floated in the dim lantern light, their direction appearing whimsical but secretly influenced by the merest movement of air. Mallory watched them dance until he heard the footsteps.

A chain of black-robed figures entered the room, passing from his right, in front of him and then circling the pentagram. They were all silent, only their robes scraping across the rough earthen floor made a sound reminiscent of the crinoline rustle of ball gowns. Mallory counted more than a dozen and still they came. The room was filling with shadows, each figure's face obscured by the hooded cowls of their cassocks.

But two Mallory recognized immediately. Lili and the albino. The tall man led the procession, his white face visible even in the shadows of the hood. Mallory recognized Lili by her walk. She carried two children, one in each arm.

The members of the coven all seemed to know their places, for each moved directly to a point of the pentagram and stopped. Some performed small tasks. One turned up the wick on each lantern, another walked about the giant circle of the pentagram swinging an aspergillum in a long slow arc, its smoke rising, the incense pungent and sharp. The others ranged in a large circle around the pentagram, their hands clasped before them.

Two high-backed wooden chairs, the dark walnut panels carved with demonic scenes, had been placed behind the altar. Lili sat in the left-hand seat, still cradling the twelfth child in one arm but now holding the hand of the other who stood unsteadily next to her.

The albino mounted the steps and took his place at the head of the altar. He pushed the cowl back from his head and slowly surveyed the room, his eyes pausing briefly on each of the prisoners. He motioned with his head toward them, and three figures stepped from the shadows and began roughly awaking them. The boy with the Mohawk groaned and turned away when he was prodded. He didn't want to come up from his dreams. A quick injection was given and after a minute his bloodshot and dazed eyes opened. He looked around the room uncomprehendingly.

The albino raised his hands. He held a dagger and a large golden chalice. The dagger was long and ornamental, the chalice about the size of a liter, was intricately sculpted with fine craftsmanship.

A bell sounded, echoing with a dull, sullen ring throughout the huge stone cellar.

The albino lowered his arms and for the first time he spoke. He had a rich, mellow baritone, a soothing voice.

"This is a night outside time, when the veil of Isis is lifted. The covenstead meets here now to consecrate the children of our Lord in his many guises—Iblis, Chemos, Dagon, Rimmon, Thammuz, Belial, Beelzebub.

"In the name of Satan, Lucifer, Belial, and all the demons, named and nameless, walkers in the velvet darkness, harken to us. O dim and shadowy things, wraith-like, twisted, half-seen creatures glimpsed beyond the veil of time and spaceless night. Draw near, attend to us this night. Give our hands the strength to pull the crumbling vaults of spurious heaven down . . . and from their shards erect a monument to your dominion o'er a world of cowering men."

The albino pointed the dagger at a large figure standing to his right and motioned for him to come forward. The man moved quietly to stand in front of the albino. The albino stretched out his hand and ran the blade of the knife across it. The flesh opened and blood rushed forward, filling his palm. The albino pressed his bleeding palm against the mouth of the big man, who licked and sucked the open wound.

After a moment the bell sounded again. The big man turned and threw back his cowl.

Weidemeier . . . God in heaven . . . Weidemeier! The bastard had been with them all along. Kelly . . . Kelly, he probably even helped to kill his partner.

Weidemeier strode over to stand near the round-faced lawyer, his face impassive. But his eyes were gleaming with excitement.

Mallory could barely believe it, but the shock was lessened somewhat by Lili having appeared at his apartment. At this point Mallory would believe anything. . . .

Weidemeier had his eyes on the albino, who nodded his head.

The big man then moved behind each of the prisoners, shoving them off the chairs to their knees. The woman fell to her side, and he grabbed her by the hair and yanked her upright until she was again on her knees, her back straight. She began weeping and shaking her head, her sweat-clotted hair hanging down over her face.

Weidemeier didn't seem to recognize him, or he simply didn't care, Mallory wasn't sure which. But expecting to be pushed, Mallory slid off the chair on to his knees when it came his turn. The knuckles of his bound hands scraped on the edge of the chair as he moved forward, but they were already numb so it didn't matter much.

Weidemeier moved slowly back around the pentagram to the first prisoner. He stopped behind the paunchy, round-faced man and reached inside his cassock. The blade he pulled out seemed a mutation, a cross between a giant bowie knife and a hooked-beak machete.

It was an ugly weapon... its purpose clear. Every eye in the cellar was riveted on Weidemeier and the Athame, at least that's what Father Paul had called the sacrificial knife used at Black Masses.

The fine hairs on the back of Mallory's neck stiffened. The nerve endings in his skin understood what was coming. They were tingling as if the horror had already reached out and touched him with its intention.

Weidemeier looked up at the albino, who raised both his hands toward him.

"Within the head and blood resides each being's power," the albino said. "Here is centered the magical strength.

"Accept from us, oh, Iblis, these magical sacrifices prepared to give Thee body and form... The blood is the symbol of the magic of Thy word... And the all-binding milk that flows in human veins is the magical water of Thy purification... The heat of the magical blood-fire is the power of life to form, enabling Thee to manifest Thyself in pleasing shape."

The albino paused and closed his luminous eyes. In a whisper almost too soft to hear, he said, "Now, children, take the head and collect the life force."

In a movement almost too swift for Mallory to follow, the big man moved his shoulders slightly to the right and swung the Athame back to his left in a short horizontal arc.

The man's head leaped from the neck, pushed forward on the wings of a geyser of blood.

The woman next to him screamed.

The head tumbled face-forward, thudded on the earthen floor and rolled erratically like a giant yellow apple spilled from a basket. So clean was the cut that the headless body didn't move for a second, and then, slowly, it curled to the ground and lay there jerking spastically.

The woman had stopped screaming and there was a stunned absolute silence . . . except for the man's leg twitching, thumping on the ground like a dog's tail, and the sibilant rushing sound of his bladder venting itself. Steam rose from his crotch as the humid stain spread, mixing with the gently pumping blood weaving down his chest and stomach.

Weidemeier reached down and grasped the man's body by his belt and hoisted him off the ground. A woman quickly brought the large golden chalice and held it under the neck. With the heart higher than the severed neck, the blood flow renewed itself, arching into the chalice in thick bursts as the dying heart muscle desperately continued to do its job.

Mallory was so sickened he closed his eyes and turned away. He felt soiled by this obscenity. He could never wash the ghastly visions away.

But then the horror became even darker, the stain deeper. The woman carried the chalice to the albino who took it in both hands.

He held it before him, the steam rising still. "Dread Lord of Death and Giver of Life, Thou Whose Name is Mystery, let thy power crystallize in our blood."

He brought the chalice to his lips and drank.

When he had finished he held the golden chalice out, at arm's length, level with his face. His soft baritone fell to a low, throaty imprecation, "Here are your waters and your watering place. Drink and be whole again beyond confusion."

He moved to the woman who had brought him the chalice. She threw back her cowl.

The old woman lifted her face, a supplicant at the bar of salvation awaiting the host. As the golden cup lowered to her mouth she closed her eyes. Mallory saw them roll up in her head so only the whites showed. The albino tipped the chalice, and the woman drank deeply, her throat moving with the hunger as she swallowed. Her mouth came away scarlet, a tip of tongue flickering over her ripe lips, still hungry.

For the first time the albino's face seemed to soften, and the white skin took on a nimbus of hazy light. He seemed transported, as if the blood were draining magically through his own flesh, into the cup, and thence into the supplicant. He smiled down at the woman, a brief movement at the edges of his mouth.

Another robed figure moved forward and kneeled before him. The cowl was thrown back, and Mallory watched as a young girl, no more than sixteen or seventeen, opened her lips to the craving.

The next was a young boy, tall and gangling, just beyond puberty.

The following was a middle-aged man, balding with

a puffy face, his eyes covetous. He seemed the most eager of them all.

And so the albino fed his flock.

Lili watched from the shadows, still clutching the twelfth child in her arms. Another baby clung to her skirt, its hand hooked into the dark folds of her robe like a tiny white claw.

In an apparent show of honor, the albino moved over to where she stood and stopped in front of her. She readily drank, moving her lips forward to prolong the moment. When she had had her fill she bent down to the one year old clinging to her side and kissed it full on the mouth, passing part of the mouthful of blood to the child. She did the same to the infant in her arms, the twelfth child. The baby opened its mouth like a hungry bird while she dribbled the remainder onto its lips. When it was finished the twelfth child gurgled and reached up to her lips, pointing, inserting the tips of his fingers into her mouth, wanting more.

Smiling, she kissed the baby's blood-stained fingers and patted his hand as she took them out of her mouth.

Mallory watched the scene with horror, magnetised by the incongruent mother-infant contact.

Everything was askew, upside-down, a terrifying Möbius strip that twisted the world, warping reality; horror converted into loving care, murder and death into ecstatic ritual. He felt as if he were going out of his mind.

When everyone had sipped from the chalice, Weidemeier moved to the next kneeling victim. The young woman was weeping, imploring them to save her, but her sobs were cut short as Weidemeier mercilessly brought the Athame down on her neck.

The same ritual was followed. He lifted her from the waist, and her heart's blood filled the chalice. Each of the coven drank.

The woman's body was dragged away from the pentagram and thrown next to the man's. The bodies were stripped and left naked on the floor.

With the sacrifice of the third victim, the air reeked with a cesspool of human odors, the redolence of terror and violent death. The whole cellar began to stink of blood, urine, feces and vomit.

It was an *abattoir,* a butcher shop with twisted purpose and without elegance.

The room was steaming with blood.

Horror upon horror. Mallory thought he would go mad before death came. As Weidemeier worked his way around the five points of the pentagram, and the bodies were dragged away, panic rose in him, bringing a shivering, icy fear with it.

For the first time he looked over at the pile of headless corpses. The dead, pastel bodies, still ruddy pink but turning a porcelain bluish-white with an occasional scarlet throat showing, lay in a pile like a painter's discarded pallet.

The teenage boy next to him was still grinning stupidly, as if the game was everything they had promised him. His eyes were half-closed most of the time, but he looked up in surprise and wonder when the man next to him was beheaded. Mallory could see that his pupils were dilated. Whatever the drug was it had to be powerful to overcome the stark and ugly reality around him.

The boy was still grinning, looking up at Weidemeier when his head was lopped off, rolling a short distance and coming to rest with the orange Mohawk flat against the ground. The swastika had been slashed through its center, and only half of the tattoo could be seen on the stump of his neck. A single, long and delicate silver earring also shaped like a swastika swayed beneath the lobe of his ear.

The blood drinking ritual was repeated, but this time more rapidly, each member only sipping once.

Then he was suddenly next. The slaughtering had been brought quickly to him. Nausea swept up and he didn't even try to fight it. There was no hiding from this insanity, no help but to throw it up, reject it from his core. A stream of vomit propelled itself up from his gut, fouling the front of his clothes and warmly collecting in his lap. His nose ran with bilious acids and tears brimmed over from his closed eyes.

Oh, my God, my God, what a waste. What a terrible, insane waste. So cheap, so cheap. He had never seen life as such a spendthrift thing. Precious, he had always thought it precious, a gift to be cherished, to be nurtured.

But here it was wantonly being squandered . . . for God knows what insane reason.

Mallory felt Weidemeier move behind him, the big man's body rustling in his heavy black robes. He could smell the sweat from Weidemeier, a rancid male body odor mixed with the blood that had splattered onto his executioner's hands. Weidemeier was breathing heavily, and he could feel it hot and rapid falling on the top of his head.

His heart was pounding with such force that the bones of his chest ached.

He lifted his head and looked up at Lili, wanting to make eye contact, wanting to have her watch him die. Would she show any emotion?

She was standing between the altar and door, at the head of the pentagram, and wasn't even looking in his direction. All of her attention was on the baby and the child clinging to her skirts.

He heard Weidemeier move behind him, positioning himself for the blow. His hands had no feeling, just a quiet tingling, but his knees ached from kneeling for so long. He tried to ignore it. Mallory hoped he wouldn't lose control of his bowels and soil himself. It was a natural reaction of the body to trauma, but he preferred to die with some dignity. The smell of his vomit was bad enough. It was a small thing and he concentrated on it, willing his sphincter and bladder to be faithful.

He kept his eyes open, still watching Lili, wondering if she would even think of him as he died, when across the line of his vision a Coleman lantern cartwheeled in a crazy, spinning arc like a juggler's flaming baton. But there was no one to catch it here, and the flip-flopping fiery lantern exploded as it crashed at the base of the altar. Great tongues of liquid flame shot out in every direction, licking everything it touched and leaving a burning trail behind.

Screams and howls of pain and fear burst from those closest to the altar, where the flames were the thickest. Within seconds three of the robed figures were rolling on the floor, their black gowns laced with fire. Another, the old woman, her body untouched, was screaming hysterically. The whole of her head was in flames. She beat wildly at her hair with both hands, crying and wailing in fear.

Chaos broke as another softly-turning bottle of flames came arcing through the air, bursting into an expanding circle of fire. An echoing wail, shrill and desperate, mixed with the cries of pain as one after another robed figure burst into flames and was consumed by the fire.

The smell of burning hair and flesh raced in every direction, billowing out from the wildly thrashing bodies.

Another flaming torch loped into the room, and another, before Mallory could break away from his role as stunned witness. The room was now engulfed in flames. Hardly a person was untouched by the fire.

Mallory twisted around, expecting Weidemeier to still be there, his executioner's sword ready to strike. But Weidemeier was rushing toward the doorway, howling at the top of his voice, the sword above his head ready to strike.

And there was Father Paul calmly standing near the doorway, using his little cigar lighter to fire up another Molotov cocktail made from the kerosene bottles. As Weidemeier lurched toward him, Father Paul threw the lit bottle directly in front of the big man. He immediately burst into a pillar of flame and began twisting and turning, howling like a wounded bear. Agonized wails came from the six-foot tower of fire as Weidemeier's flaming arms and hands beat at the fire eating his chest and head.

Father Paul turned, lit another fire bomb and threw it, crying out at the top of his voice—"I exorcise thee, unclean spirits, in the name of our Lord Jesus Christ; be thou rooted out and put to flight."

Father Paul, dressed in one of the cult's robes, stood with his legs apart lighting and throwing one fire bomb after another, all the time yelling out his exorcism— "Satan, enemy of the human race, root of evils, fomenter of vices, cause of discord, and instigator of griefs . . .

"I adjure thee, by the Judge of the living and the dead, by the maker of the world, by Him who hath power to send thee to hell, by this servant of God who returns from the bosom of the Church, swiftly depart with thy fear and the torment of thy terror."

As those of the cult rushed at him, he incinerated them before they even came near. To Mallory, the screaming old man seemed like Moses on Mount Sinai raining fire down on the sinning Israelites.

Lili, who had backed away from the burning old woman, was now slapping at small spots of fire that had landed on her robe. She snuffed it out by folding the non-burning part of her robe over it, then clutched at the one year old, lifting it into her free arm and ran toward the cellar door, a long stream of flame rushing to cut her off.

The albino had been standing at the altar when the first fire bomb exploded, instantly covering him in a shroud of fire. He had not moved when it happened, but stood quietly, his hands folded in front of him, his head bowed. For a moment Mallory thought he would turn and walk away, a human torch walking in the midst of an inferno. But he slowly folded down onto his knees, his burning hands sliding onto his thighs. He squatted there like a Buddhist auto-da-fé, his soft, parchment-pale flesh curling into charcoal. After a moment the flaming pyramid fell forward into a smoldering heap. He had not made a sound as he died.

By now the cellar was engulfed in flames, most of it concentrated around the altar. The thirty-foot pentagram was a single great bonfire, five black-robed figures curled up like charred fetuses inside the fiery cocoon.

Mallory had still not moved. The kerosene fed flames spread across the floor like burning water, blue and red fire ballooning up from the ground.

Gray streaks of smoke and fumes snaked outward from the flames, rushing along the floor as if searching for something to touch.

Mallory gagged and struggled to his feet, but his knees gave way and he fell forward, a pool of fire scorching his face. He smelled his hair begin to burn and he rolled over, away from the flames. But his hands were still tied behind his back and his legs numb from lack of blood. He began trembling uncontrollably, but then started rolling over and over, trying to escape the spreading flames.

A flash of searing heat ran up his left leg, and he screamed, pulling his legs away. The fire was spreading faster than he could roll, and he didn't have time to try and struggle to his feet. He turned over on to his belly and began scrambling away, the smoke choking and blinding him.

Hands were suddenly beating at his legs, then pulling him across the dirt floor toward the door. Father Paul rolled him over and grabbed him under both arms. He lowered his head next to him and croaked hoarsely in his ear. "Help me, you're too heavy to carry."

His breath was tainted with whiskey.

Mallory struggled up on to his knees and with Father Paul's help made it to his feet.

"No time to untie your hands..." he said. Half pulling him and half holding him up, he dragged Mallory toward the door. The whole cellar was a raging inferno, the belly of a furnace.

By the time they stumbled through the door Mallory was moving better. The screams dwindled, but the smoke was streaming out of the cellar behind them in great billowing clouds as they ran for the stairs.

Father Paul was coughing heavily, holding his chest with one hand, but still he clutched at Mallory's shirt with the other and tried to pull him up the stairs. Mallory ran with his burning eyes closed, stumbling on every step, his hands behind his back. The whole cellar was now a giant oven, the heat flowing after them and scorching their exposed skin.

An explosion shook the foundations of the house,

and the stairs trembled, the wood beneath their feet swayed, screeching like a wounded animal, ready to collapse.

"The other boxes of kerosene..." Father Paul gasped. "The fire must have reached them... We must get out before it reaches the oil tank and gas lines."

Father Paul burst through the kitchen door and fell forward on the floor. He groaned and grasped his side above the bruised ribs. Mallory bolted through the door right after him. He knelt next to the old man, blinking his eyes, trying to get them to work again. Christ, he wished he could rub them.

"Come on," he said. "We're almost there."

Father Paul struggled up, and they lurched across the kitchen and through the mudroom.

The night air hit them clean and hard. They sucked in great gulps of cold air, their lungs ballooning hungrily.

Mallory leaned over, laboring to breathe, clearing his lungs of the smoke and soot. Father Paul had his hands on his hips and was leaning backwards, his head toward the sky and his mouth open. They were both gulping like beached fish.

The house behind them groaned and hissed, a creature being eaten alive from its belly out.

Mallory turned and looked at its dark hulk. The flames were not yet visible. But there was something appropriate about the place feeding upon itself.

Father Paul moved behind him and began to untie his hands.

"Thanks," Mallory said. He began to rub them together, still watching the house, remembering what he had experienced inside its cellar.

A hot, tingling sensation suddenly shot through his hands. He and Father Paul turned and walked away, out into the field. The old man was holding his side still.

316

Mallory would retape it as soon as he could.

As they walked the crisp, fresh February air filled him, recalling him to life, bringing him back up from the bloody pits.

Never again would he forget to wonder at still being alive.

Epilogue

They stood outside in the field watching the house burn. The fire built slowly, with smoke rising from around the baseboards, seeping out of the cellar. Then the ground floor windows began to shine, first hesitantly, then with an angry glow. Flames began reaching higher until finally the whole house was blazing, each window a crimson wound in its side. The house was fixed in silence as it died, a form with no connection, no contacts to the world at large. It stood alone, sputtering sparks high into the black halo of sky above it.

Nisi dominus aedificaverit domum, Father Paul said quietly. "Unless the Lord builds the house, the builders labor in vain."

The night was almost over with a lemon dawn just beginning to color the eastern horizon. But it was still cold, and the night's chill picked at their exposed skin like tiny needles. The field was crusted with sprinkling of frozen frost, a sugar icing on the dark chocolate earth.

As they watched their own breaths smoked from their nostrils in the chill air.

"You know there's a Greek saying," Father Paul

muttered, "'The dead are in the truth. It is the living in the lie.' I've often wondered if that isn't the truth of it all."

Weary to his core, Mallory couldn't think of anything to say. His mind was as numb as his body. He simply stared at the scarlet ruin a few hundred yards away.

After a while he asked, "How did you find me?"

"Process of elimination. I don't know why, but when you weren't home I just knew you'd gone off and done something foolish. I had a terrible feeling you were in trouble. And that meant if they had you, it was at either Bowker's or the farm. When I got there and saw what was going on the only thing at hand were Molotov cocktails I made up from the box of kerosene bottles. I'd had plenty of experience with those as a boy in Ireland so I made up a few cocktails and began pitching."

Still unable to take his eyes from the flaming house, Mallory said softly, "Thanks, my friend. You know, I still can't believe these last two weeks actually happened. And Lili . . ."

He stopped, unable to articulate his feelings.

"She escaped," Father Paul said, not looking at Mallory.

Mallory shook his head. He knew.

"I saw her robe. In a pile, smoldering at the bottom of the cellar stairs."

"I know," Mallory said. She had gone with two of the children. The youngest. With the twelfth child and another. He wondered what she was going to do now?

As if reading his thoughts, Father Paul said, "I suppose she will continue. Raise the children and still prepare the way for the Anti-Christ."

Mallory turned and regarded the old man. His face was haggard, etched with charcoal and smoke. He looked like he had just scratched his way back up from hell. "Yes, I suppose she will. 'A madman with a great cause?'" he said quietly.

"Yes," Father Paul answered, pulling the collar of his jacket around his throat. "A madman with a great cause! But also with two frightening children who will someday grow up."

The old man was silent for a moment. Then he said, "You know, boyo, we Irish aren't the eternal optimists like you Protestants. Oh, no, we Catholics are realists, we feel the gravitas of earthly tribulations, the mournful pull of sentiment, of human misery and desire, of life itself. And I wonder how this poor old world can resist Satan's seductive games. Oh, no. I think she'll be heard from again . . . and so will the children."